MYST: THE BOOK OF D'NI

M Y S T

THE BOOK OF D'NI

RAND MILLER

with david wingrove

NEW YORK

Text and Fill © 1997, Cyan, Inc.

Illustrations by Tom Bowman

Cover design © 1997, The Leonheardt Group

Designed and typeset in Centaur by BTD/Ann Obringer

Printed in the United States

Library of Congress Cataloging-in-Publication Data

Miller, Rand.
    Myst, the book of D'ni/Rand Miller, with David Wingrove.—1st
ed.

        p.   cm.
    ISBN 0-7868-6161-4
    I. Wingrove, David.   II. Title.
PS3563. I4199M973   1997
813'.54—dc21   97-23999
                                                      CIP

First Edition
10 9 8 7 6 5 4 3 2 1

TO THE DEDICATED TEAM AT CYAN

ACKNOWLEDGMENTS

EVEN AS WE BRING YOU THIS THIRD BOOK, WHICH FURTHER uncovers the D'ni and their history, we realize that we have merely scratched the surface of this fascinatingly rich civilization, but have added a crucial piece to this ever enlarging puzzle. And this latest effort that we now present to you could have only been possible with the continuing effort of a core group of dedicated individuals.

It is again our pleasure to have uncovered more of these historic and stunning past events of a civilization that continues to live and to teach. Yet this work would not have been possible if not for the assistance of Chris Brandkamp, Richard Watson, and Ryan Miller along with the long hours spent by our friend, David Wingrove. This particular task of discovery was especially rewarding to each of us.

So it is again to these four friends that I extend my sincerest thanks.

RAND MILLER

MYST: THE BOOK OF D'NI

PROLOGUE

A SEABIRD CALLS. THE UNKNOWING

ONE STANDS AT THE RAIL.

PEACE. THE CIRCLE CLOSED. THE LAST WORD WRITTEN.

—FROM THE KOROKH JIMAH: VV. 13245-46

THE CAVERN WAS SILENT. A FAINT MIST DRIFTED ON THE surface of the water, underlit by the dull orange glow that seemed to emanate from deep within the lake. Vast walls of granite climbed on every side while overhead, unseen, unsensed, a solid shelf of rock a mile thick shut off all view of stars and moon.

Islands littered the lake, twisted spikes of darkness jutting from the level surface of the water, and there, on the far side of the cavern, one single, massive rock, split yet still standing, like the splintered trunk of a tree, its peak hidden in the darkness.

Beyond it lay the city, wreathed in stillness, its ancient buildings clinging to the walls of the cavern.

D'ni slept, dreamless and in ruins. And yet the air was fresh. It moved, circulating between the caverns, the distant noise of the vast rotating blades little more than the suggestion of a sound, a faint, whumping pulse *beneath* the silence.

The mist parted briefly as a boat slid across the waters, the faintest ripple marking its passage, and then it, too, was gone, vanished into the blackness.

It was night in D'ni. A night that had lasted now for almost seventy years.

In the streets of the city the mist coiled on the cold stone of ancient cobbles like something living. Yet nothing lived there now; only the mosses and fungi that grew from every niche and cranny.

Empty it was, as though it had stood thus for a thousand years. Level after level lay open to the eye, abandoned and neglected. A thousand empty lanes, ten thousand empty rooms, a desolate landscape of crumbling walls and fallen masonry everywhere one looked.

In the great curve between the city's marbled flanks lay the harbor, the shadows of sunken boats in its glowing depths, and across the harbor's mouth a great arch of stone, Kerath's Arch, as it was known, its pitted surface webbed with cracks.

Silence. A preternatural silence. And then a sound. Faint at first and distant, and yet clear. The tap, tap, tap of metal against stone.

High above, in the narrow lanes of the upper city, a shadow stopped beneath a partly fallen gate and turned to look. The sound had come from the far end of the cavern; from one of the islands scattered on the lake out there.

Mist swirled, then silence fell again.

And then new sounds: a whirring, high-pitched mechanical screech, followed by the low burr of a power drill. And then the tapping once again, the sound of it echoing out across the water.

K'veer. The noises were coming from K'veer.

Two miles across the lake and there it is, the island rising like a huge black corkscrew from the glowing lake, its once crisp outline softened by a recent rockfall.

Coming closer, the noise grows in volume, the sound of drilling constant now, as is the clang, clang, clang of massive hammers pounding the stone. The island shakes beneath the onslaught, the carved stone trembling like a sounding bell.

But no one is woken by that dreadful din. The ancient rooms are dark and empty. All, that is, but one, at the very foot of the island, down beneath the surface of the lake. There, deep in the rock, lies the oldest room of all, a chamber of marbled pillars and cold stone, sealed off by an angry father to teach his son a lesson.

Now, forty years on, that same chamber is filled with busy men in dark, protective suits. Their brows beaded with sweat, they toil beneath the arc lights, a dozen of them standing between the two big hydraulic props, working at the face of the wall with hammer and drill, while others scamper back and forth, lifting and carrying the fallen stone, stacking it in a great heap on the far side of the chamber.

A figure stands beside the left-hand prop, looking on. Atrus, son of

Gehn, once-prisoner in this chamber. After a while, he glances at the open notebook in his hand, then looks up again, calling out something to those closest to him.

A face looks up and nods, then turns back. The message is passed along the line.

There is a moment's pause. A welcome silence.

Walking across, Atrus crouches between two of the men and leans forward, examining the wall, prising his fingers deep into the crack, then turns and shakes his head.

He stands back, letting them continue, watching them go to it with a vengeance, the noise deafening now, as if all of them know that one more push will see the job through.

Slowly the chamber fills with dust and grit. And then one of them withdraws and, straightening up, cuts the power to his drill. Turning, he lifts his protective visor and grins.

All about him the others stand back, looking on.

Atrus returns to the wall and, crouching, pushes his hand deep into the crack, edging this way and that, feeling high and low. Satisfied, he eases back and, taking a marker from his pocket, stands, drawing an outline on the stone. The outline of a door.

At his signal, one of the drill men steps forward and begins to cut along the mark.

Swiftly it's done. A dozen hammer blows and the stone falls away.

The stone is quickly cleared, and as the rest look on, Atrus steps forward one last time. He holds a cutting tool with a chunky barrel the thickness of his arm. Placing the circle of its teeth about the circle of the lock—a circle that overlaps the thick frame of the door—he braces himself, then gently squeezes the trigger, letting it bite slowly into the surface. Only then, when the cutter has a definite grip on the metal, does he begin to push, placing his whole weight behind it.

There is a growling whine, a sharp, burning smell, different in kind from the earlier smells of stone and dust and lubricant. And then, abruptly, it's over. There is the clatter of the lock as it falls into the corridor beyond, the descending whine of the drill as it stutters into silence.

Setting the drill down, he raises his visor, then pulls the protective helmet off and lets it fall.

ATRUS STRAIGHTENED AND, WITH A SINGLE MEANINGFUL glance at the watching men, turned back to face the doorway. Forty years he had waited for this. Forty long years.

Placing his booted foot against the surface, he pushed hard, feeling the metal resist at first, then give.

Slowly, silently, it swung back.

A good D'ni door, he thought, *with good stone hinges that never rust. A door built to last.*

And as the door swung back he saw for the first time in a long while the empty corridor and, at its end, the twist of steps that led up into the house, where, long ago, his father, Gehn, had taught him how to write. Where he had first learned the truth about D'ni. Yes, and other things, too.

Irras came and stood by his shoulder. "Will you not go through, Master Atrus?"

Atrus turned, meeting the young man's eyes. "One should not hurry moments like this, Irras. I have waited forty years. Another forty seconds will not harm."

Irras lowered his eyes, abashed.

"Besides," Atrus went on, "we do not know yet whether D'ni is occupied or not."

"You think it might be?" The look of shock on Irras's face was almost comical.

"If it *is*," Atrus said, "then they will know we are here. We've made enough noise to wake the dead."

"Then maybe we should arm ourselves."

"Against other D'ni?" Atrus smiled. "No, Irras. If anyone's here, they will be friends, not foes. Like us, they will have returned for a reason."

Atrus turned back, looking toward the steps, then, brushing the dust from his leather gloves and boots, he stepped through, into the dimly lit corridor.

PART ONE

RIVERS OF FIRE. EVEN THE ROCKS BURN.

AN ISLAND RISES FROM THE SEA.

DARK MAGIC IN AN ERRANT PHRASE.

THE PEOPLE BOW TO THE LORD OF ERROR.

—FROM THE EJEMAH'TERAK, BOOK SEVEN, VV. 328–31

SEABIRDS WHEELED AND CALLED IN THE AIR ABOVE THE BAY, a flutter of white above the blue. It was hot, and, looking at the village, Marrim drew her hair back from her face, then gathered the braided strands together, fastening them at the nape of her neck. But for her father she would have had it cut like a man's long ago. After all, she did a man's job, why should she not wear her hair like a man's? But she was loathe to upset her father. It was hard enough for him to understand all the changes that had come to Averone, let alone comprehend the urge to explore and understand that this had been woken in his youngest daughter.

From where she stood, on the promontory, the whole of her small world was open to her gaze. For all her childhood it had been enough. The six great circular lodge houses, the river, the broad fields where they had planted the crops, and, beyond them, the woods where they had hunted and played. World enough, until Atrus and Catherine appeared.

Now she could barely imagine how it had been before they'd come. How she had ever survived without this urge in her, this need to know.

And now, almost as suddenly as it had begun, it was to end. Only that morning they had dismantled the last of the workshops and cleared the ground where it had been. So Atrus had promised the elders of the village when he had first come here, yet Marrim could not understand why it had to be. They had come so far so quickly. Why *did* it have to end? For certain, she herself could not easily return to being what she was. No. She had changed. And this world, while it still drew her emotionally, was no longer big enough for her. She wanted more. Atrus's Books had opened her mind to the infinite possibilities that existed, and she wanted to see, if not all, then at least *some* of those possibilities.

And yet tomorrow they would be gone. Atrus and Catherine, and all they stood for.

There had to be a way to prevent that. Or if not, a way of going with them. If only Atrus would ask. But even then there were the elders—her father among them—and they would never agree. As much as they liked Atrus, they did not welcome the changes he had brought to Averone. They saw the excitement in their children's eyes and to them it was a threat. Atrus had understood that. It was why he had agreed to destroy all that he had built here once it had served his needs. But he could not destroy what was in her head. Nor the seeds he had planted in the heads of others, such as Irras and Carrad. Marrim knew they shared her frustration. They, too, felt constrained now by this tiny world of theirs.

She let her thoughts grow still watching the movements down below her, in the village. Each of the great lodge houses had four large doorways, at north, south, east, and west, the massive entrances framed by the polished jarras trunks—cut from the largest trees in the woods. As she looked, three people emerged from the south doorway of her own lodge, their figures tiny against the great boles of the ancient trees; yet she recognized them at once.

Atrus stood to the left, the distinctive lenses that he wore pulled down over his face, his long cloak hanging loose in the windless air. Beside him, in a long flowing gown of green, stood Catherine, her hair tied back. Facing them, talking to them, was her father.

She groaned. Doubtless her father was asking Atrus not to interfere. And Atrus, being the man he was, would respect her father's wishes.

Her spirits low, she began to walk back down to the village, heading toward the river, away from her own lodge and the three figures who stood there debating her future. And as she walked she remembered the first time she had seen Atrus and Catherine, that morning when they had, so it seemed, stepped from the air and into their lives. Wide-eyed, the villagers had come out from their lodges to stare at the two strangers, while the elders quickly gathered to form a welcoming party.

She remembered how difficult that first meeting had been, with neither party able to speak the other's language. And yet even then Atrus had found ways to communicate with them. His hands had drawn pictures in the air, and they had somehow understood. He wanted their help. She remembered the gesture clearly: how he had put his arms straight out toward the elders, palms open, and then slowly had drawn them in, as if to embrace something to his chest.

In the days that had followed, she had barely let them out of her sight, hovering at the back of a circle of curious youngsters who had followed the two strangers everywhere they went. And slowly she had begun to pick up the odd word or two until, emboldened by familiarity, she had dared to speak to the woman. She remembered vividly how Catherine had turned to face her, the surprise in her eyes slowly turning to a smile. She had repeated the words Marrim had uttered, then gently beckoned her across.

So it had begun, four years ago this summer.

Marrim smiled, recalling the long hours she had spent learning the D'ni tongue, and afterward—in the library on Chroma'Agana—how she had sat at her books long into the night, learning the written script.

Even now she had not mastered it fully. But now it did not matter. For tonight, after the feast, they would be gone, the Linking Book burned, that whole world of experience barred to her, *if* the elders had their way.

The thought of it filled her with dread. It would be like locking her in a room and throwing away the key.

No, she thought. *Worse than that. Much worse.*

IRRAS FOUND HER CROUCHED ON THE RIVERBANK.

"Marrim?"

She glanced up at him, then returned her gaze to the surface of the water.

"Marrim? What is it?"

She answered without looking at him. "You *know* what it is."

"Look, I know you're disappointed, Marrim, we all are, but it can't be helped. The elders only let us help Atrus on the understanding that once he made the breakthrough that was it."

Marrim was silent. She picked up a handful of pebbles and, one by one, began to throw them into the slow-moving stream.

Irras watched her a moment, combing his fingers back through his dark, fine hair. Then, sighing. "Come on, Marrim. Don't spoil things. You knew this day would come."

"I know," she said. "But it's hard. I mean, it's not like going hunting, say, or fishing. There, no matter how far you venture, you come back and you're the same, unchanged. But the journey *we've* been on . . ."

Irras was silent for a long time, thinking about what she'd said, then he shrugged. "You'll be okay. You'll settle again."

"Maybe . . ."

Irras stared at her, surprised by the uncertainty in her voice.

Yet before he could speak again, to reassure her, Carrad came running up, his broad chest rising and falling from his exertions, sweat beading the big knuckle of his skull.

"Irras! Marrim! You're wanted! Atrus has called a meeting!"

Marrim looked down. No doubt he wanted to thank them and say good-bye before the feast, because there would be no time for informal farewells later on. But right now she didn't feel like farewells.

"I saw him," she said, "speaking to my father."

Carrad nodded. "Mine, too."

She looked up. He at least understood what she was feeling, she could see it in his eyes.

"I wish . . ."

"What?" she said gently, brought out of herself by the sight of his suffering.

"I wish we'd never started this."

Yes. But it was too late now. It would have been best for them all if they had never learned about D'ni and Books and all the rest of it, but now . . .

Irras's voice broke into her thoughts. "*Well?* Are you going to keep Atrus waiting?"

Marrim looked to Carrad, then back to Irras. In appearance the two

young men were like rock and wood, the one so broad and solid, the other
so agile and slender; but on the inside they were much alike.

"No," she said, knowing that whatever she was feeling, it was not Atrus's
fault: He had been as good as a father to them, after all. "You're right, Irras.
Let us not keep Master Atrus waiting."

THE HUT WAS THE LAST OF THE NEW BUILDINGS TO REMAIN
standing, and in an hour or so it, too, would be gone, the dark earth beneath
its floor raked over, as if nothing had ever been there on the site. Looking
at it, Atrus sighed. They had had happy times here, working, laughing,
teaching the young people how to use their quick and nimble minds. He
would miss that. Indeed, it was only now, at the end, that he realized just
how much he was going to miss it.

Atrus turned, looking to Catherine. She was crouched, packing the last
of their books into a knapsack. He watched her a moment, the familiarity
of her shape, her every movement, ingrained in him. There were lines at her
neck now, and a fine web of lines about her eyes and mouth, but these only
made her more dear to him. The D'ni blood in him made him age the tiniest bit slower than she, and there was always the consciousness that one day
he would be alone, without her by his side, but that only made him savor
each moment that much more.

She glanced up, noticing him watching her, and smiled. Then, seeing the
concern in his eyes, she stood and came across.

"What is it?"

He hesitated, then. "I wish there was another way."

"Is that why you want to talk to them?"

He nodded.

"And what will you say?"

"I don't know. But I feel I ought to say something. As it is, I feel as if we're simply abandoning them." He raised a hand. "I know we agreed to all this long ago, but I didn't know then how I would feel at the end."

"I know . . ." There was a sadness in her face that mirrored his own. "But at least they got to see D'ni."

"MARRIM, IRRAS, CARRAD . . . COME IN."

There was an awkwardness about Atrus's manner that was strange. It was almost as if the years between his arrival and his imminent departure had melted away, leaving them all strangers again. The three young Averonese also moved awkwardly as they stepped into the shadows of the hut, unable to meet their friend's eyes, their every gesture a denial of what was happening. This was difficult for them. More difficult than anything they'd ever done.

Marrim, particularly, seemed eclipsed. She was usually so bright, so full of life. Catherine, watching her from where she stood behind her husband, felt her heart go out to the young woman. It would be hard for her to stay here. There was such a hunger in her for new things, and what was new in Averone?

"Friends . . ." Atrus said, as they sat on the long bench facing him. "I . . ." He made a tiny noise of exasperation, then, leaning toward them, his hands extended in exhortation, said, "I wish this wasn't happening. I wish . . ."

They were watching him now.

Atrus's voice, when it came again, was subdued, as if he understood that even uttering these words might not help. "I wish you could come with us. I wish that more than anything."

Catherine saw the small, shuddering movement in each of them. The words had touched them. It was what they wanted. Wanted more than anything. And somehow, strangely, it helped them to know that Atrus wanted that, too.

Marrim looked from side to side to her friends, then spoke. "We understand."

"Yes." The single word sounded bleak. It all came down to this. Atrus had given his word, and he could not break it. Indeed, he would not be the man he was if that were possible. To be what one said one was . . . that, to Atrus, was of the essence. And he had instilled that into these young people. What one said, what one wrote—these things mattered. As much as life and death.

"I wanted to give each of you something," Atrus said gently. "To remember us by."

Atrus stood and went across, lifting three small parcels from the table at the side. Catherine had noticed them earlier and guessed what they were. Books. D'ni Books.

He returned, then leaned across the table, setting a parcel before each of them, then sat again, waiting for them to open them. But none of them made even the vaguest movement to unwrap the gifts.

"Well?" Atrus said after a moment, clearly trying to understand what was going on. "Have I done the wrong thing?"

It was Marrim who answered him. "We thank you for the gifts, Master Atrus, but we cannot accept them. We have finished with all that now, and we must settle here, in Averone."

But Catherine saw the look of longing in her eyes, quickly suppressed, and felt almost giddy at the thought of what they were doing here. Atrus and she had not even *begun* to imagine the effect they would have on these young people.

She looked away, unable to bear it any longer. Yet even as she did there was a knock on the door.

Atrus looked up, even as the young Averonese turned in their seats.

The door swung slowly open.

"Gevah!" Atrus said, standing and giving a tiny bow.

The old man looked about him, taking in the situation at a glance, then, with a nod to Atrus and Catherine, he stepped inside, closing the door behind him.

"Forgive me for intruding," he began, "but I have come direct from a meeting of the elders."

Catherine saw the three young people deflate at the words. If there had been any glimmer of hope, it had died in that moment.

"They asked me to come at once," Gevah continued, "before a great mistake was made."

Atrus blinked, then. "You can tell the elders that I will keep my word. These presents are but a token. I . . ."

"You misunderstand me, Master Atrus," Gevah said, interrupting him. "The mistake I am talking of is not yours but ours. *You* have been as good as your word. No, we have discussed the matter at length and are of one mind. The link must remain open."

Atrus simply stared at the old man. The young people were also staring, but their eyes were bright now and there were the ghosts of disbelieving smiles on their faces.

"Averone must remain Averone," Gevah said, "so it is right that the workshops should be pulled down. But there have been other changes. Changes that cannot be pulled down and raked over."

Gevah looked at the three young people who were sitting there and smiled.

"Oh, we are old, but we are not stupid. We have eyes, yes, and imaginations, too. We see how you have changed, and we are proud of you, just as Master Atrus is proud of you."

Catherine could contain herself no longer. "Then they can come with us? To Chroma'Agana? And D'ni?"

Gevah turned to her. "On one condition. That they return here, one month in two, to serve as teachers to our young, to pass on the skills they have learned."

And now, as one, the three jumped up, whooping elatedly and hugging each other, crying with joy. Even old Gevah was included in their hugs.

When things had died down, Atrus asked, "What made you change your mind, Gevah?"

The old man smiled. "The fact that you did what you had promised you would do, and without protest. It made us think. It made us see how much we had to lose if you were gone."

Atrus stood, then came round the table and embraced the old man. "Then let it be so. We shall take great care of these young people. And they will return, to pass on what they know. They will make you doubly proud of them, Gevah."

"I know," the old man said, stepping back, his eyes dwelling long on the three young people. "In fact, I am certain of it."

IT WAS VERY LATE WHEN ATRUS AND CATHERINE RETURNED TO their stall in the great lodge house. Now that the link was to remain, the feast had been a merry one, all of their young helpers in such a mood that it was hard to believe that they had all just volunteered for yet more years of long and grueling work.

Settling down beside Catherine, Atrus yawned, then gave a small chuckle.

"What now?" Catherine whispered, snuggling in to his side.

He looked up at the great raftered roof of the lodge house high above and grinned. "The look on Marrim's face when she finally opened her present," he whispered. "Why, you'd have thought I'd wrapped up the sun itself and given it to her!"

Catherine nodded thoughtfully, then. "She's a hungry one. Starving for knowledge and for strange exotic places. Oh, I know that hunger, Atrus."

"Yes," he said quietly, conscious of the hundreds of sleeping Averonese surrounding them. "And now she'll have a chance. We can teach her, Catherine. Teach her how to write."

"Yes . . ."

Atrus was silent for a long time after that. He lay there on his back, his arm curled about Catherine, unable to sleep, staring up into the dark, thinking about what lay ahead.

The breakthrough to D'ni was only the first step. The real work had yet to begin—the gathering in of the Books, the searching of the Ages. It would be a slow, laborious task.

Catherine must have sighed, though she was unaware of it. Atrus lifted himself up onto one elbow and looked down into her face. "What is it?" he whispered.

She met his eyes. "What if no one survived? What if we're alone?"

"We won't know—not until we've tried. But I can't believe there aren't some D'ni somewhere. Can you?"

She smiled, calmed by his certainty. "No."

"Good," he said. "We'll worry about all that in the morning."

"MARRIM! MARRIM! LOOK AT THIS! HAVE YOU EVER SEEN THE like?"

Marrim squeezed past Irras then stopped dead, astonished by the sight that met her eyes.

"Books!"

The long, low room was filled to bursting with books: on shelves on the walls, in piles on the floor, and on both desks; even stacked up on the tall-backed chair that rested behind the bigger of the desks. More books than she had ever dared imagine. Why, she could spend years in this one room alone and never read half of them!

She turned, excited, to find Atrus standing there.

"Master Atrus . . ."

He stepped past her, looking about him.

"This was my father's room," he said. "His study."

Atrus walked across and lifted something from among the books on the desk—an elaborate-looking pipe. He lifted it to his nose and sniffed, then placed it back, a strange expression on his face.

"He must have been a clever man," Irras offered.

Atrus turned. "Clever . . . yes." But he said no more.

"There are Books here," he said after a moment, his pale eyes narrowed. "D'ni Books. There might be functional Ages in some of them. Marrim, go through the shelves and the piles on the floor. Gather them together. But don't be tempted by them. Some of these worlds are dangerous. That's why we use the suit, remember? Your task is to locate them and bring them to me. Afterward, when all are gathered in, we can decide which ones to visit."

The two youngsters nodded.

"By the way," Atrus said, "where's Carrad?"

"With Catherine," Irras answered. "They found a boat. They're trying to repair it."

"Ah . . ." Atrus nodded, but Marrim, watching him, noticed how distant he seemed.

Atrus was silent a moment, then: "My father was a secretive man. Maybe he has hidden things somewhere in the room. Search everything. The walls, the floors, everything." He paused. "You know what you're looking for?"

"We know," Marrim said.

"Good." Atrus nodded, then quickly left.

Marrim turned full circle, excited once again now that Atrus had gone. "All these books," she said, looking at Irras. "Just imagine . . ."

CATHERINE LOOKED ACROSS AS ATRUS CAME DOWN THE STONE steps into the lamp-lit cavern.

"Marrim *said* you'd found a boat," he said, his voice echoing slightly in that enclosed space.

"Yes," she said, glancing to her side, where Carrad was busy repairing the hull of the ancient craft, his closely shaven head bobbing up and down as he worked. "It needs a little care and attention, but Carrad knows all about making boats."

"Good." Atrus stepped down onto the quay. The lamp on the wall behind him threw his shadow across the bright surface of the water. He stood there saying nothing, but something in his manner told her that he wanted to talk.

Reaching beside her, she touched Carrad's arm. "I'll not be long." Then, straightening up, she went over to Atrus.

"Come," she said. "Let's go outside."

The main cavern was dark and silent. "Sepulchral" was the word that sprang to her mind; like a single great building that had been long abandoned by its gigantic owners. Sitting there on the stone ledge, looking out across the still, flat surface of the water toward the ancient city, Catherine understood for the first time why Atrus had been driven to return.

"It must be difficult for you, coming back here."

"I was only a child," he answered, his eyes looking past her toward the great twist of rock on the far side of the cavern. "I didn't understand just how much he had twisted things in his mind. I had to unlearn so much that he taught me. I thought I'd thrown him off, but his shadow is everywhere here. I wasn't so conscious of it when we made the breakthrough, but today, standing in his room, I could almost see him . . ."

"Then maybe that's why you're here. To throw off his shadow."

He was silent a while, then: "What I *really* fear is that he's already destroyed all of the Books."

"Why should he do that?"

"It's just something I remember him saying. He used to warn me against using the Books. He said they were unstable and that it would be dangerous to venture into those Ages. But that was a lie. Those Books were all proper Books, approved by the Guilds, checked regularly by the Maintainers. They would have been carefully written—*designed* to be stable. And he would have known that. So why warn me about them unless he didn't want me going into them and finding other D'ni?"

"Yes, but that doesn't mean he *destroyed* them."

"Maybe not. But I know how he thought. He had no respect for them. And on our Book searches, though he never brought back anything but blank Books, he always noted down where the Books were."

"You don't know that."

"I fear that we'll look and look and find nothing, because there'll be nothing to find. You know the depth of his malice, Catherine. You of all people should know that he was quite capable of something like that. Even so . . ."

Atrus turned, the sentence incomplete. Catherine looked up and saw that Marrim was standing in the doorway.

"What is it?" Atrus asked, going over to her.

"This," Marrim said, handing Atrus a notebook. "I found it tucked away at the back of one of the drawers."

He stared at it, amazed. "But this . . ."

". . . was your father's," Catherine said, stepping up beside him. She opened it, flicking through the pages quickly, then handed it back.

"Maybe it's here," she said.

Decades of understanding between the two made him understand her at once. "His journals?"

"One of his journals," she said. "You say he kept a record of the Book searches. Well, maybe it's here. If so, we'll know where to look. It could save us weeks."

"Yes." Yet as Atrus looked back at the notebook his face darkened.

"Shadows . . ." he said.

"Yes," Catherine answered him. "But these shadows might just cast some light."

SENSING THAT ATRUS NEEDED TO BE LEFT FOR A TIME, Catherine took the three young Averonese back to Chroma'Agana, then returned alone.

She found him in his father's study, seated at Gehn's desk, the notebook open before him.

Atrus looked up as she came in and sighed. "It's all here," he said. "Diaries, observations, notes to Ages he was writing. And other things."

"And the maps?"

He shook his head. "Catherine? . . . Have you ever read of the Great King?"

"No . . . Unless they mean Kerath."

"I don't think so. My father's notes are unclear, but it appears he existed long before the late kings."

"What is that?" she asked, reaching out to take the notebook.

"My father's notes on the myths and legends of D'ni. Some of it's quite detailed, other parts, like the mention of the Great King, are vague. From the notations at the back of the book it seems that Gehn trawled all kinds of sources. It's a regular hodgepodge of fact and rumor, but a lot of it reads like old wives' tales. You know the kind of thing . . . fireside tales, invented to make children's eyes pop!"

Catherine was turning the pages, reading an entry here, an entry there. "So why the interest in this Great King?"

"Because I've never heard mention of him before, and because he was supposed to have made various prophesies."

"Prophesies?"

"Again, it's vague. But there are one or two instances scattered through-out the book. Here . . ." He took the book back and quickly searched through the early pages, returning it to her a moment later. "That entry there, in green ink."

Catherine read it through, then looked up at him. "It's strange, certainly."

She closed the book, then set it down. "I don't think anyone can see clearly what lies ahead."

"Nor I."

THEY MOORED THE BOAT AT THE FOOT OF THE GRANITE STEPS and carried their equipment up. Behind the great sweep of marbled flag-stones that bordered the harbor was an open space that had once been a great square. There they set up camp, clearing away the debris, then placed a ring of lamps about them, the ancient fire-marbles burning brightly in that perpetual twilight.

Standing at the foot of the great curved slope of buildings that rose level after level, climbing the cavern's massive walls, Marrim felt a mixture of awe and sorrow: awe at the scale on which the D'ni had once built; sorrow that she had not witnessed it in its living splendor.

It was strange, of course, for she was used to the shadows falling downward—the natural shadows of a sunlit world—whereas here everything was underlit, the faint glow from the water giving the whole place an eerie feel. Everywhere she looked was ruin. Ruin beyond anything she had imagined possible. Cracked walls and fallen masonry. And here and there huge pits, large enough to swallow up whole mansions. Strange mosses had begun to grow in the cracks, and here and there an odd lichen splashed subdued color on a rock.

Overall it had a strange, desolate beauty, and when Atrus came and stood beside her, she asked him what had happened to cause such devastation.

Atrus had never spoken to them of this, and, listening to the tale—a tale Atrus's grandmother had first told him long after the event—Marrim found her imagination waking, so that she could almost see the dark cloud slowly fill the cavern, and, afterward, Veovis and his ally, A'Gaeris, as they walked through the stricken alleyways of D'ni, their cart of death pushed before them.

When Atrus had finished, Marrim turned to him. "Master Atrus . . . why didn't they come back?"

"Perhaps they did."

Yes, she thought. *And saw this. And hurried back to the Ages in which they had found safe haven, knowing that D'ni was at an end.*

Catherine, who had been organizing the laying out of the bedrolls, now came across. "Shall we go and have a look?" she asked, gesturing toward the nearby streets.

"Marrim?" Atrus asked, turning to her. "Would you like to come with us?"

Marrim nodded, surprised that he'd asked. "Are we to begin the search?"

"Not today. Tomorrow, maybe, once things are better organized. I just thought you might like to look about a little before we begin in earnest." He reached down and, picking up one of the lamps, handed it to her. "Here, Marrim. Light our way."

Marrim took the lamp and, holding it up, led them on, across the littered square toward a crumbling stone archway that marked the entrance to the lowest of D'ni's many districts.

"This is Kerathen, named after the last king," he said, pointing up to the symbols carved into the partly fallen lintel of the arch. "This is where the D'ni boatmen once lived, and the traders and innkeepers."

"And A'Gaeris," Marrim said, staring through the arch wide-eyed, as if at paradise itself.

"Yes. And A'Gaeris."

THEY WALKED FOR AN HOUR, THEN STOPPED, RESTING ON THE balcony of a two-story house, the windows of which were on a level with the top of the great arch that formed a giant gateway to the harbor. Looking down from there, Atrus recalled the first time he had stood there, with his father, in what seemed several lifetimes ago.

Even Marrim was subdued now. And not surprisingly. The sheer extent of the devastation was overwhelming. It was enough to eclipse the brightest spirit.

"It's too much," Catherine said quietly. "We cannot repair *this*."

But Atrus shook his head. "It only seems too much. We have a whole lifetime to work at this. Not only that, but we shall find others to help us in the task."

Marrim, who had been looking out across the lake, now turned and looked to him. "How many people were there, here in D'ni, Master Atrus?"

"A million. Maybe more."

The thought of it clearly amazed her. "And all of them could write?"

"It depends what you mean. The D'ni were highly literate, but few could write Ages. That was something the Guilds taught. One would have needed to be a Guildsman to do that."

"And the women?"

Atrus looked to Catherine and smiled. "I know of only two women who ever learned to write."

THE NEXT FEW WEEKS WERE HECTIC. IN THE ABSENCE OF HIS father's charts, Atrus drew up detailed maps of the harborside districts, then divided his young helpers into teams of six. Two of those teams, led by Marrim and Irras, went out into the streets and alleyways of lower D'ni to search for Books; another, under Carrad, began the task of raising the sunken boats from the floor of the harbor and repairing them; and a fourth, headed by Catherine, went back and forth between the harbor and K'veer, bringing back food and supplies from Chroma'Agana and Averone. The fifth team, supervised by Atrus himself, began the job of clearing a storehouse for whatever Books were found, while he, in whatever spare moments remained, worked on maps of D'ni.

At first progress was slow. There were few big houses in the lower levels, and thus few private Book Rooms, and they quickly discovered that the public Book Rooms had already been plundered by Gehn and most of the Guild Books destroyed, just as Atrus had feared. Even so, by the end of the second week they had a total of thirty-four Books. Finished with the maps, Atrus began the task of reading and cataloging them.

Marrim, returning from a long and fruitless search of the Ne'weril district, went in to see Atrus, who was sitting at his makeshift desk in the storehouse.

"Forgive me, Master Atrus," she began, "but why are we waiting?"

"Waiting?"

"To begin the search of the Ages."

He smiled tolerantly. "I understand your enthusiasm, Marrim, but this is not something to be rushed. We need to have some idea of the scale of the venture before embarking upon it. Meanwhile there is much to do here. We have to build up a stock of blank Linking Books, and ink and writing materials. Unless you know a way of returning from an Age *without* a Linking Book?"

A faint color came to Marrim's cheeks. She bowed her head.

"Let us gather in every Book we can find," Atrus went on. "*Then* we can decide which to visit. You see, some of the Books are damaged, Marrim. Pages are missing or have been torn or burned. Others are clearly old and I'd guess were little used by their owners, even though they bear the Maintainer's inspection stamp. What we need to find are newer, more healthy Ages, for it is in those that we are most likely to find our survivors."

"And have we found any such Ages yet?"

"Two. But it might well turn out that the Books we find in these lower districts were all visited—and corrupted—by Veovis and his ally. It may be that only those from more distant, higher districts remained untouched. That is why I am taking great care to mark on the maps where each Book was found and the circumstances of its discovery. Such details might prove crucial when we come to organize the next stage of our search."

"Then ought we not to be searching the higher districts first?"

Atrus laughed. "Is that what you wish to do, young Marrim?"

She nodded.

"Then that is what you *shall* do." He turned and searched among the papers on his desk until he located one of the maps he had finished only the day before. "Here," he said, handing it to her, "this is where my grandfather and his family once lived. Jaren was a Guild district. If there are Books anywhere, they will be there. But take supplies enough for several days, Marrim, unless you fancy trekking back down to the harbor every night."

"And you, Master Atrus? Won't you come with us this once?"

He stared at her, surprised by her request, then nodded. "Perhaps I will come along. This once."

THOUGH HE HAD BEEN ON MANY BOOK SEARCHES WITH HIS
father, Atrus had never stood within these walls, never walked among these
strangely familiar rooms, and now that he did he wondered just why Gehn
had not brought him here.

Anna. That was why. It reminded Gehn too much of Anna.

He walked on, aware for the first time in his life just how strong the
connection was between himself and this ancient place. A connection of
blood. And though he was only one part in four D'ni, that did not dilute
what he felt.

No wonder Gehn became obsessed.

"Atrus?"

He turned to find Marrim watching him.

"This was my grandfather's room," he said quietly, indicating the desk,
the walls of books. "And *his* father's before him."

She nodded, then: "We've found the Book Room."

"Ah . . ." He steeled himself against bad news. "And?"

"There's a Book."

"Just one?"

Marrim nodded.

Atrus was silent a moment. His grandfather, Aitrus, had been the owner
of two Ages. One, Ko'ah, had been handed down over eight generations, and
was the family retreat. The other, Gemedet, named after the complex three-
dimensional game played by the D'ni, had been written by him and the ahrotahntee, or "outworlder," who in time had become his grandmother, Anna.

The Book Room was downstairs. The door of the room was smashed,
the shelves on the walls ransacked long ago. The faint yellow-brown residue
that was everywhere in D'ni, and that he had always assumed was natural to
the place, here lay thick upon everything.

On a podium in the center of the room a Book lay open, the faint ghost of a palm print over the dulled descriptive panel. He went across and stood, his hands gripping the edge of the podium as he stared down at the page.

Ko'ah. This was the Book of Ko'ah.

Of course. He remembered now. His grandfather, Aitrus, had taken the other Book with him when he'd returned here after the fall of D'ni, so that Veovis could not get to Anna and the child.

Atrus looked up, feeling giddy. The long years seemed to wash over him, as if, in that instant, he *was* his grandfather.

"Are you all right?" Marrim asked, concerned for him.

"Yes."

But that wasn't entirely true. For a moment he had glimpsed his grandmother, Anna, in her final illness, Catherine by her bedside, the old lady's pale, flecked hands caged within Catherine's younger, stronger fingers, and recalled what she had told him then about those final days. And as he recalled that moment he felt a strong, almost violent urge to *see* Ko'ah, to link to it and see with his own eyes where his father, Gehn, was born; where Anna had nursed him through that first, almost fatal illness.

He raised his hand over the page, shadowing the ghostly imprint.

"Master Atrus?"

Atrus looked up, startled from his reverie. If he had moved his hand the tiniest bit it would have brushed the surface of the page. Reaching across, he closed the Book, then turned, looking at Marrim. "You'd best look after this."

Atrus stepped back as Marrim came across and, taking the long-handled cutters from her belt, snipped the chain that connected the Book to the podium. He watched her carefully lift the Book and slip it into her knapsack with that same reverence he had seen her exhibit with all the Books.

Marrim turned to face him again, smiling, ever enthusiastic, her pale, oval face framed by the vivid blackness of her long, thick braided hair. "Where now?"

"Let's leave here," he answered her, looking about him one last time. "Let's go and find the others."

IRRAS PAUSED IN THE SHADOWED HALLWAY, FROWNING. Something was different. And then he understood. The colors. The colors here were brighter, more vivid.

He realized with a start what it meant.

Reaching out, he touched the wall, then drew his fingers back, sniffing at them. Clean. The wall was clean.

Irras spun around, holding his lamp out. "Gavas! Meer! Come quickly! I think we've found something!"

They rushed up, then looked about them, puzzled.

"What?" Meer asked. "What have you found?"

"Look about you," Irras answered, amused now. "What do you notice that's different?"

It was Gavas who saw it first. "The walls . . . the floor . . . they're *clean!*"

Irras nodded. "And if they're clean, what does *that* mean?"

"That someone's . . . cleaned it?" Meer offered. And then his mouth fell open.

"Exactly!" Irras said, beaming now. "Someone's been here before us. Someone must have come here and *cleaned* the walls and floors." He half-turned, lifting the lamp high once more. Everywhere they looked it was clean.

"Go back," he said, gesturing to Gavas. "Find Master Atrus and bring him here at once. He'll want to see this for himself!"

THAT NIGHT ATRUS CALLED A SPECIAL MEETING. WHEN ALL were gathered, he came out into their midst, the Book they had found in the great house in Jaren—the Book of Bilaris, as it was called—under his arm. He looked about him and smiled.

"So?" Catherine asked, preempting him. "Are we going to visit this Age?"

Atrus smiled. "Yes. But not yet. First I need to study the Book more carefully."

"But what about the signs?" Catherine said. "The cleanliness of the house, the book of commentaries we found . . . there are D'ni in that Age."

"That may be so," Atrus conceded, "but for the sake of three or four days, I'd rather be certain all is well. Remember, caution is *everything*. For the lack of caution, D'ni fell. We must not make the same mistake. In all likelihood, the people on this Age—on Bilaris—are survivors from the fall. And from the cleanliness of the house, it would seem that they share our aspirations; they, too, would like to see D'ni rebuilt to its former glory. But . . . just as D'ni fell, so might many of these Ages have fallen. We do not know. Seventy years is a long time, even for a D'ni. Much can change in that time."

He paused, looking about him again. "Then so it shall be. I shall prepare a Linking Book. Four days from now, we will link through. Myself, Marrim, Irras, and Meer. Catherine will stay here with Carrad, in case anything goes wrong."

"And in the meantime, Master Atrus?" Carrad asked.

"The work goes on," Atrus answered him. "There are Books to be found, boats to be repaired, quarters to be built."

"And food to be eaten," Carrad said, reminding Atrus that they had not yet had supper.

Atrus laughed, for the first time that day relaxing. "Trust young Carrad to think of his stomach at such a time!"

Carrad feigned a hurt expression, but like all there, he knew they had taken a huge step forward, and as Atrus looked about the circle, he saw how each face mirrored that same realization.

Survivors! Cautious as he was, Atrus, too, believed they would find them in Bilaris. There were D'ni in the Ages. They had only to be patient now and they would find them!

THAT NIGHT CATHERINE AND ATRUS DECIDED TO RETURN TO Chroma'Agana. Catherine had been back several times, but for Atrus it would be the first time since they had set up camp in D'ni, six weeks before.

Rowing across the dark and silent lake, he watched the city slowly recede, its details blurring into the great wall of rock, and felt himself relax.

K'veer was silent, empty. Lighting a lamp, they made their way up the great twist of ancient steps and into his father's study where the Linking Book awaited them. There, Atrus hesitated.

"What?" Catherine asked, amused. She knew that look.

In answer he went across to the shelves beside the desk and took down his father's notebook, slipping it into his knapsack, which already held the Book of Bilaris, the book of commentary, two blank Linking Books, a pot of special D'ni ink, and a pen.

"You need to rest . . ." Catherine began.

"And I *shall* rest," he said, tightening the cord, then throwing the bag over his shoulder again. "But I also have to work. We're close now, Catherine."

"I know. But you must ease off. You'll be ill."

Atrus laughed. "For a moment you sounded just like Anna. . . ."

He fell silent, realizing just how true that was. Why, if he closed his eyes, he could see in memory the two of them standing together under the trees on Myst island, more like mother and daughter than two strangers from separate worlds.

Long ago that memory, for Anna had been dead for nearly thirty years.

Shadows, he thought, surprised by how fresh her loss still seemed. *How strange that the past could cast such deep shadows on the future.*

Shaking off the mood, he stepped across and, with a smiling glance at Catherine, placed his palm upon the open page.

ATRUS LIT THE FIRE, THEN STRAIGHTENED. THROUGH THE OPEN door of the cabin he could see the moonlit lawn, edged by tall Oreadoran oaks, and, through the trees, the sea like a sheet of shimmering, beaten metal, stretching away into infinity.

It was a beautiful night. The kind of night that made Atrus feel young again; as young as when he'd first met Catherine. So it was whenever he returned here after a long absence.

Catherine was in the library at the far end of the island. She had gone there almost as soon as they'd arrived, the Book of Bilaris under her arm, while Atrus, who had given his solemn word that he would rest, had sat upon the shore, barefoot, staring out into the distance as the sun went down and the tide slowly ebbed.

He stepped outside, into the freshness of the night, then turned to look along the rocky spine of the island, his vision traveling along the narrow path toward the long, low shape of the library and the workshops and laboratories beyond, the connected buildings climbing the gentle slope of the hillside like steps, the textured stone a silvered gray beneath the moon.

He was tempted to call out to Catherine and ask her to come and walk with him, but he knew that she did not like to be disturbed when she was working. In that she was like him. Even so, he began to walk in that direction, hoping that perhaps she would look up and see him and, setting aside her work, come out and join him under the open sky.

Looking about him he realized just how much he loved this place. Its peacefulness spoke to the depths of him. Its sounds were like the sounds of his own body. Here he felt complete.

Yes, and it was strange how he needed to go away before he realized that.

It was like Catherine. All those months of separation had, he knew now, been necessary. To teach him her worth.

Atrus looked up at the night sky, wondering, not for the first time, just *when* he was. From his studies of the star charts in the observatory, he had worked out that he was in a very different part of the galaxy from the planet he knew as Earth—or its equivalent—if one even existed in this Age. But it was more difficult to tell just how far he was from it in time, for when one linked there were no limits. The mind-staggering vastnesses of Time and Space were irrelevant. *Congruity*—the matching of word and place—was all that mattered.

Or, as his grandfather, Aitrus, had explained it to his grandmother, Anna: "These Ages are worlds that do exist, or have existed, or shall. Providing the description fits, there is no limitation of time and space. The link is made regardless."

Atrus stopped, a smile lighting his features as he remembered how young Marrim's face had filled with wonder when he had first explained it to her. And still, when he thought of it—when he really thought about it—he would feel that same wonder fill him. It was an astonishing ability to possess. Little wonder that his father, freed from the restraints of D'ni society and lacking the true humility of his D'ni peers, had thought himself some kind of god. It was clear now why Anna had taught him as she had—avoiding the same mistake she had made with Gehn.

Careful not to make the same mistake, his first lesson to his own students—to Marrim and Irras and Carrad and all their fellows—was this: One did not *make* the Ages to which the words linked. A far greater force than the D'ni had made those, yet it was easy to be deluded into thinking so, for the universe was so vast, so all-encompassing, so infinite in its variety of worlds, that almost anything one wrote had its counterpart in reality.

Unstable worlds. Worlds that were living hells. Or the beautiful, "impossible" worlds that Catherine once wrote.

Moving past the Eye Pool, Atrus swiftly climbed the grassy slope until he stopped, not ten yards from the door to the library. The door was open, and from where he stood in the darkness, he could see Catherine, seated behind the great oak desk, the Book open before her, one finger tracing the lines of D'ni symbols as she read.

Atrus smiled and walked on, taking the path that led round to the right, past the side of the library and out onto the cliff path. Ahead of him the great Anchor Rock was a shadow against the greater darkness of the sky. Beyond it lay a thousand miles of emptiness.

He walked out onto the pale stone, the sea fifty feet below him, the great muscular shape of the Anchor Rock above him and to his left. Standing there, he thought of his father and of the notebook they had found in the study on K'veer. It had told him little that he did not already know or suspect, yet, reading Gehn's words at this distance from events, he had, against all expectation, been impressed by his father's intellect, and had found himself wondering what Gehn might have become had D'ni *not* fallen. And that thought had spawned others. Was it *really* Gehn's fault that he had become what he'd become? The destruction of his hopes at such an impressionable age had clearly traumatized the boy, yet could everything be accounted for by that? What of the cruelty in his father, that *twisted* aspect of Gehn? Was that a product of events, or was it something natural in the child that, through circumstance, had been encouraged rather than controlled?

It was impossible to say. All he knew was that he himself had been lucky. Lucky to have had Anna during those formative years of his upbringing— to have been taught by so good and wise a teacher.

And then there were his own sons . . .

He pushed the thought aside, then turned, hearing soft footsteps just behind him.

"Catherine?"

"Let's go," she said. "Tonight."

"Tonight?" He laughed, then turned slightly, looking at her. "But I haven't written the Linking Book yet."

Her face, silvered in the moonlight, was smiling strangely. "No. But I have." And she handed him the slender book, enjoying his surprise.

THEY LINKED TO A LARGE ISLAND, THREE-QUARTERS COVERED in forest. There was a clearing beside the cave and a path led down between the trees, but otherwise there was no immediate sign of habitation.

It was mid-morning by the look of the sun in the sky, and it was warm with the suggestion that, as day drew on, it might grow hot.

They quickly searched the cave, looking for a Linking Book, but found nothing.

Now they went down, following the footworn path. Leaf shadow kept them cool as they went, but even so, by the time they reached the clifftop they were beaded with perspiration. A perfect, white sand beach lay thirty feet below them.

"It's beautiful," Catherine said, looking out across the scattering of islands that lay like emeralds upon the azure of the bay. "But where are they?"

There were no buildings. No boats or jetties. Nothing but the path to suggest anyone had ever been here.

A bird called from high up in the trees. Atrus turned and looked up at it, putting a hand up to shield his lenses from the sunlight that glittered on their surfaces.

"Let's try the other end."

They walked back, taking their time, relaxing in the sunlight. Passing the clearing once more, they went on, leaving the path, winding their way between the great, straight boles of the trees until they stood on a shelf of bare rock, overlooking a vast expanse of ocean.

"This can't be right."

"Why not?" she asked, turning to look back through the trees. "It conforms with the Book."

"I didn't mean that. I mean, where are they? They have to be here somewhere. It makes no sense unless they are."

"Then let's search the island."

But a long and thorough search of the island found nothing. The island was uninhabited. Even the path, now that they looked properly at it, was partly overgrown.

"Maybe it's the wrong Book," Catherine suggested, sitting down wearily on a rock overlooking the island-scattered bay. It was hot now and she fanned herself slowly as she looked up at Atrus.

"It's possible," he answered, stepping up onto the ledge above her, "but then what about the book of commentary?"

"A false trail? To make us think they were here?"

"But why?"

"Because they were afraid. And because they wanted to safeguard where they really are?"

"I suppose it's possible." But Atrus's eyes stared out at the perfect, un-spoiled shapes of the islands as if to decipher some mystery. He wiped the back of his hand across his brow, then turned to her again.

"Let's get back," he said. "There's nothing for us here."

IT WAS SAID THAT THE GREAT KING WAS HAUNTED BY DREAMS, and that those dreams were filled with strange, inexplicable visions that the Great King then wrote down in a large notebook bound in bright golden leather. Or so Atrus's father, Gehn, had written. But Marrim knew better than to trust what Gehn had written. She had heeded Atrus's warning to her when Catherine had lent her the notebooks: *"My father had the tendency to twist facts to suit his vision of the world."* Even so, she could picture it vividly: the old man waking, his brow beaded with sweat, his hands trembling as he reached out to write down what he had seen in the darkness of his dreams.

Even if it wasn't true. Even if, like much that was in Gehn's notebooks, it had been exaggerated down the years, there must still have been a core of truth; some story, some actual event, that had spawned all of the subsequent tales about the Great King, like the speck of grit in an oyster shell about which the pearl subsequently grows.

Marrim closed the book and looked up. Lamps blazed about the camp. Just across from her, Irras and Carrad sat facing each other, Irras's dark head pressed close to Carrad's polished skull, the two of them deep in conversation, while a number of other helpers looked on, listening attentively. She knew exactly what they were talking about, for there was really only one topic of conversation at the moment. The visit. The upcoming trip to Bilaris.

She smiled. Like all of them, she was excited by the prospect of venturing into another Age. D'ni was astonishing, certainly, but partly because it was also a gateway to so many other worlds, so many other ways of living. She glanced across at the great stock of Books that were piled up in Atrus's makeshift library and felt her head swim at the thought of what they were.

She had been blind to the reality of the universe surrounding her. She had thought her tiny world—that world of lodge house and fishing boats, of hill and stream and island—the sum total of existence. But now she knew. Whatever it was possible to imagine *could* exist.

In theory, anyway.

Marrim stood, then walked across, remembering her conversations with Catherine; recollecting what Catherine had said about the Books *she* had written. They must have been something to see.

As she came closer to the circle, Irras looked up and smiled at her, indicating that she should take a seat beside him, but she did not feel like sitting down. She felt restless. Eager to get on.

Resting her hand briefly on his shoulder, she walked on, leaving the young men to their talk. At the harbor's edge she paused, staring out across the darkness of the lake.

At first she wasn't sure. Then, with a huge grin of delight, she turned to the others.

"They're coming!"

Irras hurried across and stood beside her, squinting out into the darkness, until he, too, made out the dark shape of the boat. Moment by moment that shape grew larger, clearer. Catherine turned in the prow and, seeing them, hailed them across the water.

Marrim answered, her voice echoing back from the great levels of stone that climbed the cavern walls behind her.

She knew almost at once that something was wrong. She could see it in Atrus's face. Catherine was as cheerful as ever, but Atrus was withdrawn.

As he climbed up onto the quayside, Atrus beckoned Irras, then, without waiting for him, turned and walked over to the makeshift library, disappearing inside.

Irras was with Atrus barely two minutes. When he emerged, he was frowning, as if he'd been told something he didn't want to hear. He brushed past Marrim as if she wasn't there. She turned, meaning to follow him, but Atrus called out to her.

"Marrim! A word . . ."

She went inside.

"Here," he said, glancing up and holding out a folded piece of paper. "You'll need provisions for a week."

Marrim unfolded the paper, then looked back at him. It was a map of one of the upper districts.

"There's still a lot to be done," Atrus said, "so we'd best get down to it. I want all the Books collected in."

She understood. They weren't going. The trip to Bilaris had been canceled.

"We must complete the search," Atrus said, opening his notebook and reaching for a pen. "Only then will we know the full extent of our task."

"We'll go tonight," she said.

He looked up at her. "It's all right, Marrim. Tomorrow will do."

Marrim nodded, then backed away, but it was only when she was standing outside, the paper held loosely in one hand, that it really hit her.

We aren't going. After all that, we're not going!

There was a moment of disappointment, and then Marrim looked at the map again and her determination was reborn. They would find all of the Books there were to find. And among them there would be Books that worked—that linked to functional Ages. And in those Ages, surely, there would be survivors.

But first it was up to her to find the Books.

Marrim slipped the map into her pocket. Tomorrow? Forget "tomorrow." She would gather her team together and begin the search tonight.

PART TWO

A BURROWING WORM BLINKS IN THE SUNLIGHT

AND PULLS HIS EYES DOWN OVER HIS EYES.

EARTH'S MOUTH STEAMS. DEEP VOICES GRUMBLE.

TIME DRAWS A JAGGED LINE UPON THE SAND

IN WHICH THE WOMAN WAITS.

—FROM THE KOROKH JIMAH, VV. 21660–64

THE BROAD LEATHER SPINES WERE OLD BUT WELL CARED for, the blues and reds, the blacks and yellows and greens of the ancient Books embossed with D'ni symbols that were faded yet still readable. Row after row of them crowded the shelves of the storeroom, overspilling into a second great room: 787 Books in total—all that remained of the tens of thousands that had once graced the great houses and common libraries of D'ni.

Two large desks had been pushed together in one corner of the newly added room, on which were stacked a huge pile of Kortee'nea—blank Books—they had unearthed, to their astonishment, beneath the fallen stones of one of the common libraries.

Seated at one of those desks, his head down, patiently toiling into the night, Atrus was unaware of Catherine's approach until he felt her hands upon his shoulders.

"Haven't you finished yet, my love?"

"Two more lines," he said, indicating the Linking Book he had been working on, "and then I'm done."

To one side of him, beyond the ink stand and the glowing orange lamp, was a small pile of Linking Books—five in all—that he had prepared already.

It was four months since their trip to Bilaris and they had all worked hard. All of the Books were gathered in—yes, and cataloged and read. The six most likely had been selected by Atrus and Catherine, after a long and sometimes heated debate, and now they were almost—*almost*—ready to go.

A month back, belatedly fulfilling his promise to the elders of Averone, Atrus had sent his young helpers home, to teach the new generation, taking the time, in their absence, to make his final preparations.

Tomorrow they would return, and a new phase of the reconstruction—a painstaking search of the Ages—would begin.

"You have the draft letter?" Catherine asked, easing past him to sit on the edge of the desk.

Atrus reached across and, rifling among his papers, came up with a single sheet. He handed it across, then watched as Catherine quickly read it through.

She looked back at him. "That should do."

"You don't think it too formal, then?"

"No. It has the right tone, I'd say. Dignified without being self-important."

He laughed at that. The letter was an introduction of sorts, as well as being a statement of intent. And when his teams went into the Ages, they would each take copies of the letter, ready to present, if and when they made contact with survivors.

"I'll make some copies, then," he said, taking it back from her, "and seal them using my grandfather's ring."

Catherine stared at him a moment, then, changing the subject, said, "You've missed her, haven't you?"

Atrus hesitated, then nodded. They were talking, as ever, of Marrim. "It's strange, Catherine. Marrim was always so quick, so enthusiastic, but something's changed since we came here. She's grown."

"Hungry children grow when fed," Catherine said, covering his hand with her own. "You should begin teaching her. That copy of the *Rehevkor* we found. . . . You should give it to her, Atrus."

The *Rehevkor* was the ancient D'ni lexicon; the principle teaching tool for D'ni children. Atrus himself had learned the D'ni language from it.

"You think so? You think she's ready?"

Catherine grinned. "She was ready months ago. But first things first. Finish the Linking Book, then come and get some sleep. Tomorrow will be a long day."

STEPPING THROUGH THE OPEN DOORWAY, MARRIM STARED INTO the shadows of the schoolroom. Through the windows on the far side she could see the bay, the sun setting over the water. In an hour she would be gone. To Chroma'Agana, and thence to D'ni.

And then?

The thought of going—of visiting the Ages—thrilled her, yet at the same time she felt a deep regret that she had to leave here. Before now it had been easy, for there had been nothing for her here—except, of course, her family—but this last time things had changed. Now she had a reason to come back.

Marrim walked to the desk at the front of the room. It had all been crudely, hastily fashioned, to the orders of the elders, yet it had served its purpose well. A hundred or more children had crowded into this room by the end, eager to hear her and learn from her. And she, for her part, had been as eager to teach them.

It had been a wonderful four weeks, all told, yet now that it was over she found that she had missed Atrus and Catherine, missed them more than she cared to say. With them *she* was the pupil.

She grinned, remembering those smiling, eager faces crowded into the room in front of her, the sea of enthusiastic hands, the openmouthed wonder as she told them stories about the D'ni.

Maybe that had been wrong, for her brief from the elders was to teach them useful skills—reading and writing and the use of numbers—but it would have been lean fare indeed had she not seasoned it with tales.

She smoothed her hands over the surface of the desk, then, knowing she had come here for a purpose, crouched down and began to take her things from the drawers, slipping them into her knapsack.

Last of all she removed her journal from the bottom drawer, pausing a moment to open it and read the last few entries. She had noticed how Atrus wrote everything down, keeping a daily record of events, but she had never thought to do the same until two months back, when, on a search of one of the midlevel houses, she had come upon an unused notebook. Since then, she had made the time each evening to set down her thoughts about the day's activities, to *reflect* on what she'd done. And now that she did, she understood the purpose of it. If she were a boat, making her way across life's water, then the journal was her compass. It let her steer her course. For how could she know where she was going without a reference to where she'd been.

Which made it only all the more curious that Atrus's father, Gehn, had not seen that. Reading his journals, she had found it strange how little Gehn had reflected on the world about him. Gehn's was not, as she understood it, a true intellectual curiosity, he was interested only in forcing the world to fit his first conception of it: a conception warped by his youthful experiences and the unbridled power of the art of writing.

Marrim closed the notebook and slipped it into the sack, then looked about her again. Even in the last few minutes the shadows in the room had deepened. In a moment the sun would sink below the horizon and it would be night. And she would be gone from here again.

She had already said her good-byes, her mother clutching her tearfully, her father taking her hands and squeezing them—as much emotion in that as in all her mother's embraces. Now Irras and Carrad awaited her at the clearing in the wood. But still she stood there, reluctant to leave while one shred of light remained.

At such moments there was no logic to events; one had to go with the feeling.

The sun's last light threw a bar of red across the open doorway to her right. Into that light now stepped a child. A young girl.

Marrim blinked, as if she had imagined it, but the child was still there, looking across at her, the dying light reflected in the moist pools of her eyes.

"*Allem?*"

Allem slowly came across. From close up Marrim could see she had been crying.

"You will come back, won't you, Marrim?"

Marrim knelt, embracing her. "Of course I will."

"You promise?"

THE BOOK OF D'NI • 55

"I promise. Now go. Your father will be angry if he knows you are here."

The girl nodded but did not pull away. "I had to come. You've meant so much to us."

Marrim sniffed. "And you . . . I enjoyed teaching you. You were good pupils. You made it easy for me."

The girl looked up. "Can I come with you?"

"Come?" Marrim went to shake her head, but Allem spoke again.

"I don't mean now. I mean later. When I'm grown up."

Again Marrim made to shake her head, but then, relenting, she nodded. "Yes, Allem. When you're older."

ATRUS AND CATHERINE WERE IN THE LIBRARY ON CHROMA'- Agana to greet them, as first Irras, and then Carrad, and finally Marrim linked through.

"Well . . ." he said, stepping back. "All is prepared. When the teams link through we can begin."

The other team members would arrive tonight, but Atrus had wanted his team leaders back earlier to brief them.

"Which Ages did you finally chose, Master Atrus?" Irras asked. He had helped Atrus catalog the Ages.

"Six in all," Atrus answered. "I've chosen old worlds to begin with. Family Ages of some solidity."

"Will we be using the Maintainers' suit?" Carrad asked.

"Not this time," Atrus said, yet he glanced at Catherine as he did so, as if this had been a topic of debate between them.

They linked through to K'veer. There Gavas awaited them with a boat. Marrim greeted him, then took her seat in the stern, staring past the overhang of rock into the cavern beyond.

As they rowed out under the ledge and onto the lake, Marrim glanced at

Atrus and, seeing him watching her, looked away, smiling to herself. It was so good to see him again. So good to be back. She had enjoyed her spell teaching, but this was her real work. *This* was where she belonged.

That morning's briefings were long and highly detailed. Atrus was leaving nothing to chance. He had prepared information for each of the team leaders, giving them details of the terrain, the names of the families who had owned the Ages, and, as a precaution, basic points of D'ni etiquette. Last of all he handed them copies of the letter of introduction he had penned. Marrim stared at hers a moment, studying the dark green seal that had the imprint of a D'ni letter at its center, then slipped it into her jacket pocket.

The afternoon was spent in preparation, making up backpacks for each team member, with all-weather clothes and sufficient food. It had been decided that they would camp out in the Ages, if necessary, with one team member remaining at the link point, ready to get a message back to D'ni at a moment's notice.

"I don't expect trouble," Atrus said, explaining the decision, "but we had best prepare for it."

Even so, he would not let them take any weapons into the Ages. Their intentions were peaceful, and should the worst come to the worst and they were taken prisoner and searched, he did not want their captors finding anything upon them that might suggest otherwise.

"The Ages themselves are harmless. The Maintainers were careful to ensure that. And the survivors, if there are any, will undoubtedly be D'ni. They may not welcome you at first, but they will certainly not harm you."

THEY SLEPT THAT NIGHT IN D'NI. IN THE MORNING THEY ROSE early, while the lake was still dark, and gathered in the space before the makeshift library.

A month previously, Atrus had had them carry down six of the big stone pedestals from one of the common libraries. These were now spaced out along the harbor front. A lamp had been set up above each, to illuminate the tilted lecterns on which lay the open Books, their descriptive panels glowing softly.

At a word from Atrus, the six teams of four lined up before their respective pedestals.

Atrus looked down the line of tense, nervous faces. Then, without a further word, he placed his hand against the panel and linked.

In less than a minute it was done. They stepped up, one by one, to the lecterns and disappeared, like ghosts vanishing into the air, leaving the harbor front empty, even as the lake began to glow with the faint light of morning.

MARRIM STOOD AT THE CENTER OF THE DESERTED VILLAGE AND looked about her, her vision darkened. It was six hours now and they had found no sign of life. The plague, it seemed, had taken them all.

The first sign of it had been in the cave. There, in a heap upon the floor beside the Linking Book, they had found two skeletons, their bones intertwined, their cloaks, rotted by damp, tearing like spiders' webs beneath her touch.

Veovis, she thought, and in her mind she saw Veovis and A'Gaeris, masked, their own hands gloved to protect them from contagion, placing the palms of the dead men onto the Book.

It was horrifying, yet it had been as nothing beside the other sights she'd witnessed. She had gone inside one hut only to find a whole family—mother, father, and their two young children—wiped out, their bones stretched out on the rotting mattress, their fleshless fingers linked in death.

That small, tender sign of affection in the midst of this horror had unhinged her momentarily. Until then she had been able to harden herself against it, to remind herself that this was what Atrus had warned them might await them. But *that* . . .

The disappointment seared her. She had not realized just how much of herself she had gambled on this venture.

"Lerral! Allef!" she called, stirring herself.

She watched the two young men step from the big meetinghouse at the far end of the central space, and saw at once the darkness in their eyes.

"Come," she said, walking over to them. "Let's go. There's nothing here for us."

SIX WORLDS AND NOT A SINGLE SURVIVOR.

Atrus had wanted to go back—to pack fresh provisions and have another, more thorough search of those two Ages where they had found nothing at all, not even bones—but Catherine had persuaded him against it.

"Never mind," Atrus concluded, when all else had been said. "We'll try again. We are certain to be more successful next time round. This time, I'll just check one."

"Yes. We need something to raise their spirits, Atrus. They're feeling very despondent."

"This one, I think." Atrus showed her the cover. It was the Book of Aurack. "It looks as likely as any other. I'll write our link back tonight. Tell Marrim and Carrad they can come with us. Oh, and Meer and Gavas, too. We'll take six through this time. It'll speed the search."

Catherine leaned across, kissing him on his bearded cheek. "Good. The news will cheer them."

"IS EVERYONE READY?"

Atrus looked from face to face, his eyes questioning theirs. Then, satisfied with what he'd seen, he smiled and placed his hand against the glowing panel.

Aurack was hot. Stepping out from the linking cave, Marrim raised her hand to her brow instinctively, shielding her eyes against the sun's fierce glare. Atrus was up ahead of her, standing on the edge of the escarpment, his special D'ni lenses pulled down over his eyes, their surfaces opaqued.

"Empty," he said as Catherine stepped up beside him.

"It only *looks* empty," she answered him. "Why, you could hide a hundred villages in that."

He glanced at her, conscious of the others listening. "Do you think that's what they've done?"

"It's possible. After what happened to D'ni, it would make sense to take precautions."

"Maybe," he conceded, "but how are we going to find them?"

Marrim, coming up onto the ledge, saw at once what Atrus meant. What lay below them, covering the landscape from horizon to horizon, was no wood as she had experienced it on Averone, but a forest, a thousand square miles or more of densely packed trees; an ocean of green in which you could hide forever and never be found.

"Why don't we light a fire?" she said.

Atrus looked at her. "If all else fails, we shall. But if they're here, I suspect they'll not have gone too far from the linking cave. They would want to know if anyone came through into their Age."

"You mean to make a physical search of that?" Catherine asked, gesturing toward the great sprawl of the forest.

"Only part of it. Once we've made our search for the Linking Book, we'll split up. Each take a small section of it."

"What if someone gets lost?"

But Atrus had thought of that. He'd packed special dye-markers in every knapsack. They were to use these to mark the trees they passed.

"To prevent confusion, I've given each of you a different color." He turned, looking at the three young men. "Carrad and Meer, you'll take part in the first sweep. Gavas, you can be our anchor man here on the escarpment. If anything goes wrong, send up a fire flare."

Gavas nodded, hiding his disappointment well.

"Good. Then we'll concentrate our search on this side first. There's a river down there—you can see it winking between the trees—so that might be a good site for an encampment. We can make our way down, then split up on the riverbank."

Atrus looked about him. "First, however, let's spread out and search this area. The Linking Book, if there is one, ought to be somewhere nearby."

THE RIVER WAS A BROAD BAND OF GREEN, GLIMPSED BETWEEN the straight dark boles of the trees off to the left. Out there, on the river's bank, it was swelteringly hot, swarms of exotic insects feasting on anything or anyone who strayed near, but here, beneath the branches of the trees, it was much cooler, the insect life less voracious.

Marrim paused to spray the bole of a tree, then turned, looking about her. The forest was alive with sounds, with the buzz of insects, the endless cries of birds, and the rustle of unseen creatures as they hastened away from her approach.

Even though it was much cooler here, it was still humid, and Marrim stopped frequently to mop her brow, her clothes sticking to her uncomfortably. It never got this hot on Averone, even during the dry season, and that, as much as the alien life-forms, was beginning to get to her. It was an hour since they had split up at the river, and she had seen nothing at all to indicate that there was any kind of intelligent life in this Age. But each time she thought that, she reminded herself of what it had looked like from the escarpment—how huge an area it was they were searching—and she felt her-self spurred on again.

She had grown used to the way the ground beneath her gave with each step, a thousand years of leaf fall forming a thick, dry carpet of mold be-neath her feet. She had even grown used to the strange quality of the light beneath the leaf canopy, its pellucid greenness that had at first made her think herself at the bottom of some great ocean.

Marrim scratched at her arm. The bites were heavily swollen and formed a small mountain range of red blotches from her exposed elbow to her wrist. She smiled now, but at the time she had thought they were going to eat her alive!

They had known that Aurack was a big, primitive world, but it was strange that Atrus hadn't mentioned the insects. Then again, his briefing hadn't mentioned a thing about the heat, either, so maybe they had come at an exceptional time—at the height of a hot season, perhaps, or in the midst of a heat wave. But somehow she wasn't convinced. Nothing here looked as if it didn't belong in this heat. This was quite clearly a tropical environment.

She moved on, marking her way as she went, then stopped, whirling about 180 degrees. There had been a cry: a high, inarticulate screech.

Hurrying, she began to make her way back the way she'd come, follow-ing the trail of marked trees.

Carrad and Catherine were waiting at the meeting point beside the river as she half ran, half walked toward them. Atrus arrived a moment later.

"Who was it?" he asked, looking from one to the other for an explana-tion.

"I thought it was you," Catherine said, puzzled now.

Atrus turned, looking back into the trees. "Where's Meer?"

They heard a crashing in the trees. Relieved, Carrad laughed. "Here he comes now!"

But the crashing stopped as suddenly as it had begun, and in the silence that followed, there was no sound of anyone making their way toward them.

"Let's go," Catherine said, touching Atrus's hand. "His is the blue trail. It should be fairly easy to follow."

They went in again, more cautiously now, Atrus leading them, Carrad at the back, his shaven head moving this way and that as he surveyed the jungle close at hand.

The trail snaked inward, then followed a dip in the land down into a hollow. There, abruptly, it ended, in the middle of a small clearing.

Insects buzzed and whined in the sultry heat.

Atrus went from tree to tree, then stopped, looking about him, perplexed.

Marrim bent down and picked something up. It was a piece of torn cloth. At first she didn't understand, then it hit her. She held it against her own cloak. The match was perfect.

"Atrus . . ."

She handed him the piece of cloth and watched as his eyes registered its significance.

"He may have snagged it against something," Atrus said, meeting her eyes. But that wasn't what he was thinking.

"Here!" Carrad said, from the far side of the clearing. "It looks like something was dragged through the bushes at this point."

They went across, the four of them standing there, staring silently at the broken branches.

Something had *been dragged through the bushes.*

Turning back, Marrim began to see things she had missed first time round. The way the ground seemed churned up on one side of the clearing. She walked over, then stooped, poking here and there with her fingers.

A wet stickiness greeted her. She raised her hand and gasped. Blood! Her fingers were covered in blood that had seeped down through the leaves.

Catherine, standing next to her, knelt down and took her hand, turning it and studying it.

"Meer?" Atrus called, cupping his hands and yelling into the thick undergrowth beyond the clearing. "*Meer?* Where are you?"

But there was no answer. Nothing but the flap of wings and the high, plaintive call of a hidden bird.

ARMED, ATRUS AND CARRAD HAD LINKED BACK TO AURACK AND returned to the clearing, working their way through the undergrowth, following the trail of broken branches until they had come out beside a waterfall. There, in the mud at the edge of the stream that ran away from the fall, were tracks.

The tracks of something large.

Wary, they followed the trail down the narrow valley until they came upon what they had feared they would find: fragments of Meer's torn and bloody clothes. Of Meer there was no sign, but the tracks led on, and there were clear indications that the beast had settled here to make his meal before moving on, dragging its prize with it.

Carrad, seeing the sight, had crouched and groaned, utterly distraught. But Atrus had merely stood and looked, his pale eyes carrying the full weight of his grief.

"Come," he said at last. "Let's go back."

Back in D'ni, Atrus got out the Book of Aurack once again and read it through. Finally, he closed it and, looking up, shook his head.

"I don't understand," he said. "It has the Guild of Maintainers stamp. There ought to be no creatures like that in Aurack."

"Then someone must have captured it elsewhere," Catherine said.

"But why go to all that trouble? Why not simply go straight to the world the creature comes from?"

"Perhaps because that was too dangerous," Catherine answered. "I've been thinking about it, Atrus. These were D'ni, right? Scholars and Guildsmen, builders and stonemasons, inkmakers and archivists, not hunters. In which case, Aurack would be a perfect place for the more timid of them.

The only threat would be the beast they had released for their sport. Or beasts, if my guess is correct, for this creature cannot have survived seventy years without others of its kind to breed with. I guess they would release them and kill them within days. Then, when the Maintainers came to inspect the Age, there would be no sign of them."

"Maybe," Atrus conceded. "But whatever the truth is, one thing is certain: We must take greater precautions in the future. No one must venture alone in the Ages. And we must make the teams bigger. Only two teams, perhaps, of ten or twelve. Yes, and we must arm them."

ATRUS TOOK CHARGE OF THE NEXT EXPEDITION. TWELVE OF them were to make the link, the first two armed. If there was any exploring to be done, they were to keep in teams of three, and each team leader carried a fire flare, to be used at the first sign of any trouble.

A long week had passed since Meer's untimely death—a week in which Atrus and Catherine had returned to Averone to break the news to Meer's parents—and now, as they stood before the podium, there was a very different mood—of sobriety rather than excitement—about the job at hand.

"All right," Atrus said quietly. "It's time."

Carrad and Gavas went through first. A moment later Atrus followed them.

The linking cave was long and low, but sunlight from a crevice high up to one side made it seem less oppressive than it would otherwise have seemed. The air was fresh and there was a faint moistness to the air.

"Islands," Marrim said, stepping through after Atrus. "I can smell islands."

Atrus nodded. There were indeed islands, if the Book was accurate, but that wasn't what Marrim had meant. She could smell the sea. And other things. It was like Averone. That same mixture of scents.

They climbed up onto a shelf of rock. Below them the land fell away. A long slope of waist-high grass ending in the silver-blue line of a sunlit shore. And there—immediately visible from where they stood—a village, nestled about a small, natural harbor.

Seeing it, Atrus felt the heavy burden he had been carrying these past months lift from him. For the first time in weeks he smiled.

"Come," he said, looking about him at their eager faces. "Let us go down and greet our cousins."

THEIR LAUGHTER WAS SHORT-LIVED. THE VILLAGE WAS deserted. Even so, there were signs that it had recently been occupied. Everything was well tended, the fences in good repair, the pathways swept.

Inside the cabins the beds were made and clothes lay pressed and folded in the wooden cupboards. The shelves were well stocked, the utensils clean and polished. Three fishing boats lay anchored in the harbor, their pots and nets neatly stowed. Everywhere one looked one could see the products of a small but industrious society. Yet of the people there was no sign.

"They must have seen us emerge from the cave," Gavas offered. "Seen us and run away."

"No," Marrim said. "There wouldn't have been time. Besides, where could they have got to?"

It was true. The village was at the end of a narrow promontory. The only way they could have left and not been seen by Atrus and his party was by sea.

Atrus walked over to the harbor's edge and, shielding the top of his D'ni lenses with one hand, stared out to sea.

"We'll wait," he said, a strange confidence in his voice. "We'll set up camp and wait."

THE BOAT APPROACHED SLOWLY, LONG POLES HAULING THE inelegant craft through the water until it was positioned just outside the harbor's mouth. The craft lay low in the water; a broad-keeled, capacious vessel with more than a dozen separate structures on its long, flat deck, so that it seemed more like a floating village than a normal boat. Those on board were clearly wary of the newcomers and there were heated discussions on board before one of them—an old man, solemn in appearance, D'ni lenses covering his pale eyes—stepped up to the prow and hailed them.

"Ho, there! Who are you and what do you want?"

Atrus raised an arm and hailed the graybeard. "My name is Atrus, son of Gehn, grandson of Aitrus and Ti'ana, late of D'ni, and these are my companions."

There were audible murmurs of astonishment from the craft. The elder, however, seemed unimpressed. "You say you are late of D'ni. Yet D'ni is fallen. As for your father, I have never heard of him. Yet the names of your grandsires are well known to me, if such is true."

"It is true. And we mean you no harm. We wish only to talk."

"So you say," the old man replied, then turned away.

For a long while there was no further word from the old man as he engaged in a long, murmured discussion with his fellows—a dozen or more of them crouched in a huddle at the center of the boat—then, finally, he came back across and hailed Atrus once again.

"It is decided. I will talk with you, Atrus, son of Gehn."

And with that he stood back, allowing two of the younger men to lower a small rowboat over the side of the vessel. He climbed into this and, with a gesture to those aboard, took up the oars and began to row for the shore. As he did so, the men aboard the larger vessel leaned heavily on their poles, beginning to move the craft out into the bay.

As the rowboat nudged against the harbor wall, Carrad hurried down to help the old man tie up, but he was waved away with a suspicious glare.

Carrad moved back, letting the elder pass him on the steps.

Atrus hesitated a second, then stepped forward, bowing respectfully to the stranger, who had stopped less than five paces from him. From close by he seemed not as old as he'd first appeared and Atrus realized with a shock that he was wearing the cloak of a D'ni Guildsman. An old, much-mended cloak.

"So," the old man said, "you are Atrus, eh? My name is Tamon and I am Steward here. In D'ni I was a Guildsman. A stonemason. But that was long ago. Now tell me, Atrus, why are you here?"

"I am here to ask you to come back," Atrus answered, meeting Tamon's eyes unflinchingly, seeing how the other sought to find something there.

"Back?" Tamon asked.

"To D'ni."

Tamon's laugh was dark and full of sorrow. "To D'ni, eh? But D'ni is a ruin."

"Is," Atrus agreed. "Yet it need not be. If enough can be found, we might yet rebuild it."

"And that is your task, Atrus? To find enough to rebuild D'ni?"

Atrus nodded.

"Then speak, for it seems we have much to talk of." Tamon half-turned, looking back at his vessel, which had now edged far out into the bay, then turned back, meeting Atrus's eyes, his own filled with a cautious fear behind their D'ni lenses.

THEY TALKED FOR MOST OF THAT AFTERNOON, TAMON questioning Atrus closely. Afterward, Atrus stood on the jetty, watching old Tamon row away, his tiny boat disappearing into the late evening gloom. He expected to have his answer later that night, but two whole days were to pass before the Guildsman returned. During those two long nights, while Atrus and his party cooled their heels, distant lights—campfires—could be seen twinkling on a smudge of island far out in the center of the lake.

It was late morning on the third day when Tamon climbed the harbor steps wearily.

"So?" Atrus asked, concealing any impatience he felt.

"We have decided we will talk with you," Tamon answered. "Others will come at high sun. They will listen to what you have to say."

"You are still in doubt?"

"Not I," Tamon said, "but you must understand, Atrus. We have been much alone here, and some of the younger men have never seen a stranger. But come . . . let us eat and talk and then, perhaps, decide what shall be done."

TAMON HAD NOT KNOWN ATRUS'S GRANDFATHER, YET HE HAD much to tell Atrus about the circumstances leading up to the fall of D'ni, things not even Anna had told him.

"There were many who blamed her for everything. In those final hours they cursed her name, as if Veovis and that foul philosopher had had no part in it," Tamon concluded, even as he offered his pipe across the table to Atrus.

Atrus accepted the stubby, ornately carved pipe, then, out of politeness, took a tiny indrawn breath of the acrid smoke. Tamon, watching him, smiled, showing a set of pearl white, perfectly formed teeth.

"Strong," Atrus said, trying not to cough. His eyes watered.

Catherine, seated beside Atrus, accepted the pipe from him. Tamon watched her through half-lidded eyes. It was clear that he was not used to women who were quite so forward in their ways. As she handed the pipe back to him he frowned, not knowing he did so, then looked away quickly, lest what he was thinking conveyed itself to Catherine.

Yet Catherine, looking on, saw everything. These people had lived so openly these last seventy years that they had lost whatever social masks they'd once possessed. What they were was written clearly on each face: their hopes, their fears, yes, and especially their suspicions, all could be read, as in a book.

But of this she said nothing.

"And you, Master Tamon?" she asked. "Did you blame Ti'ana?"

"Not I," the old man said, and Catherine could see he meant it. "Oh, I thought her strange, I don't deny. But she was honest. Anyone with a pair of eyes could see just how honest she was."

"Then come back with us, Master Tamon," Atrus said, leaning toward him. "Help us rebuild D'ni. It will take time, I know. A long, long time, perhaps. But time is what we D'ni have plenty of."

Tamon stared back at him, then shrugged. "I must talk some more with my own people. Discuss things with them further. Only then . . ."

"I understand," Atrus said. "Yet in your deliberations, remember this. There will be other survivors. Hopefully many. And they will make the task easier for us all. Every extra pair of hands will make a difference."

"I see that," Tamon said. Then, changing the subject, he turned and clapped his hands. At the signal, two young boys—barely out of their infancy—came across and, bowing, presented themselves to Atrus and Catherine.

"My grandchildren," Tamon said, smiling proudly at them. "Arren, Heejaf . . . say welcome to the good people."

The two boys bowed, and then, in perfect D'ni, bid their guests welcome and good health. Atrus grinned and clapped his hands loudly, but Catherine, watching the old man, seeing how proud he was at that moment, knew, even before he had discussed the matter with his fellow villagers, what the answer would be.

IT WAS ONLY LATER THAT THEY LEARNED OF THE OLD MAN'S tragedy.

Nine days after the fall of D'ni, his son, Huldref, had volunteered to link back, to try to discover what had happened and whether it was safe to return. He had promised he would be back within a day with news, but Huldref had never returned. Doubtless he had succumbed to the plague that had claimed so many other victims. And Tamon and his wife had been left to grieve.

That night, however, the mood of Tamon and his people was much brighter. News that D'ni was to be rebuilt had stirred the survivors and they were eager to get back and help. Packing what they would need, they prepared to link back to their home Age—an Age many of them, far younger than old Tamon, had never set eyes upon.

"We shall return to D'ni," Atrus said, taking Tamon's hands, "and prepare things for your people. There are makeshift shelters and beds. Enough for all of you."

"Then let us meet again tomorrow, Atrus, son of Gehn," Tamon said, his old hands gripping Atrus's tightly. "Tomorrow. In D'ni."

But Atrus was to have one further surprise. As the disorientation of the link back to D'ni wore off and he looked about him at the harborside, he shook his head, trying to clear his vision. On the far side of the square, a whole village of tents had sprung up. And people! There were people everywhere Atrus looked, sitting on their packs outside the tents, or standing in groups, talking. Seeing him, they fell silent, looking to him expectantly.

"Gavas?" Atrus called, looking to his young helper, even as Catherine and Marrim linked through. "What is going on here?"

"Atrus?" a voice asked from behind him. "You are Atrus, I assume?"

Atrus turned to find himself facing two men, in their thirties; a small, rather rotund man with disheveled hair, and a taller, dark-haired man with huge dark eyebrows and a frowning face. From their pale eyes he knew at once who they were.

The first of them—the one, he presumed, who had spoken—offered his hands.

"I am Oma," he said, "from Bilaris. And this is my brother, Esel."

"WELL," SAID ATRUS, ONCE THEY WERE ALL SEATED ABOUT THE desks in the makeshift storehouse, "when did you get here?"

"Six hours back," Esel answered. "Just before you last linked."

Atrus narrowed his eyes. "You saw that?"

"We witnessed everything," Oma said, getting in before his brother could speak again, one hand nervously combing through his lank, disheveled hair. "From the very start. We saw you . . ."

"We saw you, on K'veer," Esel said. Unlike his brother, he sat very still, like a statue, his face formed into what seemed a permanent frown. Indeed, looking at the pair from where she sat at Atrus's side, Catherine could not think of two men who looked less like brothers.

"You've been watching us all the time?" Atrus asked.

"Most of the time," Oma conceded. "We weren't sure."

"So what made you change your mind and join us?" Atrus asked.

"Intuition," Esel said.

Atrus waited, and after a moment Oma explained. "Things *felt* right. We watched what you were doing and there seemed no harm in it."

"We talked a long while," Esel added, "back in Bilaris, and we . . ."

"About that," Atrus interrupted. "We visited your Age. There was nothing there."

"So it seems," Oma said, a faint smile on his lips. Again his fingers raked through his lank hair. "After D'ni fell our father thought we should take precautions. He decided that we should move from the main island. We built dwellings on the smaller islands . . ."

"On the far side of them," Esel added, "where they couldn't be seen from the main island."

"So that's it!" Atrus said, sitting back and steepling his hands, the mystery solved. "And your father . . ."

"Died twelve years ago," Oma said, looking down.

"I'm sorry," Atrus said.

"He was a Guildsman," Esel said, after a moment. "A Master in the Guild of Archivists. He taught us."

"And it was your idea to come back?" Catherine asked, speaking up for the first time.

Again the two men looked to each other.

"Our father never wanted us to," Oma said. "Oh, he came back several times himself, but the mere sight of what had happened here would always darken his spirits. In the end he stopped coming."

"But you came back," Catherine prompted, "after his death."

"Yes," Esel answered. "Our people looked to us, you see. On Bilaris . . . well, there was no future on Bilaris."

"And there's a future here, you think?" Atrus asked.

"Yes," the two men answered as one, then grinned—the same grin from two very different faces. And suddenly Catherine could see that they were indeed brothers.

"We want to help you," Esel said.

"There are many craftsmen among us," Oma added, "stonemasons and technicians."

"That's good," Atrus said. "But how many of you are there?"

"The number will be no problem," Esel said, sitting forward slightly. "We can live under canvas until more permanent quarters are available. And we can bring food from Bilaris. Fruit and fish. And fresh water."

"Excellent," Atrus said. He was about to say something more, but Catherine spoke again.

"Forgive me, Oma and Esel, but what exactly do you do?"

Oma looked to his brother. "We are . . . historians."

"Of a kind," Esel said quickly, a strange look of censure in his eyes.

"*Of a kind?*" Catherine asked, watching him closely.

"Of the self-taught variety," Esel said, looking directly at her.

Again, there was that openness about him that she had seen in Tamon earlier. The loss of masks. As if, in being forced to live away from D'ni and its intense social pressures, they had all shed several layers of skin.

"Then you are among fellows," Atrus said, "for we have all been forced back upon our own resources since D'ni fell. There is no shame in being self-taught, only in not seeking learning in the first place."

"Well spoken," Oma said, grinning once more. But beside him Esel just stared at Catherine, unaware that he was doing so.

WHEN TAMON AND HIS PARTY FINALLY ARRIVED THE NEXT morning, they began to organize what part each would play in the coming reconstruction. It was generally agreed that the overall planning would be left in Atrus's hands, but that Tamon, as a former member of the Guild of Stonemasons, was to be placed in charge of the actual stone-working.

There was a need, of course, to create sufficient living quarters for those returning from the Ages—for they had already outgrown their harborside site, but it was also felt that some kind of gesture was necessary: something that would symbolize the rebirth of D'ni. It was Tamon's task to come up with a suitable scheme, something that would raise their spirits but not divert too much time and energy away from more practical measures.

By late afternoon he returned, his eyes twinkling. "The old Inkmakers Guild House," he said, in answer to Atrus's unspoken query. "I've just come back from it, and it seems relatively undamaged. Nothing structural, anyway. There are a few cracks, of course, and a few of the internal walls have come down, but otherwise it appears sound."

"Then that's where we begin," Atrus said, looking about him at the gathered helpers, who numbered more than a hundred now. "But the search must go on. Until all the D'ni are home."

There was a great murmur of agreement from all sides. Smiling, Atrus turned back to Tamon. But Tamon had turned and was staring up once more at the massive pile of ruined stone that climbed and climbed into the darkness of the cavern's roof, and as Atrus looked, he saw the old man's eyes fill with uncertainty and knew he would have to be a pillar of strength in the days to come.

To see them through. To make sure they do not turn back.

"You must tell me what tools you'll need, Master Tamon," Atrus said, speaking as if he had seen nothing. "And men. What will you need? A dozen?"

Tamon turned back, switching his attention back to the practicalities once again. "Oh, not as many as that. Eight should do it. After all, we must not neglect our other duties."

"No," Atrus agreed, holding Tamon's eyes a moment, letting his own certainty register on the old man. "One step at a time, eh?" he said, and, stepping close, touched the old man's shoulder briefly. "One step at a time."

PART THREE

INNER AND OUTER MEET IN A FACE ON A PAGE.

DEEP LINES AND ANCIENT EYES, MIRRORED.

THE DOOR IS OPEN. THE STRANGER COMES.

BLACK FLIES THE CLOUD BEHIND THE NEWCOMER.

—EXTRACT FROM GEHN'S NOTEBOOK,
ATTRIBUTED TO GERAD'JENAH (UNDATED)

Marrim raised the visor of the protective helmet and looked across to where Atrus looked on, his own face similarly shielded.

"Well?" she asked. "Is it okay?"

Atrus stepped forward and crouched, examining the slab of stone.

The room they were in was small and enclosed—its thick stone roof distinguishing it from every other building on the harbor front—and it was hot. Very hot. The fierce orange glow from the corner forge colored everything in the room, seeming to bleed into the air and melt the edges of objects. Beneath the thick leather clothing she wore, Marrim felt extremely uncomfortable. Her neck and back were slick with sweat, but she did not complain. After all, she had volunteered for this job.

"It looks good," Atrus answered, straightening up. "A nice straight cut. We can chip out the rest."

She smiled. If Atrus said it was good, it was good. He didn't mince words when it came to such matters. Either a thing was done properly or it wasn't worth doing—that was his philosophy.

Marrim went across and pushed the forge door closed, then reached up, taking one of the medium-sized hammers from the rack on the wall. She would chip it out right now, herself, before Master Tamon returned.

"Hold," Atrus said. "Not too eager now."

"But . . ."

"There's no rush," Atrus went on. "It will not harm if you wait until Master Tamon comes back. Besides, he'll want to check this for himself."

That much was true. Old Tamon did not let a thing pass without checking it. And sometimes—just sometimes—that could be wearing on the nerves. But Marrim did not argue. She put the hammer back, then, crossing to the door, slid back the bolt and stepped outside, into the cooler air.

She pulled off her helmet, then turned. Atrus was watching her from the doorway.

"What did your father say?"

"My father?"

"About your hair."

Five weeks back, before she had returned to Averone, she had cut her hair short. Not conscious she was doing so, Marrim reached up, her fingers brushing the fringes of her dark hair where it lay against her neck. "He . . . didn't say."

"No?" There was a tone of surprise in Atrus's voice, but he did not pursue the matter.

Marrim glanced at him, then looked away. "I practiced, you know. Cutting stone, I mean. I took a hammer and some chisels with me when I went back . . . and a mask."

"And gloves, I hope."

She smiled. "And gloves. I'd sit on the rocks, on the far side of the island, and chip away. I'd carve shapes in the stone."

Atrus was watching her earnestly now. "You wanted it that much, eh?"

Marrim met his eyes. "To be a stone mason? Yes. It seemed of the essence of what you D'ni are. You live in the rock. You know it better than anything else."

"Even writing?"

She nodded. "Even that. I mean, the writing's wonderful—astonishing, even—yet it seems almost secondary to what the D'ni really are. Or were. When I watch Master Tamon at work, I seem to glimpse something of how it must have been."

"Yes," he said, clearly pleased by her understanding. "It took me a long time to take in. Yet the two processes have much in common, Marrim. Both require long and patient planning. Before one makes a single cut, or writes a single word, one must know why. One must have clear in mind not just that single part, but the whole, the *totality* of what one is setting out to achieve."

"What your grandmother called the bigger picture?"

Atrus laughed. "Who told you that? Catherine?"

Marrim nodded, smiling now.

"And how goes the writing?"

"Slowly," Marrim answered, her face clouding a little. "I'm afraid I'm not very patient."

"Nonetheless, keep at it. Like all things, patience will come."

Seeing the dismay in her face, Atrus smiled. "You think patience an innate quality, Marrim. Well, perhaps for some it is. But for most of us it must be learned. It is a life skill that must be acquired if one is to succeed."

"You think so?"

"Oh, I know so. Look about you now. What do you see?"

Marrim turned and looked. The square beside the harbor, which, when they'd first arrived, had seemed so vast and spacious, was filled with makeshift dwellings, forming a kind of village beneath the steep-sloping levels of the city, while to one side, surrounding the library where Atrus worked, was a collection of workshops and storehouses.

Six months had passed since they had encountered the first survivors and much had changed for the better. It helped also that there were more than twelve hundred of them now, yet Marrim did not expect that number to increase by much. In a week—maybe less—the last of the Ages would have been searched, and they would know finally just how many had survived.

Not enough, Marrim thought, dismayed despite the signs of industry that surrounded her. She did not know how many Atrus had expected, but she was sure it must have been more.

Looking up, beyond the busy harbor front, she saw at once the scale of their problem. Compared to the ruin that surrounded them, their little hive of activity was as nothing. So many empty streets, so many fallen and abandoned houses.

Patience. . . . No wonder Atrus counseled patience.

Yet maybe he was right. Maybe patience could be learned. Maybe the task was not beyond them.

"Well?" Atrus prompted, when a minute had passed and she still had not answered him. "What *do* you see?"

"Stone," she answered him, meeting his eyes. "Stone, and rock, and dust."

THAT EVENING THEY HELD A MEETING IN THE LIBRARY. Catherine was there with Atrus, as were Master Tamon, Oma, Esel, Carrad, and Irras. Marrim was the last to arrive.

Coming straight to the point, Atrus drew a big leather-bound Book toward him and opened it.

The descriptive panel glowed.

"Twelve Books remain," Atrus began. "This, the Book of Sedona, is probably the least dangerous of them. Even so, when we explore this we shall need to use the Maintainers' suits."

Atrus paused, then. "Sedona is a very old Age. Thousands of years old. Maybe even older. The language used is of a more antiquated and formal kind than we are used to. Oma and Esel have given up a great deal of their valuable time to help me . . . *translate* the Book. We think we know what most of it means, and what kind of Age we're likely to encounter, but we cannot be sure, so we shall wear the suits as a precaution."

"And the other eleven?" Tamon asked.

"The Guild of Maintainer seals on those are either broken or missing, and it is difficult to ascertain just whether those Ages were in use at the time D'ni fell. The only way to be certain is to make rigorous checks."

"Using the suits," Tamon concluded.

"Exactly," Atrus said. "But first Sedona. The suit is ready. We shall link in the morning. You know the routine. We've practiced it often enough these past months. Tomorrow we do it for real. Marrim, Carrad, Irras. You will report here at sixth bell, along with Oma and Esel. I shall be here to greet you."

"Are you going to come, too?" Marrim asked, surprised.

"If it's safe," Atrus said. "I was there at the beginning. I think it only right I should be there at the end."

THE CELL WAS A GREAT SQUARE OF A ROOM, A DOZEN PACES TO a side, the jet-black walls coated with a layer of impervious matter—part stone, part chemicals—that sealed it hermetically. A narrow doorway, set deep into the end wall, was the only exit from the cell, and that led directly to an air lock, beyond which was a second sealed room, almost identical to the first—a fail-safe devised after one particularly gruesome accident.

The rooms differed in two respects alone. The first was that this cell— known simply as the Link Room—was further divided by a double wall of floor-to-ceiling bars that formed a tiny cell within a cell; thick rods of special D'ni rock known as nara spaced a hand's width apart, the two walls separated by less than an arm's length. In the center of that double wall, flush with it, was set a small revolving cage, the only entrance to that smaller cell.

The floor of the inner cell was a mere two paces square and lined with nara. A big semicircular machine of stone and brass was suspended some ten feet up, capping it like a roof, coiled armatures and other strange devices extending from its dark interior. This was the decontamination pod.

The second difference was the alcoves—eight in all, four to the left, four to the right—that were recessed into the walls on either side of the doorway. These were deep and heavily shadowed, and housed the eight protective suits that stood like huge mechanical sentries, their shiny surfaces untarnished by age.

So it was. So the Guild of Maintainers had designed it four thousand years earlier, founding their design upon long centuries of experience and many a fatal mission.

In theory, nothing could go wrong. No matter what was brought back from the Ages, it could not escape these cells. The bars prevented anything dangerous, whether it be desperate natives or aggressive beast, from breaking into D'ni, while the seals and air lock dealt with the ever-present threat of contagion.

For seventy years the cell had lain in total darkness, but now it was bathed in light from the great overhead lamps; a clean, almost sanitized light. In that penetrating glare Atrus and his fellows toiled, dressed in special lightweight suits, the impervious cloth a rich dark green, the bright red lozenge of the Guild of Maintainers crest, with its symbol of an unblinking eye above an open book, prominent on every chest. These suits were very different from those in the alcoves, one of which they were now removing from its recess, four of them hauling the incredibly heavy suit along the grooved runners in the floor.

Finished, they stood back, admiring it.

The protective suit had a brutal, almost mechanical appearance. It stood at the center of the laboratory, empty, like the casing to some giant insect, its chest and arms studded with strange appendages. The jet-black overlapping plates of which it was made had a polished, metallic look, yet there was no element of metal in their manufacture. The suit was made of stone—of a special lightweight stone named deretheni, not as hard as the legendary nara, but tough enough to handle the job for which it was intended.

Special hydraulics—slender rods of the same molecularly altered stone—gave the suit a degree of flexibility, but not enough for its wearer to turn quickly or to run. Not that that mattered. The wearer would need neither to turn nor run, only to look out through the polarized visor and take in, in the instant he was there, what the Age looked like.

Right now Gavas was putting on the inner suit, Oma helping him to attach the various straps and buckles, the two of them talking quietly, running through the routine for the dozenth time that morning.

The suit was ancient—according to the records it had been made by the Guild of Maintainers more than a thousand years ago—yet it looked brand new. Like everything the D'ni made, the environmental verification suit had been built to last.

Everything was ready. Or almost so. It remained only for Atrus to attach the last of the sampling devices, put the Linking Book inside the glove, and set the timer.

Once that was done, Gavas could climb into the suit and be sealed in.

Atrus consulted with Catherine a moment, then turned and looked across.

"Are you ready, Gavas?"

Gavas smiled. "As ready as I'll ever be."

"Good."

Atrus reached down and picked up the two special books—tiny, "stone-bound" volumes less than a sixth the size of a normal Linking Book—then slid them into the special compartment in each glove.

The first would link Gavas to Sedona, the second would link him back. Both worked on the same principle. A thin, inert membrane overlay each page, rendering it impossible for Gavas to link—until he pressed a stud on the back of the right-hand glove, which would release a vial of harmless gas that would, in turn, dissolve the membrane and bring his palm into contact with the page.

At that moment he would link. And at that selfsame moment the timer would be activated.

For the first two seconds on the other side a similar membrane would overlay the page of the Linking Book in his left-hand glove, preventing him from linking back. But then the timer would do its work, the tiny vial of gas would be released, and Gavas's palm would press against the page once more.

After two seconds, Gavas would link back, whether he was conscious or not. Alive or dead.

Two seconds. It was all they could risk first time out. Yet it was time enough for them to find out all they needed to know about the world on the other side of the page. The suit's sampling devices would tell them what the atmosphere was like, how hot it was, and whether there were any signs of life. And unless it was so bright that the visor completely blacked over—which it was designed to do, to save Gavas's eyes from frying in their sockets—he ought to get a good glimpse of the Age.

The deretheni plates of the suit would insulate him against the fiercest heat, while the suit's hermetic seals would ensure that no noxious substances leaked through to poison him.

Carrad and Oma helped Gavas climb into the outer suit, then began to seal him up, each of the catches snapping shut with a resounding clunk. As they went across to fetch the massive helmet, Gavas gave one final look about him, smiling nervously. They had drilled for this many times now, but this was the first time any of them had done it for real.

Only Atrus seemed unaffected by the tension of the moment, and as he came across to give Gavas his final instructions, his very calmness put them all at ease.

"Remember, Gavas. Your job is to look. Don't think, just *see*. I'll do the thinking for you when you get back."

It was not the first time Atrus had said this, but Gavas nodded as if it were.

Atrus stood back, letting Carrad and Oma lift the helmet, with its heat-resisting visor, up over Gavas's head, fastening it into the brace about his neck. Satisfied, they tightened the six great screwlike bolts that held it in place. That done, they began to work their way down the suit, from neck to toe, checking each one of the special pressure seals. Satisfied, they stepped back.

The gloves were last. Now they only had to move him over to the cage. He could have walked there, but it was quicker for them to push him along the grooved track and close the barred door behind him.

There was a great hiss of hydraulics and then the tiny cage turned a full 180 degrees. It clunked into place, bolts emerging from the floor to secure it. Only then did the barred door open once again, allowing Gavas to step out slowly, awkwardly, into the inner cell.

Wearing the suit, Gavas had little room to maneuver. Slowly, very slowly, he turned, until he was facing Atrus again.

All was ready. There was no reason for any further delay. Atrus looked to Gavas and placed his left hand over the back of his right, miming the signal. Gavas nodded, then—the motion of his arm exaggerated by the suit—copied the motion.

The suit seemed to shimmer in the air, then it was gone.

Inside the cell there was a nervous exchange of looks. Only Atrus stared straight ahead at the now empty cage.

One beat, two beats, and it was back.

The heat exploded into the room, as if someone had opened a furnace door. With a fierce crackling the whole suit seemed to convulse as it dropped the temperature gradient, the air about it steaming as the automatic extinguisher flooded the chamber with an enormous hiss.

There was a great groan from every side. Immediately, Carrad and Irras rushed to the chamber, wishing to help as the heavy layer of retardent boiled on the surface of the suit. They moved to step through the cage to help him, but Atrus called them back.

"No!"

They stood there, horrified, watching, knowing there was nothing they could do but wait while, slowly, the stone hardened as it cooled—the wet foam smothering the darkening surfaces. But now it was warped and twisted. The limbs stretched like wax, the body of the suit partly crumpled into itself, the helmet misshapen.

Catherine moved to speak when the silence had become unbearable, but stopped short when a faint groan came from within the suit.

Carrad quickly opened the floor drains purging the chamber. Irras flung wide the chamber door and selflessly went about extricating Gavas. Minutes passed as the others anxiously waited—their rehearsed duties and ready supplies would prove to be enough to spare his life, this time.

They carried Gavas away, his wounds being carefully tended prior to returning him to Averone for recovery.

"A nova," Atrus answered quietly. It had to be. Nothing else could have generated the temperatures or pressures capable of melting a suit.

Gavas had stepped straight into the heart of an exploding sun.

ARIDANU WAS NEXT. A NEWER AGE, BUT LACKING A GUILD of Maintainers stamp. They had found the Book, partly damaged, in one of the upper district houses. It seemed okay, but that lack of a stamp worried Atrus.

As Carrad and Irras helped Esel climb into the E.V. suit, the door at the far end of the lab hissed open and Marrim hurried in.

"I'm sorry I'm late, Master Atrus," she said, clearly relieved to see that Esel had not yet linked.

Atrus looked up from where he was working and nodded.

Marrim hastened across, moving between Carrad and Oma to slip something over Esel's neck.

"What is it?" Esel asked quietly. He had already inserted his arms into the suit's voluminous sleeves and so could not reach the delicate pendant.

"It's a charm," Marrim said. "For luck."

Esel glanced across at Atrus, but Atrus was busy, making a final check of the apparatus they would use to analyze the samples.

"Thanks," Esel said quietly, clearly touched by her gesture.

Marrim stood back, then watched as Carrad and Irras went about their work. Satisfied, they moved back, letting Atrus take over.

"Are you all right in there, Esel?"

There was a muffled response, barely audible. The right-hand glove flexed and unflexed—the signal that all was well.

"Good," Atrus said. He turned, looking to the others, who at once began to move the bulky suit toward the cage.

As Esel stepped out, then turned to face them, the cell fell silent. There was a tension in the room that had not been there before.

All was ready. Once again, Atrus looked to Esel and placed his left hand over the back of his right, miming the signal. Esel nodded, then nervously copied the movement.

The suit shimmered in the air, then it was gone.

One beat, two beats, and it was back.

No flames, no smoke . . .

Thank the Maker, Marrim thought, seeing Esel's head move through the clear glass of the visor.

At once they swarmed about him, gloved hands reaching through the bars to pluck things from him, divesting the suit of its various sampling devices, even as, overhead, the great machine slowly descended, a fine mist of spray beginning to rain down over the suit, cleansing it.

Only Atrus spoke, questioning Esel about what he'd seen.

"What's it like?"

"Beautiful!" The word was clear despite the muffling effect of the helmet. But what he said next was less easy to make out.

"What's that?" Atrus said, straining to hear.

"People," Esel answered, that single word again quite clear. His eyes shone, a broad grin split his face. "There are *people* there!"

THEY LINKED THROUGH AN HOUR LATER, AFTER THE ANALYSIS of the samples had confirmed what Esel had seen.

Aridanu was a lush and beautiful Age; a world of huge trees and peaceful lakes. They linked into a clearing overlooking one of those lakes, an ancient wood and stone village nestled into the fold of hills just below them. Smoke rose from a dozen chimneys. As Atrus and his party walked down, men stepped from the cabins to greet them, openhanded and smiling.

When several dozen had gathered, children milling about their feet, they made their introductions. Their spokesman, a man named Gadren, took Atrus's hands firmly, a broad smile on his face. "We knew you would come back. When we saw the suit . . ." He laughed. "Why, it half frightened the children to death!"

"I'm sorry," Atrus began, but Gadren waved his apology away. "No, no . . . We knew at once what it was, and you were right to take precautions. This is an old world."

"And beautiful," Atrus said.

"Yes . . ." Gadren looked about him thoughtfully, then. "You come from D'ni, I take it?"

"We do."

"And how *are* things there?"

"We are rebuilding."

"And are there other . . . *survivors?*"

"More than a thousand."

Gadren's face lit at the sound of that. "A thousand." Then, more seriously. "And you want us to return, yes? To help you rebuild?"

"You are welcome. Yet the choice is yours."

"And has anyone said no?"

Atrus hesitated. No one had actually said no. But in three instances there had been a promise to "come later"—promises that had not yet been kept.

"You must do as you see fit," he answered finally. "If you are happy here . . ."

"Oh, we are happy, Atrus. Never happier. Yet happiness is not everything, is it? There is also duty, and responsibility. I love this place, true enough, but I was a Guildsman once, and I swore oaths to stand by D'ni to the end. When D'ni fell I felt the obligation had lapsed, but if it is to be rebuilt . . ."

"You need time to discuss this among you?" Atrus asked, looking about him at the villagers, noting how few of them were older than himself.

Gadren smiled. "There is no need for that. The matter was settled long ago. If D'ni calls, we will answer." He gripped Atrus's hands again. "We shall give what help we can."

LATER, WHEN THEY WERE ALL SITTING IN GADREN'S CABIN
talking, someone mentioned the old man who lived alone on an island on
the lake.

"An old man?" Atrus asked, interested.

"His name is Tergahn," Gadren's wife, Ferras, said before her husband
could speak, "and he keeps bitterness for a wife."

"He lives a hermit's life," Gadren said, frowning at his wife.

"Hermit indeed," Ferras said, making a face back at her husband. "If we
see the old stick once a year that's oftener than most."

"Is he D'ni?"

"Oh, indeed," Gadren said. "A fine old gentleman he must have been. A
Master, I'd guess, though of what Guild I wouldn't know."

"You didn't know him, then?"

"Not at all. You see, he was passing our house when it all happened. The
great cavern was filling up with that evil gas and there was no time for him
to get back to his own district. My father, rest his soul, saw him and asked
him in. He linked here with us."

"And afterward? Did he not try to return?"

Gadren looked down. "We did not let him. He wanted to, but my father
would let no one use the Linking Book. Not for a year. Then he went himself. After that, no one went."

"And the Linking Book?"

"My father destroyed it."

Atrus thought a moment, then stood. "I would like to meet this Tergahn
and talk with him. Try to persuade him to come with us."

"You can try," Ferras said, ignoring her husband's frown, "but I doubt
you'll get a word out of him. He'll scuttle away like a squirrel and hide in
the woods behind his cabin till you're gone."

"He's that unsociable?"

"Oh, aye," Gadren said with a laugh. "But if you're keen to meet with
him, I'll row you there myself, Atrus. And on the way you can tell me what's
been happening in D'ni."

THEIR DESTINATION WAS AT THE FAR END OF THE LAKE, OVER A mile from the village. The lake curved sharply here, ending in a massive wall of dark granite. The island lay beneath that daunting barrier, its wooded slopes reflected in the dark mirror of the lake.

As they rowed toward it, that mirror shimmered and distorted.

A narrow stone jetty reached out into the lake. From there a path led up among the trees. Tergahn's cabin was near the top of the island, enclosed by the darkness of the wood. It was silent on those slopes. Silent and dark.

Standing just below the cabin, staring up into its shadowed porch, Gadren cupped his hands to his mouth and hailed the old man.

"Tergahn? Tergahn! You have a visitor."

"I know."

The words startled them. They turned to find the old man behind them, less than ten paces away.

Tergahn was not simply old, he looked ancient. His face was deeply lined, his eyes sunken in their orbits. Not a shred of hair was on his head, the pate of which was mottled with age, yet he held himself upright and there was something about his bearing, a sharpness in his eyes behind the lenses, that suggested he was still some distance from senility.

Atrus took a breath, then offered his hands. "Master Tergahn, I am honored to meet you. My name is Atrus."

The old man stared at him a while then shook his head. "No, no . . . you're far too young."

"Atrus," he repeated, "of the Guild of Writers, son of Gehn, grandson of Master Aitrus."

The old man's eyes blinked at that last name. "And Ti'ana?"

"Ti'ana was my grandmother."

Tergahn fell silent. He looked down at the ground for a long time, as if lost in his thoughts, then, finally, he looked up again. "Ahh," he said. "Ahh."

"Are you all right, Master Tergahn?" Gadren asked, concerned for him, but Tergahn gave an impatient gesture with his hand.

"Leave me," he said, a hint of bad temper in his voice. "I need to talk to the boy."

Atrus looked about, then realized that Tergahn meant him.

"Well?" Tergahn said, staring pointedly at Gadren. "Haven't you a boat to look after?" Then, turning, pulling his cloak tighter about him, he stomped past Atrus and up the slope.

"Come," he said, stepping up into the shadows of the porch. "Come, Atrus, son of Gehn. We need to talk."

THE INTERIOR OF THE CABIN WAS SMALL AND DARK. A BULGING knapsack sat beside the open door, its drawstring tied.

At the center of the room was a table with a single chair. Standing on the far side of that table, Tergahn put his arm out, indicating that Atrus should be seated.

There were shelves of books on the walls, and prints. Things that must have been there before Tergahn came.

Declining the offer of the chair, Atrus stood there, facing Tergahn across the table.

"Forgive me, Master Tergahn, but I sensed just now, when I mentioned my grandfather's name, that you knew him."

"I knew *of* him. He was a good man and an excellent Guildsman." Tergahn stared at Atrus intently a moment. "Indeed, you're very like him now that I come to look."

Atrus took a long breath. "We came here . . ."

"To ask us to return?" Tergahn nodded. "Yes, yes, I understand all that. And I'm ready."

"Ready?" For once Atrus could not keep the surprise from his voice. "But surely you'll want time to pack?"

"I have already packed," Tergahn answered, indicating the bag beside the door. "When I heard the boat coming and saw you on it, I knew."

"You *knew*?"

"Oh, yes. I've been waiting a long time now. Seventy years in this cursed place. But I knew you would come eventually. Or someone like you."

"And all this?" Atrus, gesturing toward the books, the various objects scattered on shelves about the room.

"Forget them," Tergahn answered. "They were never mine. Now come, Atrus. I will not wait another hour in this place."

THE FINAL SEARCHES TOOK MUCH LONGER THAN THE EARLIER ones. As Atrus had foreseen, the majority of them proved to be dangerous, unstable Ages, and the E.V. suit found much further use. But there were successes. One Book in particular—an old, rather decrepit volume for which Atrus had held very little hope—yielded up a colony of three hundred men, women, and children. This and a second, much smaller, group—from a Book that had been partly damaged in the Fall—swelled the population of New D'ni to just over eighteen hundred souls. On the evening of that final search, eight weeks after they had linked into Sedona, Atrus threw a feast to celebrate.

That evening was one of the high points of their venture, and there was much talk of—and many toasts to—the rebirth of D'ni. Yet in the more sober atmosphere of the next morning, all there realized the scale of the task confronting them.

When a great empire falls, it is not easy trying to lift the lifeless carcass back onto its feet. Even if many more had survived, it would have been difficult; as it was, there were not enough of them to fill a single district, let alone a great city such as D'ni. At the final count there were 618 adult males, and of them a mere 17 had been Guildsmen.

Atrus, making his final reckoning before beginning the next phase of the reconstruction, knew that one thing and one thing only could carry them through: hard work.

Each night he fell into his bed, exhausted. Day after day he felt this way, like a machine that cannot rest unless it is switched off completely. Each night he would sleep the sleep of the dead, and each morning he would rise to take on his burden once again. And little by little things got done.

But never enough. Never a tenth of what he wanted to achieve.

One morning Atrus wandered out to see how Master Tamon was faring. Tamon had cleared most of the fallen masonry from the site, exposing the interior of the ancient Guild House, and now he was about to begin the most delicate phase of the operation: lifting an internal wall that had come down in what had been the dining hall. The fallen wall had smashed through the mosaic floor in several places, revealing the hypocaust beneath it. Master Tamon's problem was how to clear away the massive chunks of fallen wall without the damaged floor collapsing beneath his team as they worked.

After much consideration, he had decided that this was a simple mining problem—an exercise in shoring up and chipping out—and therefore he had called in "Young Jenniran," a sprightly ninety-year-old who had been a cadet in the Guild of Miners when D'ni fell. When Atrus arrived, the two men were standing, their heads together, on one side of the site, a sheet of hand-drawn diagrams held between them as they debated the matter.

"Ah, Atrus!" Tamon exclaimed. "Perhaps you can help us resolve something."

"Is there another problem?"

"Not so much a problem," Jenniran said, "as a small difference of opinion."

"Go on," said Atrus patiently.

"Well . . . Master Tamon wishes to lift the wall and save the floor. And

I can see why. It's a very beautiful piece of mosaic. But to do so, we would have to get beneath the floor and prop it up, and that will take days, possibly weeks, of hard work and involve considerable risks for those undertaking the task."

Atrus nodded. "And your alternative?"

Jenniran glanced at Tamon, then went on. "I say let's give up the floor. Let's drop weights on it and smash the whole thing through, then clear up the mess. It will not only save us precious days but cut out any risk of injury."

"But the floor, Atrus! Look at it!"

Atrus looked. He could see only the edges, and they were covered in a fine layer of dust, but he had seen the diagrams of the Guild House and remembered this mosaic well. It would be a great shame to lose it. Then again, Jenniran had a point about the safety element, and the floor *was* badly damaged as it was.

And then there was so much else to do. So much to clear away. So much to repair and make good. Thinking that, Atrus made his decision.

"Can I have a word, Master Tamon?" he said, laying an arm about the older man's shoulders and turning him away.

THE FLOOR GAVE WITH A HUGE CREAKING SIGH. THERE WAS A deafening crash that echoed all about the cavern.

Dust rose in a great choking cloud.

Studying the scene through his visor, Atrus felt a moment's regret. As the dust began to clear, there was a murmur of surprise from the watching helpers. Something was wrong. The hole was much *deeper* than they had imagined it would be . . . and longer. Atrus blinked, then raised his visor, staring into what appeared to be some kind of hall beneath the old Guild House, two rows of massive pillars flanking it.

He turned, looking to Tamon.

"Master Tamon . . . is there anything in the plans?"

Tamon looked mystified. "Nothing. At least, nothing like *that.*"

"The hypocaust . . ."

But Atrus could see that the ancient heating system that ran beneath the ancient Guild House had collapsed and whatever it was lay *beneath* that.

"Well," he said, after a moment's reflection. "I guess we'd best bring lamps and investigate."

"Go *down* there?" Master Tamon asked.

"Certainly," Atrus said, intrigued by what he could glimpse within that shadow. "Those pillars seem strong enough."

"We should check them first."

"Of course . . ." Atrus looked about him, calling to this one to bring this, that one to do that—organizing them; being the hub about which they all revolved. Yet even as he orchestrated it all, in his mind he was already down there, poking among the shadows, trying to piece together the mystery.

"MARRIM! MARRIM! COME QUICKLY! THEY'VE FOUND SOMETHING beneath the Guild House!"

Marrim had turned at the first hearing of her name. Now she set aside the book she had been reading and stood.

"*Beneath* it?"

"Yes," Irras said, coming up to her, breathless from running. "We . . . broke through the floor of the old dining hall and there was a chamber underneath it.

"Well?" he said, after a moment. "Aren't you going to come and see?"

"I've work to do," she said, and it was true. She was teaching some of the younger children basic D'ni, and she had to prepare the work for tomorrow's lessons, but this *was* important.

"Okay," she said. "Just to look. Then I must get back here."

"Come on then!" And with that, Irras took her hand and half dragged her across the square and beneath the arch, heading for the Guild House.

By the time they got there, a number of ladders had already been lowered into the hole and lamps set up along one side. Atrus, Tamon, and Jenniran stood in a huddle some ten feet away from the overhang, Jenniran holding up a lamp as they stared into the chamber, where several of Tamon's helpers were checking the pillars for any signs of cracking.

Seeing what was beyond them, Marrim felt a ripple of excitement. It was magnificent, like the entrance hall to a great palace. The walls and pillars appeared to be of beautifully colored marble, and, farther in, the floor looked like a polished mirror.

She was still staring when Esel and Oma hurried up. There was a moment's stunned silence as they took in the sight, then Oma spoke.

"It *has* to be."

"Why?" Esel asked.

"Because what else *could* it be?"

"But they're only stories. You said so yourself."

"Maybe. But even myths are based on something. And maybe *that's* the something."

"What's that?" Atrus called from below.

"It was in one of my grandfather's books of D'ni legends," Oma said, walking over to the edge and addressing Atrus. "There were several mentions of a Great King and of his temple, and of a hall of beautifully colored marble."

"And you think this might be it?"

"They were only tales," Esel said apologetically. But Oma shook his head.

"That is exactly how it is described. The two rows of massive pillars. And at the end of the hall there's a great doorway, surrounded by a circle of stars."

"So the book says," Esel quickly added.

Atrus nodded thoughtfully. "All right. Come down, all of you. Let's see if Oma is right or not."

ATRUS LED THE WAY, UNDER THE LIP OF ROCK AND INTO THE
great chamber, his lamp held high, the fire-marble burning with a fierce
white light that seemed to emphasize the purity of the colors in the stone.

The rows of pillars on either side of the hall went on endlessly, it
seemed, each pillar so huge that to Marrim, walking between them, it
seemed as though they walked in the halls of ancient giants. Deep, deep into
the rock it went. And then, suddenly, there it was, the far end of the chamber, and there—just where Oma had said it would be—was a huge doorway, set within a great circle of stone, a dozen broad steps leading up to it.

They approached, stopping at the foot of the steps, looking up at that
massive doorway.

"Stars . . ." Atrus said.

"Then this is it," Tamon, who stood beside him, agreed. "The Temple
of the Great King."

"Maybe he's inside," Oma said excitedly. "Maybe this is his tomb. If
so . . ."

Atrus looked to him. "Was there anything else in the tales that we should
know about, Oma?"

Oma hesitated, then shook his head. "Nothing that I remember. Only
those mentions of the prophecies."

"Yes," Marrim said, "but they were in Gehn's notebook. In view of how
much else he wrote was suspect, we can't be sure that they were all true."

"I agree," Atrus said. Then, turning to Irras, he added, "Go up and examine it."

Irras climbed the steps. For a time he was silent, examining the edges of
the great door meticulously, then he looked back at Atrus.

"It looks as though there *was* a real door here, at some stage, but it's been
sealed up. And a very efficient job, too, by the look of it."

Atrus looked to Tamon. "We could *sound* it. If there *is* a chamber behind that, then it will show up on a sounding scan."

Tamon nodded, suddenly enthusiastic. "There were machines in the Miners' Guild House. If they're still there, we could use those."

Atrus smiled. "Excellent. Then arrange it, Master Tamon. Meanwhile, we'll set up lamps in here. And Oma . . ."

"Yes, Atrus?"

"Bring me the book you spoke of. Your grandfather's book. I would like to read those passages myself."

ATRUS LOOKED UP FROM THE PAGE AND FROWNED. NOTHING WAS clear. Everything was hearsay and rumor. Of dates and names and facts there was nothing. Even so, those two lines where the chamber was described had a powerful effect. They seemed to give some credence to the rest, for if *they* were true . . .

He felt the soft touch of familiar hands on his shoulders.

"Atrus?"

"Yes, my love?"

"Aren't you coming?"

"In a moment . . ." He hesitated, then half turned, looking up at her. "Those passages in my father's notebook . . . wasn't there a mention of a great library?"

"There was. But not in connection with the Great King."

IT HAD TAKEN EIGHT OF THEM TO HAUL THE CAPSULE UP THE makeshift tracks and position it on the platform, alongside the door. Now Master Tamon sat at the controls of the large crystalline craft while Jenni-ran read from the Guild manual.

"Forgive me, Master Tamon," someone said, pushing through the crowd of watchers at the foot of the steps, "but might I have a word?"

Tamon turned, about to make some bad-tempered comment, when he saw who it was.

"Why, Master Tergahn, I . . ." Then, "Of course. Come on up. If you know *anything* that might help . . ."

The old man slowly made his way up the steps until he stood at the rear of the sounding capsule. He looked about him, then nodded to himself. Tamon stood, indicating that Tergahn should take his place. The old man did so, once more looking about him, familiarizing himself with the controls. He gently felt each knob, each switch, recalling their function. Reaching out, he grasped the headphones and pulled them on.

"You know how to operate that, Master Tergahn?" Atrus asked, stepping up.

"We'll see," the old man answered without turning; laying one hand gently, respectfully on the long metal shaft of the sounder.

Tergahn closed his eyes then gently eased the shaft down and to the left, pressing on the pearled handle as he did. At once a single, pure note grew in the air. Yet even as it formed its perfect shape, the tone clear and clean, Tergahn twitched the end of the shaft. At once the note died.

And returned, *changed* from the rock.

Tergahn's eyes slowly opened. He looked to Tamon, then, nudging the shaft a little to the right, closed his eyes again and gently pushed down on the shaft.

A second note grew, slightly stronger and higher than the first. And once again, even as it formed, Tergahn killed it.

Again there was an echo from the rock. Different this time. Much lower than the sound that had come back the time before.

Atrus watched, closing his eyes each time a note sounded; trying to make out some discernible difference in what came back. And indeed, there did seem to be some kind of pattern to what he was hearing.

Twenty, thirty times Tergahn sent a signal into the rock. Then, finally, he sat back, nodding to himself.

"I'll need to make more soundings . . . a lot more. . . but . . ." Tergahn swiveled round on the seat. "There is definitely a hollow behind that wall. A void of some kind. But how big it is is much harder to tell. My ear was never trained to make distinctions of that kind."

Atrus nodded. "We should discuss things and hear all sides before we choose to act. If it's sealed, there might be a good reason *why*."

"Wise words," Tergahn said. "If the D'ni chose to seal that chamber and erase all mention of it from their history, then perhaps they had a reason for doing so."

"I agree," Atrus said. "We should discover if anything more is known of the Great King and of the events surrounding the sealing of his Temple. Maybe one or another of our company heard some tale at their mother's knee that might add to the sum of our knowledge, scant as it is. Until then, we should do nothing rash.

"I shall call a meeting," Atrus went on. "Tonight. In the meantime, Master Tergahn, if you would continue with your soundings?"

Tergahn nodded, no flicker of emotion in his deeply lined face. "I shall be guessing at best."

"Then guess your best guess. And if there is anything else you need, give instructions to young Irras here. He can be your legs."

Tergahn nodded tersely, then turned back, returning to his task.

Atrus watched him a moment, then turned away. "Come," he said to Catherine, as he began to make his way down the steps. "We have a meeting to arrange."

"SO." ATRUS BEGAN, ADDRESSING THE SMALL GROUP GATHERED in his room that evening after the meeting, "it all comes down to hearsay."

"And what is written in your father's notebook," Catherine added.

"Yes," Atrus said. "And that is little enough." He paused, then: "Even so,

I think we might take a look and see what's on the other side. But caution must be our byword. Once Master Tergahn has completed his soundings, we shall make a sample drilling and push a scope through and see what's to be seen."

"And then?" Carrad asked.

Atrus smiled. "And then, if all is well, we shall breach the seal and go inside."

BACK AT THE DOORWAY, MASTER TERGAHN HAD FINISHED HIS soundings. As Atrus returned, he was sitting on the bottom step, papers scattered about him, hunched forward over a chart, writing.

Atrus stopped several paces from him. "Master Tergahn?"

The old man looked up, then gestured for Atrus to join him. "See," he said, indicating the diagram he had been working on. "It seems to go back quite some way, but it's not very wide. No wider, it would seem, than the circle itself."

Atrus studied the diagram a moment, then looked up at the circle of stone that surrounded the doorway. "A tunnel, you think?"

"It might be."

Atrus turned. "Irras . . . help Master Tamon bring a drill from the Guild House. One of the small-bore machines with a sealed end. The kind we can take an air sample from. And a scope. It's time we saw what's behind there."

It took them more than an hour to set up the drill, the heavy frame in which it rested placed low down and at the center of the door. Then, with Master Tamon supervising and Atrus looking on, they began, the drill bit, encased as it was within the transparent sealing sheath, nudging the stone surface, then biting deep, the whine of the drill filling that brightly lit space beneath the old Guild Hall.

Slowly, slowly, it ate into the toughened rock. Then, with a marked change of tone—a downward whine—it was through.

Tamon signaled for the power to be cut, then stepped across to examine their handiwork. He hunched over it a moment, then turned to Atrus and nodded.

Slowly and very carefully they removed the bit, an airtight seal inside the sheath clicking shut behind it. As it did, Catherine, wearing special gloves, removed the bit and hurried down the steps to where a temporary laboratory had been set up. Immediately, Carrad and three others came across and lifted away the heavy frame that held the drill, carrying it down to the foot of the steps.

They waited twenty minutes while Catherine analyzed the air sample from the tiny capsule in the bit. Satisfied, she nodded to Atrus. "Just air. Stale air."

"Okay," Atrus said, turning to Irras, who stood nearby, the scope—a long, curiously "furred" shaft with a lens at each end and a small bullet-shaped extrusion at its tip—held against his chest, "let's see what we have here."

Irras stepped across and very carefully inserted the rod into the end of the sheath, the special seal within the sheath opening before the scope's tip, the continuous circles of fine hairs on the scope's surface, which gave it its "furred" look, maintaining an airtight seal even as the rod slid into position.

As the end of the scope clicked into place—a finger's length of the shaft protruding from the surface of the sheath—Irras turned to Atrus. "Atrus? Will you be first to look?"

Atrus nodded, then came across and, crouching, put his eye to the lens. There was a small catch on the side of the shaft where it protruded. Atrus now placed his thumb against it and drew it back.

There was a muffled pop and the surface of the lens, which had been dark until that moment, now glistened with light; light that was reflected in the pupil of Atrus's eye.

The muscles about Atrus's eye puckered. He drew back the tiniest fraction. And then he nodded.

"It's not a tunnel, it's another hallway. Smaller. Narrower, too, with pillars set into the sidewalls."

"Can you see the far end?" Catherine asked, stepping up alongside him.

"Just," he said. "It's almost in shadow. There might be steps there—it's hard to make out . . ."

"And a doorway? Is there another doorway?"

Atrus shrugged, then moved back, straightening up again. "I don't know. As I said, I couldn't make it out. Here, Marrim . . . your eyes are better than mine, you look!"

Marrim hurried across, then crouched, her eye pressed to the lens. For a time she was still and silent, then she moved back.

"I think so," she said. Then, "But there has to be, surely? I mean . . . why build all this if there's nothing on the other side?"

Oma was about to comment, but Atrus quickly interceded. "Let us waste no more breath speculating. Master Tamon, bring up the cutting equipment. Let's breach the seal. I want to see what's at the far end of that chamber."

AFTER A LONG DAY'S WORK THE HUGE CUTTING FRAME WAS maneuvered into position before the doorway, four massive bolts securing it to the walls on either side. Then, taking the utmost care, the seal was breached, six of the D'ni using handheld cutters, the ancient door prised from the stone in which it had been set. Then, and only then, was it removed, the stone sighing as it gave, a huge gust of stale air wafting out into that space beneath the rock.

The massive slab of stone was lifted on four huge pulleys and lowered— the thick hawsers straining at the weight—onto the floor of the hall. Then, and only then, when it was safely down, did Atrus turn and contemplate the inner chamber.

The fire-marble they had fired into the chamber still glowed, but shadows gathered at the edges of vision. The far end of the chamber was dark, the doorway—if door it was—hidden from view.

A dozen or more pillars ranged along each side of that narrow chamber, set back into the walls, their marbled surfaces covered with strange markings. Stepping out between them, Atrus raised the lamp, then walked over to one of the pillars. He stood there a moment, staring up at it, then turned.

"Oma . . . come here."

Oma hastened across.

"What do you make of these?"

Oma stood there a while, studying the carvings. They looked like the signs and symbols of some ancient language.

"I . . . don't know."

"Esel?"

Esel shook his head. "I've never seen their like."

"No," Catherine agreed, "and yet they look familiar."

"Familiar?" Atrus turned to her. "You think you've seen these somewhere before?"

"Yes . . . but I can't think where."

Atrus turned back, then, stepping across, reached up and put his fingers into the groove of one of the more complex characters. The cuts were deep and smooth, each edge and surface finely polished. As for the symbol itself, it had the definite, finished shape of a letter in an alphabet, yet at the same time it also suggested a picture.

Atrus stepped back, lifting the lantern, trying to see if there were any other markings farther up the pillar, but what the lamp revealed was not more markings but Books, thousands upon thousands of Books, on shelves recessed into the walls high up and back from the pillars.

No wonder they hadn't seen them at first.

Oma gave a cry of pure delight, while Esel turned, looking to Carrad, his long, frowning face filled with a sudden urgency. "Carrad . . . Irras . . . bring ladders. Quickly now!"

They were back within a minute, Irras scrambling up onto the ledge, then hurrying down again, one of the ancient, leather-bound Books clutched to his chest.

As Oma carefully opened the page, they gathered round.

"Look!" Esel said. "It's the same script as on the pillars."

"It looks very much like it," Oma agreed. "And the panel . . ."

"Do not touch it," Atrus said quietly. "There is no Guild of Maintainers seal. And who knows how old these Ages are, or if they are stable or otherwise."

Atrus stared at the page, unable to decipher that ancient script, yet there was something about it that was familiar. Looking up, he raised his lantern once again, astonished by the sight. If they were all like this . . .

He walked on, slowly, the lamp held up before him, the darkness receding before him. Wall after wall of Books met his gaze, until he felt quite overwhelmed by it all. Then, lowering his eyes, he turned away . . . and stopped dead.

Just ahead of him, through a low arch flanked by pillars, was an anteroom. He stepped through, into a small chamber with four tiny alcoves leading off. The floor was marble, the low ceiling a concave circle of mosaic. His lamp blazed in that tiny space, and as he looked about him, Atrus realized that in each alcove the character that had appeared on the very first pillar was repeated.

And at the very center of the door, the character that had appeared on the very first pillar was repeated.

Atrus stared a moment, then turned, looking back toward where the others were still huddled about the ancient Book.

"Irras! Bring Master Tergahn! Now! Tell him we have need of his services once more!"

ATRUS TOOK HIS EYE FROM THE LENS OF THE SCOPE, THEN straightened up. He nodded to himself, as if some guess of his had been confirmed, then turned and gestured for Catherine to take the sample capsule from the shaft.

While Catherine tested the air sample of the second chamber, Marrim studied the surface of the nearest pillar. Like all of the others, its surface was completely covered in the strange, ancient markings. Esel and Oma had already begun the task of copying down the symbols, and though they had progressed little beyond the first two pillars, that had not stopped them from speculating upon their possible meaning.

Oma was of the opinion that this was an early form of D'ni, if only because of its age and location, but Esel was not so sure.

Marrim, looking at them once more, was struck by how beautiful the markings were.

Catherine came across, showing Atrus the sample. "It's safe."

"Good." Atrus turned and looked across the room. "Irras, bring me a cutter."

THE BOOK WAS HUGE, MUCH BIGGER THAN A NORMAL D'NI Book, the leather of its cover as thick and hard as slate, but strangest of all was the writing, for like the carvings on the pillars it was in a language none there recognized, though aspects of it were familiar.

For thousands of years the Book had lain there, sealed into the alcove at the far end of that ancient hidden hall. Now, seeing it there, the descriptive panel on the right-hand page glowing softly in the half-light, Marrim felt something between awe and a sheer superstitious fear of it.

Atrus, careful as ever, forbade any of them to touch it. He was determined to find out all he could before they used it.

That was, if they used it at all.

"Burn it," old Tergahn said, on looking at that strange, alien script. "That's what I say. If our forefathers thought to bury these chambers and

seal the doorways up, then no good can come of it. Burn it, Atrus! Burn it, then seal these chambers up once more."

"I agree," Atrus said. "The Book is far too dangerous."

But Esel and Oma argued otherwise.

"We should copy it," Oma said. "See what sense we can make of it. In all likelihood it's related to the markings on the pillars. If we can find a clue to reading it . . ."

Atrus hesitated. "All right," he said, after a moment. "But you will take the utmost care in copying it."

"I still say burn it," Master Tergahn said, shaking his head, a sour look on his heavily lined face.

"It may well come to that," Atrus said, glancing at the old man, "but it won't harm to take a look. That is, if Oma and Esel can unlock the meaning of that script."

"Burn it," Tergahn said, more determined than ever. "Burn it now, before any harm is done."

But Marrim, watching Atrus's face, saw that Atrus was not about to bow to the old man's superstitious fear of the Book.

"I hear you, Master Tergahn, and I note what you say. But I shall burn no Book without good cause."

"Then you're a fool, young Atrus," Tergahn said, and without another word he stalked away, the sound of his footsteps fading as he vanished into the darkness at the far end of the chamber.

Atrus stared a while, then turned, looking to Oma and Esel once more. "Begin at once," he said. "The sooner we know what this means, the more comfortable I'll feel."

OMA SAT AT HIS MAKESHIFT DESK INSIDE THE INNER CELL, dressed in one of the dark-green decontamination suits, complete with gloves and visor. The ancient Book lay to his left, open, the top two pages protected by a thin transparent sheet.

From his position on the other side of the bars, Esel looked on. He, too, wore protective garb.

"Well? Is it the same?" he asked, waiting for Oma to check back in his notes.

Oma ruffled through the pages, then stopped, having clearly found what he was looking for, and read through the earlier passage. Half turning, he shrugged. "I don't know. It's *almost* the same . . ."

"Almost?" Esel's heavy eyebrows went up.

For the last hour or so the two brothers had been debating a passage partway through the text that seemed to have no correlation with the normal, expected structure of such Descriptive Books. In it, many of the earlier passages they had already translated seemed to be repeated, yet with minor changes of phrasing and emphasis.

"The changes are so minor . . . It's almost as if the writer is trying to reinforce the earlier phrases."

"Hmmm . . ." Esel frowned deeply. "Reinforcement, yes. But to what purpose?"

"To make it more stable, perhaps?" Atrus said, coming across from where he had been checking one of the big E.V. suits.

"Then why not a direct repetition?"

"Because that would be redundant. By making such subtle changes in the repeated phrases, the writer may have been attempting to make the Age he was writing *more specific.*"

Oma had turned to face Atrus. "But why not simply put in those subtleties first time round?"

"As I said. To make it all more stable. I know from experience that the more subtle you try to be, the more *specific,* the more unstable your Ages are likely to be. It was the one great flaw with the worlds my father wrote."

"Then why did the practice cease?"

"Who can say? Things change. Perhaps they felt it *was* redundant and let the practice lapse."

"Maybe," Oma said. "Yet I rather like it. That is, if it is what you think it is, Master Atrus."

"And I," Atrus said, smiling. Then, changing the subject, "Are you still having problems with the phraseology?"

Oma grinned and looked to his brother. "We were, but we think we've mastered that now. Most of the oddities are simple structural inversions in the individual sentences. They probably accord with standard speech patterns of that time."

Atrus nodded. They knew now, for certain, that the underlying basis of the ancient script *was* D'ni, for the primitive forms matched the modern ones virtually one-to-one.

"So how long do you think it will take you to complete the work?"

Oma looked to his brother. "Two days? Three at most."

"Then keep to it. And Oma . . ."

"Yes, Master Atrus?"

"You might ask Marrim and Irras to look at the characters you have not yet managed to translate. They have a fresh eye to the language, and who knows if they might not see what more familiar eyes would overlook."

"I shall prepare a page for them."

"Good. Then I shall leave you to it."

IT WAS TIME, ATRUS DECIDED, TO MAKE A DECISION.

For the best part of a day he had sat alone at his desk, reading through the translated copy of the Book.

"Well?" Catherine asked finally, taking a seat across from him.

Atrus considered a moment, then answered her. "It is phrased so strangely. Unlike the D'ni Books we are used to. There is a certain . . . *ambiguity* to it. And yet, on the surface, it seems a safe and stable world. Those reinforcing phrases would seem to make it so. Yet what if there's something we've overlooked? Some small yet crucial detail." He shook his head. "I can't risk one of our people being trapped there."

"Then do as Master Tergahn said. Burn the Book. At least that way you'll remove the temptation."

Atrus laughed. "You think it *is* a temptation, then?"

"Of course it is! The young people think of nothing else . . . talk of nothing else. Why, they are so curious about what lies on the other side of that page that they would link at once, if you gave permission, without a moment's thought for their safety."

Atrus stared at her. "I didn't realize."

"On the other hand . . ."

"What?"

Catherine looked down, a strange smile on her lips. "You or I could go."

"And take the risk?"

"Or destroy the Book."

They stared at each other a moment longer, then, with a tiny shrug, Atrus reached across and took one of the last of their small store of blank Linking Books from the side.

"Okay," he said, glancing up at her. "I'll write a Linking Book. But *I* go, understand? No one else."

"Yes, my love," she answered, watching him open the slender Book then reach across for the pen. "You alone."

WHEN IT WAS DONE, ATRUS GATHERED TOGETHER THE SMALL team who had been working on the project and told them the news. There were grins and cheers and then, strangely, silence, as the full implication of what Atrus had said sank in.

"But you can't!" Irras said. "The risk's far too great!"

"No greater than for any of you," Atrus answered, determined not to be swayed by any argument of theirs. "I've made up my mind and it won't be changed. I link through, tomorrow morning, once everything's in place. Carrad, Irras, you'll be responsible for the suit, all right? Catherine will run the laboratory. Marrim . . . you'll assist her. Master Tamon . . ."

"Atrus . . . Irras is right. You cannot go. You're far too important. If anything went wrong . . ."

"Precisely. If anything went wrong it would be on *my* conscience, and I cannot have that."

Tamon shrugged, then bowed his head.

"Good," Atrus said. "Then you, Master Tamon, have a special task. If there are . . . complications, you will take the Book and burn it. Understand me?"

"Atrus . . ."

"No arguments," Atrus said, with a finality that silenced the old Master. But looking around the circle of friends, it was clear to him that none of them were happy with the arrangements.

"Until the morning, then."

IT WAS LONG AFTER MIDNIGHT WHEN THEY RETURNED. IRRAS led the way, a veiled lamp held up before him as they made their way along the corridor that led to the Guild cell.

Just behind Irras came Marrim and Carrad.

"I really don't like this," Marrim whispered, for what must have been the dozenth time.

"You want Atrus to risk himself?" Irras hissed back at her, attempting to be angry and quiet at the same time. "There's no other way, and you know it. We must test the Age before Atrus links through."

"But Irras . . ."

"Irras is right," Carrad hissed, turning to look back at her. "We owe Atrus everything. If we were to lose him, then we ourselves would be lost."

Marrim looked down, chastised. But she wasn't finished yet. "It isn't right, going behind his back like this."

"Maybe not," Irras conceded, "but he would never allow us otherwise. You heard him earlier. He was adamant."

Marrim sighed. "Okay. Then I will go."

"You can't!" Carrad and Irras said as one.

"Why not? I'd be missed less than you two."

"Nonsense," Irras said. "I'd miss you dreadfully."

"And I," Carrad said. "But that's beside the point. Irras is going."

Irras turned, wide-eyed, to face him. "What?"

"You heard," Carrad said. "Or have you learned how to operate the suit since last we used it?"

"No, I . . ."

"Then it's decided. Unless you don't *want* to go."

"I'm not afraid, if that's what you mean."

"Then it's decided," Carrad said, and, turning back, headed swiftly along the corridor, leaving the other two to catch up as best they could.

"ARE ALL THE SAMPLING CAPSULES FITTED, CATHERINE?"

"They're all in place. And there's extra oxygen in the cylinder on your back. Just in case."

Atrus's eyes followed Catherine as she busied herself at the laboratory bench. Sensing he was watching her, she looked up. "What is it?"

"Nothing," he answered. "Are you ready?"

She nodded, her face showing no emotion; as if this were a purely routine matter.

Carrad looked to Catherine, as if about to say something, but Irras frowned at him. "Come on, Carrad. Help me with the helmet now."

And then all was ready. Slowly, like some great mechanical thing, Atrus stepped into the cage, his back to the inner cell. The door clunked shut behind him, the seals came down. Slowly the cage revolved.

"Good luck!" Catherine called.

With a clunk the bolts slid back again and Atrus stepped out, into the inner cell.

Slowly he turned until he faced them again, then, raising his right glove, he brought it down on the back of his left.

The suit shimmered and then vanished.

Marrim looked across at Catherine, seeing the tension in her, the momentary fear in her eyes, and looked down.

Two seconds later the suit was back.

At once they were swarming about it, reaching through the bars to pluck the sampling capsules from their niches, even as the decontamination unit lowered itself over the suit, spraying Atrus with a fine mist of chemicals.

"Well?" Master Tamon asked. "What did you see?"

Atrus laughed. "Rock . . . I was surrounded by rock."

Marrim, looking to Irras, gave the faintest smile.

"*Rock?*" Master Tamon queried, surprised to find Atrus so excited about mere rock.

"Yes, and there's another doorway," Atrus went on excitedly, "like this one, but it, too, is sealed. And there's a Book . . . almost identical to the one we found! In the same ancient script!"

"A Book!" Master Tamon looked about him, seeing the sudden excitement in every eye.

"Yes," Atrus said. "And if my guess is right it links back here. But come, let's get on with it. Irras, set the timer for five minutes. I want a much better look this time."

THERE WAS BARELY ROOM IN THE ALCOVE TO TURN, LET ALONE set up the portable drilling machinery, but somehow it was done. Irras, his movements clumsy in the suit, made the first test bore, alone in that distant Age, sensors on the special suit ready to activate his return should there be any sudden change in atmospheric pressure or temperature.

Slowly the drill ate through the rock, then, suddenly, it was through, the bit meeting no further resistance.

Irras drew back; then, sealing the hole, he activated the sampler. As the tiny glass bubble moved back through the center of the drilling shaft, he felt the urge to take the scope, which was in the room with him, and peer through into the space beyond. But he had his orders. They would test the sample first. Then, and only then, would they take a look.

Slotting the sample capsule into the clip on his breast pocket, Irras pressed one hand against the stud in the palm of the other and linked back.

At once Catherine stepped up and, unclipping the capsule, turned and took it back down the steps to her workbench.

Irras looked about him. For once no one spoke.

This was the worst of it—having to wait about in the suit while the tests were made. It was not that it was uncomfortable—at most there was the feeling of cushioned constraint—but at such times Irras found himself questioning Atrus's little-by-little approach and wishing he'd take a risk now and then.

Atrus came across now and smiled at him. "Did the drill bit penetrate very far, Irras?"

"A hand's breadth," he answered.

"Good." Atrus turned, looking down toward where Catherine was busy at the centrifuge. "Well . . . we'll know very soon now."

"Atrus?"

"Yes?"

"Have you thought any more about *why* it might have been sealed?"

Atrus hesitated, then shook his head.

"And Master Tergahn's view?"

All were listening now. Last night Master Tergahn had reiterated his opinion that they should leave well be, that they should burn the Linking Book and reseal the chambers.

Atrus shrugged. "I only wish we knew more about the Great King. I have a vague recollection that my grandmother, Anna, once mentioned something about it, but what it was I can't recall."

For a moment he stared away into the shadows at the far end of the chamber, as if lost in thought, then he returned and, smiling, went down the steps again to stand beside Catherine at the workbench.

"Well?" he asked.

She glanced at him, then continued with her work. "I'll need to do more tests."

"Stale air?"

"Quite the contrary," she answered. "If my results are right, the air in there is fresh. And there are living organisms in it. Pollen, too."

"Pollen?"

Catherine nodded. "Yes. Now let me get on with things, Atrus. As soon as I know something more . . ."

". . . you'll let me know. But there's definitely air? Fresh air?"

"Yes!" she said. "Now leave me to get on."

Atrus turned, then hastened up the stairs, gesturing to Irras as he went. "Okay. Let's get you back inside. Let's see what's behind that wall."

IT TOOK THEM DAYS TO CUT A BIG ENOUGH HOLE IN THE wall, the task made more difficult by the fact that they could not use the portable power tools within the alcove, and that the two men, standing side by side, had little room to maneuver. They had spent the best part of an hour laboring beneath the light of a single lamp, careful not to nudge each other as, using hammer and chisel, they chipped out the channels in the rock.

But now the job was done. Three metal hooks had been screwed into the partially cut section of the wall, and a link of chain threaded through them. Irras now held the end of that chain, the powerful hydraulics of the special gloves he was wearing maintaining a tight grip as Atrus swung the great hammer.

The section of wall gave with a great crunch, the weight of the stone making it slew to one side, but the chain restrained it, keeping it from falling.

"Are you all right?" Atrus asked.

"I'm fine," Irras said, straining to keep the thing from sliding away from him.

"Good. Then lower it slowly. I'll shine the lamp through."

Atrus reached up and unclipped the lamp, then poked it through the gap.

There was an eerie silence. The only sound was that of their own breathing. That and the grating of the stone, the click-click-click of the chain links against the edge of the wall as Irras lowered the section to the ground.

"Good," Atrus said, as the huge piece of rock came to rest against the floor. "I'll step through and secure it."

Personally, Irras would just have kicked the thing in, but Atrus was keen to do as little damage as he could. *We are explorers,* he'd said, *not vandals.*

Even so . . .

He heard Atrus's gasp, sensed as much as saw him turn and raise the lamp high.

"Atrus?"

The lamp swung back. In its sudden brightness he could see a huge chamber, not unlike the chamber back in D'ni, with row after row of broad, stone shelves climbing the walls above the pillars.

Another library.

Only all of these shelves were empty.

Irras stepped out into the chamber and stood beside Atrus, taking in the sight. Somehow those empty shelves made it seem even more desolate than it otherwise might have been. And there was dust everywhere—huge drifts of dust, like sand, covering the marbled floor, in all but one or two places.

There was a sense of great age. Of long centuries of neglect.

Atrus gestured toward the far end of the chamber. "Let's see what's down there."

They walked across, their footsteps muffled, small clouds of dust lifting, then floating like smoke upon the air.

Atrus stopped. There was a huge doorway before them. Like those in D'ni, it had a massive circle of stone surrounding it, its pale surface decorated with a ring of stars, but unlike those in D'ni, this one seemed to be ajar.

Atrus walked toward it, then mounted the steps.

It *was* ajar.

He set down the lamp, then stepped closer, peering through the crack, unwilling to shine a light through that narrow space until he knew what was on the other side.

It was dark, yet not as dark as the chamber in which he stood, and after a moment his eyes grew accustomed to the half-light within.

Another chamber, larger, grander than the library, but in ruin, a number of its mighty pillars fallen, its great arched ceiling cracked in places, revealing a cloud-strewn night of brilliant stars.

And now Irras came and stood beside him, squinting into the darkness.

"Ruins," he said quietly, unable to keep the disappointment from his voice.

But Atrus made no comment, only: "Come, let's fetch the others. It's time we explored this Age."

PART FOUR

TORN PAGES CURL AND BROWN. THE FLAMES FLY UP.

IN THE FLICKERING LIGHT A CRY.

WHO WILL LIFT THE FALLEN STONES?

WHO WILL LINK THE BROKEN CHAIN?

—FROM THE <u>KOROKH</u> JIMAH, VV. 11383–86

Atrus turned to look as, one by one, his party linked through into the alcove, then stepped out into the chamber.

They had brought with them lamps and provisions, and as Oma, the last of them, stepped through, that ancient place seemed ablaze with the brilliant light of the fire-marbles.

Concerned that they might reveal themselves to hostile eyes, Atrus had them extinguish all but one of the lamps. Then, and only then, did he lead them across to the door at the far end of the chamber.

Though the door was open a crack, long eons of dereliction had wedged it in place, such that even with four of them heaving against its carved stone face they could not budge it the smallest fraction. Eventually, it was Marrim who, squeezing through the gap, set about clearing some of the debris from beneath it.

That done they tried again, and this time managed to move it back an inch or two, allowing the rest to squeeze through.

That second chamber, which Atrus had named The Temple, was a forlorn sight. It was not long now until the dawn, and in that last hour of the night it seemed impossible that they would find anything that might justify the time they had spent investigating this mystery.

This was a dead world. Or a world so long-abandoned as made little difference.

Marrim, standing in the center of that ruined chamber, turned full circle, taking in the desolation, then looked up through one of the great cracks in the fallen ceiling at the predawn sky.

It felt, to her, as if some ancient tragedy had befallen this place. Some tale so old that even the D'ni, that most ancient of races, had no record of it.

She turned back, looking to Atrus, who stood in the midst of the others, talking quietly, then spoke. "Atrus? What happened here?"

It was not that she expected him to answer; it was just that the question haunted her. Why was there no record of this place? And why had the Books been sealed off all these thousands of years?

"I don't know," Atrus answered, coming across. "Perhaps we'll learn." He turned slightly, addressing them all once more. "We'll split into groups and explore the site. One hour. And if anyone finds anything, return here at once."

They all knew what to do. They had done this now so many times it was second nature to them. Even so, it felt different this time, and as they stepped out through the great archway at the far end of the Temple, there were exclamations of surprise.

The Temple sat at the center of a host of other buildings, on a huge plinth of stone above the rest, while about the edges of that ancient town a great wood grew, the massive trees looming over that scene of ruin.

Not a building stood undamaged. In the growing light of dawn, they could see that long centuries had passed since anyone had ventured here. Weeds grew thick over the fallen stone.

It was as if the tragedy that had befallen D'ni had also visited this place. Here, too, a great civilization had once flourished, only to crumble into dust.

"Well," Atrus said, when no one had moved for several minutes. "Shall we see what there is to see?"

"MASTER ATRUS!" MARRIM SAID BREATHLESSLY. "WE'VE FOUND something!"

Atrus turned to her. "What is it, Marrim?"

She grinned. "You must see this!"

At to the outskirts of the ruined town, there was a way that wound between the massive trees following the course of an ancient stone drainage pipe that, over the long years, had been exposed to the air and now thrust up from the earth, like the rounded back of a huge snake.

They walked atop that ancient way, until they came to a massive slab of ochre rock that climbed the air in front of them.

"Here?" Atrus queried, for there seemed no way forward, but Marrim went on, climbing the rock like a mountain goat, seeming to find handholds were there appeared to be none.

Shrugging, Atrus followed, finding it much easier than he'd thought. The rock was porous and easy to grip; even so, he felt breathless by the time he'd come to the top of it.

As Catherine came near the top, he reached down and helped her up. Only then did he turn around and look. Only then did he understand just how high up they were.

And even as he registered that fact, his mind seemed to flip and his mouth fell open in sheer astonishment as he took in what he was looking at.

They were on the edge of a great plateau, a sheer drop of maybe half a mile directly beneath them, while below them, stretching from horizon to horizon, was the most beautiful land Atrus had ever seen; a land of lush, verdant farmland, massive fields divided by meandering waterways that sparkled in the early morning sunlight. Scattered here and there amid that vast landscape were buildings — huge, beautiful buildings of gleaming white stone, each set atop a grassy mound, and each one quite unlike anything Atrus had ever seen before, with a grandeur and elegance that took the breath. Godlike they were, such that, staring at them, Atrus wondered what manner of people inhabited this land.

All this Atrus took in at a glance, yet looking more distant, he caught his breath, seeing, in the far distance, its contours veiled in mist, another huge plateau, much larger than that on which they stood, up the soaring walls of which climbed a vast city of the same gleaming stone, the whole great edifice topped by a single massive building, with great towers and gilded domes.

Even at such a distance, Atrus understood at once. Here was something far greater than D'ni; a civilization so vast and ordered that it made his schemes for rebuilding that ancient home seem futile. No wonder they had let the ruins behind him lie untended. What need had they for such when they lived their daily lives amid such splendor?

Looking out across that magnificent landscape, Atrus felt a longing he had never thought to feel. A longing to belong to the land he had first seen only a moment before. And, looking to Catherine, who stood beside him, he saw it in her eyes, too.

"It's beautiful," she whispered.

"Yes," he answered, taking her hand.

For a time they stood there, silent, lost in a haze of astonishment. Then there was a shout from below, from the foot of the rock.

"Atrus? *Atrus!* What's going on up there?"

But Atrus had turned back, staring openmouthed once more, his eyes filled with astonishment as they flitted from wonder to wonder in that vast and beautiful land.

ATRUS DANGLED IN THE HARNESS, HIS LEFT HAND STEADYING him against the rough surface of the cliff face, as he leaned across and marked the trunk. Below him was a thousand feet of tree and rock, an almost vertical drop with here and there a yawning chasm reaching deep into the shadowed interior of the plateau.

Some fifty feet up from him, yet still some way from the summit, Carrad and Irras also hung, Irras fixing the two broad straps about the trunk of the marked tree, while Carrad began to saw through the base.

Above them was a path of neatly cut stumps, reaching up to where Master Tamon was busily organizing the construction of the platform, using the trunks they had cut earlier. They had been at the task two hours now and already a skeletal structure jutted out over the edge, a skein of ropes securing it until a more permanent fixing could be made.

Young Jenniran was in charge of making and fitting the winch, while Catherine and Marrim were busy organizing food and supplies for the expedition, a dozen backpacks laid out in a neat line at the back of the clearing.

Atrus turned, spinning expertly on the rope, stopping himself with the toe of his boot against the rock face. Looking up, he studied the channel they had cut through the trees and nodded to himself. He had chosen this route because of the slight overhang, turning a natural obstacle to his advantage. It would have been almost impossible to climb down from the plateau, and certainly quite infeasible to attempt to clamber back in case of an emergency, but when the chairlift was working they could get up and down the cliff in minutes, and transport whatever equipment they needed—not to speak of its use in an emergency.

But he would need to replace Irras and Carrad soon. It would have been heavy work even on steady ground, and though they were still enthusiastic, he could see they were flagging—the slightly built Irras more than his sturdier cousin.

He called up to them, keeping his voice low enough to carry, but not strong enough to be overhead from below.

"Two more, then send replacements down."

They did not argue, merely nodded, yet he could sense their disappointment. There was nothing they liked more than a challenge, and this—the scaling of this gargantuan cliff—was a challenge. Looking down again, Atrus felt his astonishment return, renewed every time he looked. Below him the massive trees stood like vast pillars in some demented mountain hall, nightmarishly tilted to the vertical.

At the foot of the plateau, glimpsed through the heavy foliage, was a huge rock, a great spur of dark ochre, its surface bare.

Atrus narrowed his eyes, staring through his lenses at it, then shook his head. It could not be helped. They would have to stop the chairlift some way above that, before the tree cover gave way to barren rock, and run rope ladders down, because if anyone were watching . . .

He tugged on the rope, once, twice, a third time. Slowly it was let out from above. Slowly he descended, using his feet to push himself out from the rock face. This tree . . . yes, and that.

But what if they are watching us? he thought. *What if they've been watching us since we came through—waiting for us to come down? What if they're setting their ambush even now?*

It was not a fear he wished to share, but he had to face it. Whoever they were, the native people of this Age might not readily welcome intruders; even ones as peaceful as themselves.

Atrus looked at his timer. From his estimates they had another six, maybe seven hours of daylight—time enough to finish the chairlift and make the descent. But he did not like the idea of going down there just as night fell. No. They would complete the chairlift and test it. Then they would secure it at the top of the plateau and spend the night up there.

Maybe so, yet even he felt impatient at the thought. He wanted to explore this world more than any other he had ever seen, and he knew that all the others felt the same. He had seen for himself how their eyes kept going to that wondrous landscape, awed—one might almost say *stunned*—by its beauty.

They would descend tomorrow, at dawn; unarmed, yet prepared, if necessary, to fight their way back to the cliff and back to D'ni.

And the Linking Book?

He would have Master Tamon rig something up to dispose of the Book if an emergency arose. It was easily done, after all.

From above came the sound of sawing, then a call. As Atrus looked up he saw another of the great trunks lift away and then sway its slow way up the cliff face toward the platform.

Tomorrow then, he thought, and turned, facing outward once again, seeing the rich greenness of the land there just beyond the branches, below him and to either side. *Tomorrow . . .*

THAT EVENING THEY CAMPED IN THE CLEARING. THE DAY HAD been long and hard, but no one wanted to retire, and after supper they gathered on the platform, sitting there long into the night, staring silently out into the sable blackness, upon which was scattered a thousand tiny patches of glowing pearl, like stars upon the night's dark ocean.

"What do you think?" Irras asked finally.

"I think I could sit here forever," Marrim answered him, and there was a murmur of laughter at that.

"Maybe so," Atrus said, standing and stretching, "yet we should get some rest now."

"Five minutes," Marrim pleaded, then, pointing, added, "Look, the moon is rising."

And, true enough, a single, small blue-white moon was just visible above the distant horizon; the smallest of the three that this Age apparently possessed.

Atrus turned, looking across the vast, pearled darkness at that thumbnail of glowing light, entranced by the sight, then nodded. "All right. Five minutes, then."

DAWN FOUND THEM STANDING AT THE FOOT OF THE PLATEAU, IN deep shadow, the great spur of ochre rock beneath their feet.

A pleasant wood lay below them, on the far side of which was a watercourse. But Atrus did not mean to travel that way just yet. First he would send out scouts, to see what could be learned about the land and its inhabitants. For this task he chose Irras and Jenniran. He had them set their timers, then promise to be back within the half hour.

They returned with just under two minutes to spare, perspiring heavily. The land, it seemed, was prosperous and there were signs of recent activity, but they had seen not a single person.

Cautious as ever, Atrus sent out Carrad and Esel to make another sweep of the land, but when they returned half an hour later, it was only to confirm what Irras and Jenniran had reported. The land was beautiful but empty.

Taking Catherine aside, Atrus debated the matter a moment, then addressed the rest of them once more.

"If my estimates are correct, the nearest of the dwellings we saw from the plateau is a two-hour walk from here. We'll make for that, sending out scouts along the way. We have ample food and water, so our only problem will be one of secrecy. If you must talk, speak to an ear, otherwise remain silent. And keep to the trees. But don't bunch. Keep in a line behind me."

He paused, then added, "Jenniran, I have a special task for you. You will be our anchor, here at the foot of the plateau. From time to time I shall send a messenger back to report on what we have found. I need you to relay those messages back to D'ni, through Master Tamon."

Atrus turned back. "Now let us be on our way. But remember, though the land looks peaceful, we do not know the nature or customs of these people. So take care at all times."

And with that, Atrus turned, leading the way down off the rock and onto the plain below.

AN HOUR'S WALKING BROUGHT THEM TO THE MIDDLE OF AN orchard of low trees with dark red trunks whose verdant branches bore a strange purple fruit. There they rested, seated on the rich green grass that lay like a carpet between the smooth boles of the trees.

The day was hot, but it was cool enough beneath the branches. If Atrus was right, the great house they had seen from the plateau lay directly ahead, but as yet they had had no sight of it. Atrus sat there now, his measuring instruments open on the grass beside him as he wrote in his notebook.

Marrim closed her eyes and rested back on her elbows, her legs stretched out. For a time she drifted, thoughtless, her head filled with the hum of the local insects. Earlier, she had caught and studied one of them—a large, bee-like insect, its "fur" bright red with a spiraling black stripe about the abdomen—and found that it lacked a sting. But so it was here. The beauty of it, combined with the warmth of the day, washed over her like the waves of a warm ocean on a summer's day.

Oma, who had wandered away for a moment, returned to the clearing, gazing about distractedly, one of the dark, perfectly spherical fruits in his hand. Seeing Atrus he looked across and smiled.

"Oma!" Atrus bellowed. "What in the Maker's name are you doing?"

Oma blinked, then stared at the partially eaten fruit in his hand and, horrified, dropped it as if it were a burning coal. "I'm sorry, I . . ." He swallowed. "I forgot, Master Atrus."

"*Forgot!*" Atrus leaned toward him. "If you're sick, you look after yourself, you understand?

"But Master Atrus . . ."

Atrus turned his back. "All right," he said, "we'd best press on. Irras . . . scout ahead."

As Irras hurried away, they rose silently and, slipping on their packs, made their way slowly after Atrus, spread out like shadows beneath the trees.

They had not gone far when Irras returned.

"There's a path," he said. "It runs straight."

"Toward the house?" Atrus asked.

Irras shook his head. "It crosses our way."

"All right. Let's go and see."

It was a broad, well-tended path of loosely chipped white stone, raised up just above the level of the ground to either side. Small culverts, containing the narrow irrigation channels that were everywhere in this land, ran beneath it at regular intervals, while on its far side was a great field of tall, exotic-looking plants with flame-tipped flowers, and beyond that a tree-capped ridge, its foliage dense and dark. As for the path itself, just as Irras had said, it ran straight to left and right. Yet the house, if Atrus's calculations were correct, lay directly ahead.

"Maybe it curves," Esel suggested.

"It doesn't look as though it curves," Irras answered him.

"No," Atrus agreed. "Yet maybe we should follow it a while. Perhaps it meets another path, farther along."

Carrad made to climb up onto the path, but Atrus called him back. "No, Carrad. We keep to the trees."

Chastened, Carrad did as he was told.

Turning to the right, they began to walk. At first they were silent, but after a while, reassured by the peacefulness of the day, the beauty of the land through which they moved, Atrus began to talk.

"It makes you wonder," he said, pausing to turn and look about him.

Catherine came alongside him. "Wonder what?"

"What kind of people they are who tend this land."

"A generous people," she said, without hesitation.

Atrus looked to her. The rest of the party had stopped and were looking about them at the surrounding fields, fanning themselves in the afternoon heat. "You think so?"

"I do. Just look at how rich this land is. There's so much here. They can afford to be generous."

Atrus smiled. But Catherine went on. "Where there's little to go round, each man—and woman—must fight for their share. But when there's so much . . ."

"It isn't always so," Atrus said. "When I lived with my grandmother, we had little or nothing, yet I would not say we were ungenerous."

Catherine laughed. "That's different. What if there had been three or four families living in the cleft, each needing to rake a living from the little that was there? What then?"

"Maybe," he said, without any real conviction. "But I feel you're right."

They walked on, lost in the day's beauty, each with their own thoughts about the wonders that lay on every side. Half a mile farther on, the path gently climbed, crossing a small, delicately arched bridge. Beneath its single span flowed a stream; a broad blue channel that meandered gently through the fields to their right, finally losing itself among the trees far to the left.

Indeed, they were so taken by their surroundings that it was a moment or two before anyone saw the boat that was moored on the far side of the bridge.

"Atrus!" Oma hissed. "Look!"

The boat was long and broad, its prow elegantly curved, a great awning of yellow silk overhanging the deck below which rested a number of elegant-looking couches. Beneath that awning, one hand resting lightly on the supporting pole, stood a tall young man dressed in a flowing robe of lavender edged with black. His hair was midnight black and cut in a strange yet elegant fashion, and his eyes were a deep sea green. But the strangest thing of all about him was that, though he looked directly at them, he seemed not to have seen them at all.

"Do I see you?"

Atrus stopped dead. The words, spoken in a clear yet heavily accented D'ni, had come from the stranger, yet still the man did not seem to look at them.

Was he blind? Marrim wondered, seeing the lack of movement in those eyes. Or were those green eyes lenses of some kind?

Atrus took another step toward him. "Where are we?"

The young man did not seem to hear him. "Do I see you?" he repeated.

Atrus turned, looking to the others, puzzled by the young man's behav-

THE BOOK OF D'NI • 139

ior, then turned back, stepping closer, stopping no more than four or five paces from where the young man stood in the boat.

"We are from D'ni," Atrus said, speaking slowly and precisely. "We have come from D'ni."

There was a movement in the young man's eyes—a movement that wasn't quite a movement, more a reassessment. A look of understanding slowly entered those orbs that, until a moment before, had seemed sightless.

"From Ro'D'ni?"

Atrus hesitated, then nodded.

"Then come," he said, the D'ni words clear despite the strange accent. "You must be hungry after your long journey."

The young man looked about him, taking each of them in one at a time, his eyes resting slightly longer on the figure of Marrim, the eyes narrowing slightly as he noted her boyish hair.

Then, putting out both hands to Atrus, he introduced himself.

"Forgive me. My name is Hadre Ro'Jethhe, son of Jethhe Ro'Jethhe. Welcome . . . welcome to Terahnee."

THE BOAT MOVED SLOWLY, SILENTLY DOWN THE STREAM, ITS smooth passage within the channel unaided by oar or motor such that the D'ni, seated aboard the strange craft, looked about them in wonder.

Wherever they looked, their eyes found delights, as if this whole land had been sculpted—each plant and bush arranged *just so* to please the eye. The shape of the land, its textures and colorings: each element blended perfectly, with now and then a contrast—be it a brightly colored flower or a specially shaped rock—that would cause them to smile with sheer pleasure.

As for their host, though he was genial enough, he was not greatly forthcoming. Whenever Atrus asked a direct question, Hadre would answer vaguely, or change the subject, or even act as if Atrus had not spoken, and this, like his behavior in those first few moments they had met, puzzled Atrus. And yet there seemed no darker reason for it. From what Hadre did say, it seemed they were to stay at the great house that evening. Moreover, the young man made it quite clear that they were very welcome and that if there was anything they wanted—*anything*—they were only to ask and he would see to it.

They sat back, lounging against the broad, ornately decorated gunwales of the boat, entranced by their surroundings. As the boat came around a turn in the stream and, passing beneath a decorative arch, glided into a sun-lit glade—a small bowl in the surrounding hills—Atrus was surprised to find a picnic set up for them.

They climbed from the boat, amazed. A dozen couches were set up within that pleasant space, and at the center of it all a great table was piled high with food—all manner of fruits and other delicacies—that, when they finally tasted them, proved delicious beyond all belief.

Oma, who had sustained no harm from his earlier forgetfulness, now turned to their host and smiled. "This is most excellent."

Hadre smiled. "I am glad you like it, Master Oma," he said, impressing them all, for Oma had been named but once on the journey, and then only in passing.

But that was not the only instance. Hadre had only to be told something once and he remembered it.

When they had eaten their fill, Hadre ushered them back onto the boat and they continued their journey.

Once more the land opened up about them as they glided silently through an endless vista of wonders. As they came around one bend they were confronted by a great waterfall of tiny blue flowers, beneath which they passed, finding themselves a moment later within a cavernous space, the roof of which was formed by the roots of a single massive tree. And on they went, past sculpted banks of wonderfully scented blooms and out into a valley where, directly ahead of them, the great house rose like a glacier from the mound on which it sat.

"The Maker's name!" Atrus said, under his breath, not merely because the building was far bigger than he had guessed at from a distance, but because he saw now what they all suddenly saw: that what they had taken to be simple whiteness was not in fact white at all but a whole rainbow of colors within the stone, as if the whole building were one great prism. Yet the stone was not transparent; the different colors in the stone seemed to shift with every moment, as if alive.

Closer they came and closer still, and then, with a strange little rush, the channel turned, taking them through a long, low archway and beneath the walls of the building into a huge, shadowed courtyard of startlingly blue marble, about which level after level of balconies looked down, great clusters of gorgeously scented blooms—bright gold and startling crimson, jet black and emerald—trailing from them. Six massive stone ramps led up from the courtyard, each entering the house through a beautifully carved wooden gateway, beyond which were huge double doors inlaid with pearl.

"Home," Hadre said simply. Then, stepping from the boat, he turned and bowed graciously. "Welcome Atrus and Catherine. Welcome all. Welcome to the house of Ro'Jethhe."

ATRUS STEPPED THROUGH THE GREAT ENTRANCE ARCH AND INTO a hall of cool marble, at the center of which was a round pool. A circle of slender pillars surrounded it, each a distinct color, the stone sculpted to resemble the stems of flowers, each pillar blossoming where it met the ceiling, the giant petals folding outward, so that the ceiling seemed like a huge floral bed, the interplay of color delightful to the eye.

Atrus stared up at it a moment then looked to his young host. "Is all of this great building yours, Hadre Ro'Jethhe?"

Hadre turned, smiling pleasantly. "It is my father's house. And all the lands surrounding it are his."

They walked on until they stood beside the pool, looking down into its crystal depths. The pillars to either side of them soared up into the ceiling, fifty, maybe sixty feet above their heads, dwarfing them. From this close the stone, which, from the doorway, had seemed frail, now looked thoroughly solid and immovable.

Thus far Hadre had been the only person they had seen in all of Terahnee, but now two other men—smaller and more stockily built, discernibly different from Hadre, and not merely in their physical attributes—entered the hall from a narrow doorway to the left and, hastening across, bowed low before Hadre. They wore long flowing cloaks of a soft wine-red cloth, but what was most distinct about them was their silver hair—not white, but silver, like a fine wire—which was swept back off their foreheads and tied in a tight bunch at their necks.

"Master?" the elder of them asked. As he turned, Atrus noticed he had two vertical purple stripes beneath his right ear.

"Kaaru . . . Jaad . . ." Hadre said, "these are my guests. You will take great care of them and see to all their needs."

"Master!" the two men said as one, then stepped back, seeming almost to vanish as they slipped into the shadows beside the pillars.

Hadre turned back to his guests and smiled. "And now you will forgive me, Atrus, but I must tell my father the news. He will want to greet you personally."

AFTER HADRE HAD GONE THE TWO SERVANTS LED ATRUS AND his party through into a second, smaller hall where, once again, a meal had been laid out ready for them.

As in the clearing in the wood, a number of couches had been placed in a circle about the center of the room, within easy reach of the endless delicacies that graced the central table.

Having seen that they were comfortable, Kaaru and Jaad stepped back, seeming to blend once more into the shadows of the walls.

This second hall was both more modest—in its scale—and more opulent—in its detail—than the previous one. Marrim, looking about her, could not help but admire the care these people took. Each bowl, each spoon, each tiny fork, was a work of art, not to speak of the arms of the couches, or the carved panels that filled each wall between the swirling marble pillars.

Not a surface was overlooked. Even the simplest thing was decorated. Yet the overall impression was not overly decorative. There was an underlying simplicity that formed a perfect contrast with the intricate designs. Nothing was out of place here; nothing overwrought.

Looking across, Marrim saw how Atrus stared at the myriad of things surrounding him, looking from one to another with the same awed look, and knew at once that he, too, had seen what she had seen. Yet when he looked up, there was a strange, almost wistful smile on his face. Seeing it, Catherine, who had also been watching him, asked:

"Atrus? What is it?"

Atrus picked up one of the delicate spoons, tracing the molded pattern on its bowl with his thumb, then laughed; a strange, brief, haunted laugh.

"All this," he said finally. "It reminds me."

"Of Anna?"

Atrus nodded. "There was never a surface she could leave alone. It was as though the whole universe was a blank page on which she was compelled to write." He paused, then. "I sense it is the same for these people. I look around and see the same blend of simplicity and embellishment."

"They must be great dreamers," Catherine said.

"Yes, and fine craftsmen, too," Esel added, looking up from the beautifully glazed bowl he was holding.

Marrim nodded, then reached out to take the cool drink so close to hand, sipping at the blood-red liquid delicately. Like the drink she had had in the clearing, this was both refreshing and intoxicating, though not in the way that wine was intoxicating. There was such a scent to this, such an overwhelming taste, that it was as if her senses had been numbed until the moment she had tasted it.

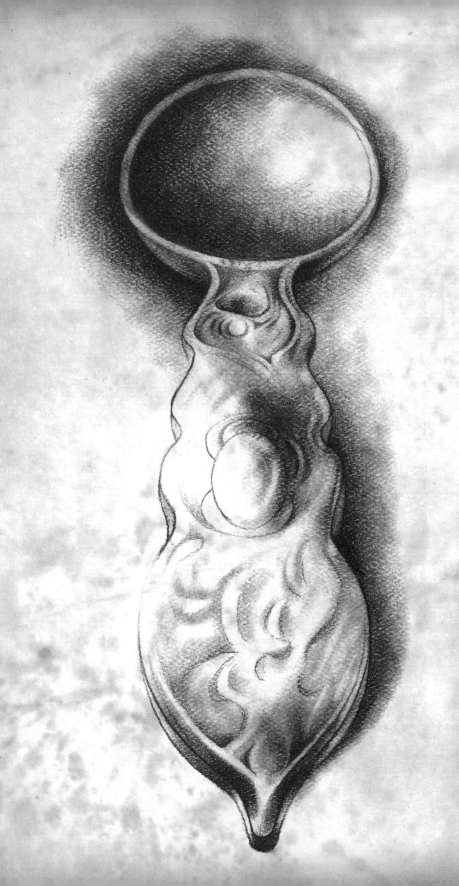

"This Hadre and his father," Irras said. "They must be very rich men to own all this. They surely cannot *all* live like this."

"On the contrary . . ." a voice boomed from the far side of the chamber, "ours is but a humble estate."

At once they were all on their feet, facing the newcomer—a handsome, elderly looking man with neat dark hair and a stern, patrician air. Yet even as that sternness registered on the mind, the old man smiled and, opening his arms, walked across and embraced Atrus warmly.

"Atrus! Friends and companions of Atrus! I am Jethhe Ro'Jethhe, and you are welcome to my house. Stay as long as you will. My home is your home."

And with this little speech complete, he walked among them, taking hands or embracing them, coming to Marrim last.

"Young lady," he said, with a slight bow of his head, as if he spoke to someone high above him in status. "I am indeed most pleased to make your acquaintance."

Marrim, both delighted and embarrassed by the sudden attention, ducked her head down, feeling a faint flush come to her neck.

And then it was Atrus's turn to thank Hadre's father for his hospitality.

"Think nothing of it," Ro'Jethhe said, with a lazy gesture of dismissal. "I am sure you would do the same were we the visitors and you the hosts."

Atrus smiled. "Indeed we would."

The old man's smile encompassed them all. "Well, then. So it is." Then, turning to Irras. "But forgive me my rudeness, Master Irras. You asked a question, and I gave you but a partial answer. Come then, let us all be seated once more, and I shall answer *all* your questions."

IT WAS LATE AFTERNOON WHEN FINALLY JETHHE RO'JETHHE clapped his hands and stood.

"Kaaru! Show my guests to their rooms!"

At once his servant was at his back, waiting to do his bidding. Turning to Atrus, Ro'Jethhe smiled. "You have traveled far, my friends. I am sure you will wish to bathe and change your clothes before tonight's entertainment."

"Entertainment?" Atrus sat forward. It was the first time Ro'Jethhe had mentioned it.

"Oh, it's nothing much. A simple thing. A few friends—local landowners—will be invited. And my sons, of course. It will be a chance for you to meet everyone."

Atrus smiled. "We thank you, Jethhe Ro'Jethhe, for your kindness."

"Not at all," the old man said, looking about him and smiling. "I am glad you are here, Atrus. You and all your party. And remember, whatever you want, you have only to ask."

The two men bowed to one another, then Ro'Jethhe turned and swept from the room, his son hurrying to catch him up.

THE BEDROOM, LIKE ALL ELSE, WAS MASSIVE. A HUGE BED— big enough, it seemed, to sleep a small village—rested in the center of a huge, high-ceilinged room. Here the pillars were thick, eight-sided things of a midnight basalt. Eight of them formed an octagon about the center of that long and airy chamber, thrusting up out of a floor that was made of wood, the broad slats of which were coated with a fine dark red lacquer inset with all manner of ingenious patterns. The partition doors were huge, paneled things, set into walls so thick they reminded Atrus of a fortress he had visited once on an ancient D'ni Age. Most impressive of all, however, was the wide balcony that led off of the room, and gave a perfect view of the surrounding countryside.

A fine silk hanging of pale lemon and blue shimmered in the late afternoon breeze as Catherine stepped beneath it and out onto the stone flags of the balcony.

"Atrus . . ."

He stepped through, joining her there at the balustrade, the two of them silent a moment as they stared out across the sloping lawns toward a copse of trees; no tree the same, the combination of colorings and textures a delight to the eye. A strange bird called, high and sweet.

Threading her arm through his, Catherine smiled up at him. "Have you ever dreamt of such a place, Atrus?"

"No," he said. "My mind reels before it, Catherine. To think that it is *all* like this."

For Jethhe Ro'Jethhe had told them that far from being a rich man, he was but a common citizen, and that there were many—the governor of the district among them—who lived in a far more palatial manner, though how that could be Atrus could not imagine, for this was luxury beyond anything he had ever experienced. Moreover, Ro'Jethhe himself had proved an intelligent and witty man, immensely cultured, quick to understand, and always generous in his comments. Atrus had warmed to him at once.

Even so, it was hard to take in much of what Ro'Jethhe said, and had Atrus not already had that glimpse of the land from the plateau, he might have counted it as boastful. Was this place *really* as big as Ro'Jethhe claimed? Two hundred million citizens! It was difficult to imagine, even though he had seen how the land stretched away from horizon to horizon. Why, if they *all* lived like this, then the wealth of this land must be truly phenomenal. D'ni, even at its height, was as nothing beside it.

While they bathed and changed, Catherine and Atrus talked further of what they had learned from Jethhe Ro'Jethhe.

Terahnee was ruled by a king, supported by a council of advisers, under which were the district governors. Yet astonishingly enough, despite the size of the kingdom, there was no equivalent of the Guild of Maintainers. *No one policed Terahnee because no one needed to.* It was that, more than anything else that they had seen or heard, that most impressed Atrus, for to him it revealed the high moral standard this culture had attained.

This was a land without wars, or theft, or fraud.

"All this . . ." Atrus said, gesturing at the mosaics, the statuary, and all the other innumerable beautiful things that surrounded them. "*All* of this is quite remarkable, yet without a moral depth it is nothing. The true, defining mark of a civilization is how its people treat each other."

"They have servants . . ." Catherine began.

"Yes, but they clearly treat them well, as I'm sure you've noticed. Kaaru and Jaad might bow their heads before their masters, yet there is nothing servile about them. Indeed, I sense an air of great pride about them."

"Do you not find that *strange*, Atrus?"

"In a land such as this? No. Some must work while others plan and organize the work. So it is in all societies. So it was to a degree in D'ni."

"To a degree." But Catherine left it there. Besides, she was not really in disagreement with Atrus. To keep a world this beautiful must take a great deal of organizing. And Atrus was right. She had never before met with such servants.

Changing tack, she asked another question that had been playing on her mind.

"Atrus? Do you think they are your kin?"

"D'ni, you mean?"

"Yes. There is the common language, after all . . ."

"That might have been acquired, or shared, maybe, back in the distant past. It's possible this was an Age that, losing its connection with D'ni, went its own way."

"Do you think so?"

"I'd say it was highly likely. For one, they do not share the visual weakness of the D'ni. As far as I have seen, they wear no lenses. And the style in which they build . . . it is as different from the D'ni as it could possibly be. Their extensive use of wood, for instance."

"True," Catherine said, "but that can be easily explained. In D'ni they had no trees. Here there are millions of them—thousands of millions. Besides, over millennia societies take different paths. We should expect such differences."

"Maybe so," Atrus said, pulling on a silken jacket that had been left out on the bed for him, "but until I know for certain that there is a link, I will not assume one. The fact that they speak a version of our language proves nothing."

Catherine was about to pursue the subject when there was a knocking at the door.

"Come!" Atrus said, turning to face the doorway.

But it was only Marrim, Irras, and Carrad. They spilled into the room, all smiles and excitement.

"Master Atrus!" Irras said. "There's a library!"

"It's huge!" Carrad added, as they left the room and hurried down a long, broad corridor, the ceiling of which seemed like the bottom of a well it was so far above them.

"And the books!" Marrim added. "You've never seen anything like it!"

Atrus smiled at that last, yet when he stepped into the deeply recessed doorway, he stopped dead, astonished.

The library was not a single room, as he'd expected. Indeed, it was not a room at all, but a great hall, with, just beyond it, a second and even a third hall, the walls of which were filled, floor to high ceiling, with books—endless leather-bound books. Enough, it seemed, to fill D'ni!

"And these are simple *landowners?*" Catherine said, voicing his own thought.

"Atrus?"

Atrus turned, surprised, to find Hadre there behind him in the doorway.

"Forgive us, Hadre. We did not mean to pry."

"There is nothing to forgive," Hadre said, smiling and gesturing that they should go through, into the library. "Whatever you wish to see. As my father said, our home is yours while you stay with us."

"You are both most generous."

"Not at all," Hadre said. "My people love to share the things of the mind. We are great lovers of books. As I sense *you* are."

He clapped his hands and at once a servant appeared in the doorway to their right. It was not Kaaru or Jaad this time, but a much older man. Even so, he wore a similar wine-red cloth, and had the same silver hair, the same striped markings beneath his right ear.

"Master?"

"You will not be needed, Duura. I will see to my guests myself."

"As you wish, Master." And with a bow, Duura departed.

"So?" Hadre said, looking to Atrus, smiling once more. "Where would you like to start?"

THE LIBRARY WAS NOT THE ONLY WONDER IN THE HOUSE. Catherine's favorite was a great hall of glass partitions filled with the most astonishing plants—in effect, a massive indoor greenhouse, whose levels and separate chambers were each lit at different times of the day from a great lens of a window that was set into the ceiling of the chamber. One could climb within the mazelike chamber into rooms, the floors and walls of which were solid glass, permitting you to believe you walked within a lush, exotic jungle, the air intoxicatingly sweet, the light like that of the primal forest on an untouched world.

Beyond that, and in total contrast, was a long gallery, the light within which seemed to have filtered down through the long centuries. There, to either side, in three long rows on walls that seemed to go on endlessly, hung what seemed like a thousand life-size portraits.

"These," Hadre said proudly, "were Ro'Jethhe."

Staring at them, at those endless variations on the same face, Atrus understood at last just how old this place really was, for all of these men had in turn been master of this house. This long, unbroken chain of fathers and sons spoke more eloquently than anything of the durability of this society.

"You say all of these were Ro'Jethhe," Atrus said. "Was that their name, or their title?"

Hadre turned to him and smiled. "When they were younger they had other names—names their mothers gave them, Just as my brother Eedrah and I have names. But when it was their time, each lost that name. You understand?"

Catherine nodded. "So you, in turn, will be . . ."

"Ro'Jethhe." He smiled. "But that will be many years from now. My father is in the prime of his life."

"Your people live a long time, then?" Atrus asked.

"Long enough," Hadre answered.

"A hundred years?" Catherine asked, knowing, because she had asked him earlier, that Terahnee's year was not dissimilar to D'ni's.

Hadre laughed at that. "No. My father is almost two hundred years old."

"Ahh . . ." Catherine met Atrus's eyes, the faintest flicker of a smile in her own, as if some point had been proven.

A bell rang, deep and low, its tolling seeming to come from the very foundations of the great building. Hearing it, Hadre turned to them and, bowing low, made his apologies.

"Forgive me," he said, "but I must leave you now. Until this evening . . ."

Hadre made to leave, then turned back. "Oh . . . and you will be pleased to learn that we shall be having a special guest at this evening's entertainment. The district governor will be attending. He has expressed great interest in meeting you."

And with that he turned and hurried from the room.

"Well . . ." Catherine said, then fell silent, noticing the servant standing to one side of them. She was sure he had not been there a moment before.

"If you would follow me," the man said, inclining his head, "I shall show you to your rooms."

Atrus looked to Catherine, his surprise mirroring her own, then he shrugged. "All right," he said, glancing once more at the long line of Ro'Jethhe ancestors that filled the walls on every side. "Lead on."

THE BOAT MOVED SWIFTLY, SILENTLY BENEATH THE PEARLED moon, the land mysteriously veiled in silver light. From where he sat in its prow, Atrus turned and looked back, past Catherine and Hadre, toward the receding whiteness of the house.

He had assumed the evening's festivities would take place in Ro'Jethhe, but on arriving downstairs at the appointed hour, they were greeted by Hadre with the news that they were all to meet up at the amphitheater, which was to the north of the house.

And so here they were, gliding along through countryside as beautiful as anything they'd seen, the stream, which had broadened to a river, winding gently through the folded hills.

In the stern of the boat, Marrim sat among the young men—Carrad and Irras, Oma and Esel—the same look of wonderment on every face. It was their habit to talk as they journeyed—to discuss things endlessly—but the beauty of the evening had robbed them all of their tongues.

Atrus looked down, smiling, knowing that he felt no less. He had been here less than a day, yet already he was half in love with this strange and wonderful land. Of all the Ages he had traveled to, none came close to comparing with this, and, not for the first time, he began to wonder who had written such a world; who had crafted the physical characteristics that had permitted such a place to develop—for if he knew anything about writing, it was that, ultimately, geography determined an Age's social structures. He would study the Book even more—surely it was written by a master of masters.

What then had happened here to create such idyllic circumstances? Was it merely the placidity of the weather, the richness of the soil, the unchanging sameness of the place that had allowed such a society to develop? Or were the decisions of men—men like himself—to account for this perfect orderliness, this astonishing flowering of a civilization?

He did not know—nor, to be truthful, did he really wish to. And that in itself was strange, for never before had he felt the edge of his curiosity blunted in this manner. Catherine, too, he knew, was happy to take things as they were, to let the flow of things carry her along.

As now, he thought, conscious of the silent movement of the boat beneath him. As the boat turned a bend in the river, his eyes caught sight of the terraced hillside just ahead of them, the levels of that terrace hollowed out in places and filled with water, so that the whole hillside was a pattern of deep shadow and brilliant, silvered light, forming the silhouette of a face—the face of a beautiful young woman.

There was a murmur of appreciation from the stern of the boat, and then a tiny gasp of surprise, for as the boat moved on, changing direction slightly, so the pattern of light and dark changed. And now the silhouette of a young man was revealed, staring back, as if at the young lady who had so briefly appeared and then vanished once more.

"Ingenious," Atrus said. "Quite ingenious."

"It is an old design," Hadre said, playing down Atrus's praise, "but popular."

"Are there many such designs?" Oma asked.

Hadre turned and smiled at the younger man. "Very many. In fact, you passed some earlier in the day, but they are far less easy to discern in the glare of daylight."

"And the water . . . how do you get the water there?" Esel asked, frowning heavily.

But Hadre had turned back to Atrus. "It is not far now, Ro'Atrus," he said. "The amphitheater marks the boundary between our lands and that of our neighbor, Ro'Hedrath. You will meet him, and his son, Juurtyri. Juurtyri, Eedrah, and I shared a tutor when we were younger."

Catherine, who had been sitting quietly throughout, now said, "You mentioned your brother earlier. Will he be there tonight?"

Hadre turned slightly, meeting her eyes. "He has been away, but tonight he will return." Hadre paused. "He has not been well. . . ." Then, smiling, "But come, we are almost there."

AS THE MUSICIANS FINISHED, MARRIM RAISED HER HEAD AND sighed. She had never heard anything like it. At first she had not understood or liked the strangely dissonant sounds with which the composition had begun, nor the oddly mathematical patterns in which it was arranged, yet as it developed and those wonderful harmonies had begun to overlay that basic pattern, she had found herself not merely moved but thrilled by the passionate complexity of the music.

Clever, she thought, then corrected herself. *No, not clever, remarkable.*

So remarkable that, while the music had been playing, she had completely forgotten where she was. And that really was amazing.

When the boat had first entered the amphitheater, gliding beneath a series of low arches, she had smiled, pleased by the way the raised bowl at the center of the amphitheater resembled a giant petal. Yet even as the boat had slowed, following a spiral twist about the center, the walls surrounding the amphitheater had seemed to shimmer and dissolve into a kind of mist. Marrim had stared, not understanding, then had clapped her hands with delight, for the walls had changed in that instant into a continuous waterfall that completely surrounded the amphitheater, the crystal water tumbling into the deep moat that ran around the shell-like structure.

Earlier, discussing things with Oma and Esel, Carrad and Irras, they had agreed among themselves that the wonders that they had witnessed on their travels must have been developed over many, many years. They had imagined a process where someone—some bright, creative sort—had originally had an idea, and how others throughout the land had then copied and developed it, refining it over long centuries until it had reached its present state. Even so, the whole thing was quite incredible. It was not simply that these people put so much thought into everything they did, it was the scale on which they worked. Nothing was too much trouble for them, it seemed.

Now, lounging among the several dozen guests—neighboring landowners and their wives and sons—the idea that some kind of magic lay behind all this was strong in her mind.

"Master Atrus?"

Atrus turned on his couch, looking to her. "Yes, Marrim?"

"Did they have music in D'ni?"

"Yes, but in truth I have never heard it. Besides, it would not compare with what we have just heard."

"You liked our music, Atrus?"

The speaker, on the couch immediately to Atrus's right, was Ro'Jethhe's second son, Eedrah. He was slighter in build than his brother and paler of complexion, yet the resemblance was striking.

Atrus turned and addressed the young man, inclining his head. "To be honest, I have never heard the like."

"Ah, yes," Eedrah pressed, "but did you *like* it?"

To Marrim's surprise, Atrus hesitated, then shook his head. "It was astonishing. So complex and so elegant, but, to be frank, I found it . . . *uncomfortable.*"

Marrim, hearing this, could not help herself. "But it was wonderful, Master Atrus! Those harmonies! The underlying patterns of the music! It was . . . *beautiful!*"

She looked about her after she had said it and saw how everyone was suddenly looking at her; how all the landowners, all the wives and children of the landowners, were suddenly staring at her, the same concentrated frown on every face. Eedrah, particularly, seemed to be watching her closely. Seeing that, she blushed.

"I agree," Catherine said, interceding. "For a moment I totally forgot where I was."

Eedrah smiled. "Why, you are in Terahnee!"

And there was laughter. The young man bowed his head and grinned at Marrim, who blushed deeper. But the moment had passed, and the conversation, which had stopped for the music, began to flow once more.

It was quickly obvious that the people of this Age loved to talk—and not merely to talk, but to debate each subject at great length and in great depth; a natural wit keeping the conversation light and buoyant even when the subject matter was profound.

Marrim, watching Atrus, saw how he suddenly blossomed in this new environment. Admiring him as she did, she had nonetheless thought him somewhat dour, a deep and taciturn man, but suddenly he was transformed, and in the cut and thrust of conversation gave as good as he got from his hosts.

And then, suddenly, the subject turned to D'ni.

"Forgive me, Atrus," Ro'Jethhe said, "but my son mentioned something about your home. About a place called Ro'D'ni. I must confess, I have never personally heard of such a place."

Atrus looked about him. "We are, indeed, from D'ni. At least, from a place known as such."

"I see," the neighbor, Ro'Hedrath interjected, "but how did you get here? By boat?"

Again there was laughter, but now everyone, it seemed, leaned in, awaiting Atrus's reply.

"The ruins . . ." Atrus began.

"*Ruins?*" Ro'Hedrath looked about him. "I know of no ruins in Terahnee!"

"But surely you must," Atrus said. "They are but half a day from here."

At this Ro'Jethhe looked to his second son. "Eedrah, have you read of any such ruins?"

The young man had been looking down. At his father's query he looked up, startled. "No, Father."

"There *are* ruins," Atrus went on. "Up on the plateau. They are screened by trees—huge, ancient trees—but they *are* there. High up. We came through there."

"Came through?" Ro'Jethhe looked puzzled.

Eedrah stood abruptly. "Forgive me, Father, but I feel . . . unwell."

"Of course," Ro'Jethhe said, waving his son away. Then, turning, he gestured to one of the stewards to go aid the young man.

Turning back, he smiled. "You must forgive him, Atrus, but he has always been a little . . . frail."

Atrus opened his mouth, about to answer—to explain just how and why they were there—but at that very moment another boat appeared from beneath the great arch on the far side of the amphitheater, breaching the flow of the falls, water spraying up in a misted arc, and entered the spiral channel, coming to rest at the edge of that central space.

Four men were seated in the body of the boat. One of them—a big, gray-haired man wrapped in jet-black furs—now stood and, stepping from the boat, called a greeting to Ro'Jethhe, who, like all the others, had risen to their feet immediately the boat appeared.

"Governor!" Ro'Jethhe said, grinning with pride as he stepped across to greet him. "Welcome to our humble entertainment."

The governor was indeed an imposing figure. He stood head and shoulders above Ro'Jethhe, who was not by any means a small man. Granting Ro'-Jethhe a brief smile of acknowledgment, he stepped past him, approaching Atrus's couch.

Atrus had stood, and now, confronted by the man, inclined his head. "Governor," he said.

"So you are Atrus, of Ro'D'ni."

There was a moment's strangeness—a kind of pause in which anything, it seemed, might happen—and then the governor reached out and took Atrus's hands in a firm grip. "Welcome to Terahnee, Atrus of D'ni."

Relinquishing Atrus's hands, the governor stepped back. "It is rare indeed that we have visitors in this land of ours, so you are truly welcome. I am Horen Ro'Jadre, governor of Ni'Ediren, and I bear a message from the king."

As he spoke the words, the governor drew a sealed scroll from within his cloak and offered it to Atrus. It was a long, impressive cylinder, covered in gold leaf, the great seal of office—an oval lozenge of bright blue wax—appended to it.

Atrus took it, then bowed his head. "I am grateful for your kindness, Horen Ro'Jadre."

"Think nothing of it," the governor said; then, turning to address all of them, he announced, "The king has invited Atrus and his party to attend him in the capital. They are to leave tomorrow." He looked about him. "Where is Eedrah?"

Ro'Jethhe smiled politely. "I am afraid he is unwell."

"Again? Hmmm . . . I wanted him to accompany our guests on their journey to the capital."

"And so he shall," Ro'Jethhe quickly said. "It is only a momentary indisposition. Eedrah will be honored to accompany them."

Horen Ro'Jadre smiled. "Good." He looked about him briefly, then walked across to take the vacant couch at the very center of the amphitheater. As he did, all returned to their couches.

There was a low chime in the air. As it faded, the light in the amphitheater changed as lamps behind the surrounding falls switched on, making the crystalline curtain of water shimmer magically. At the same time a large section of the amphitheater's floor slid aside and a platform rose from beneath.

Six young men stood on the platform, naked to the waist; perfect physical specimens who bowed, then began a routine of gymnastics that left Marrim mesmerized by their dexterity.

All was going well, when suddenly one of the young men seemed to catch the ankle of another and went tumbling over, falling heavily. He made no sound—indeed, the whole performance had been carried out in silence; a silence broken only by the thud of feet or hands on the platform, the hiss of escaping breath—and even now, as he lay there, grimacing, clearly in pain, he made no sound.

From his couch to the right of Marrim, Ro'Jethhe clapped his hands. At once the performance ended, the platform returned into the floor.

Almost at once the conversation started up again, Ro'Jethhe himself taking the lead, returning to a subject they had been discussing earlier. No mention was made of the performer's error, nor of D'ni.

They ate, and drank, and later, in a momentary pause in their talk, the governor spoke directly to Atrus once again.

"I am told by friend Ro'Jethhe that some of you wear special glasses in the daylight. May I ask why this is?"

"Of course," Atrus said. "It is a hereditary aspect of our race. Our eyes are sensitive. The daylight hurts them. And so we wear these lenses." And with that Atrus took his own lenses from his jacket pocket and, walking across to the governor's couch, handed them to Horen Ro'Jadre.

The governor studied them a while, fiddling with the silver catch at the side of the lenses, then peered through them, fascinated, it seemed, by the details of their manufacture. Then, smiling pleasantly, he handed them back.

"You will come stay with me, I hope, Atrus. On your way to the capital. It is on your route and I should welcome the chance to talk with you some more."

"That is . . ."

". . . most kind, I know." Ro'Jadre laughed. "Oh, kindness has nothing to do with it, my friend. I am curious to know more about you and your fellows."

"Then we shall be glad to stay. Oh, and governor?"

"Yes, Atrus?"

"Might I send back a messenger, to my own people, to let them know what has transpired."

"Your people . . ." The governor blinked. "Of course . . . yes, of course. You must do so at once. To let them know you are well."

Atrus bowed. "That is . . ."

". . . most kind."

And this time both men laughed; their laughter joined by all, guests and locals alike.

"Well," Ro'Jadre said, looking about him, his face filled with pleasure, "let us continue with the rest of our entertainment. Jethhe Ro'Jethhe, will you begin?"

Their host bowed his head slightly, acknowledging the invitation, then, after a moment's thought, spoke softly but clearly into the sudden, expectant silence:

"Old, but newly found. Hidden, yet in full sight. A newly hatched egg with an old cracked shell . . ."

And Marrim, looking about her, found herself amazed once more. *Riddles*, she thought. *They're playing riddles!*

THE JOURNEY BACK WAS MERRY. THEY HAD DRUNK FAR TOO much—even the normally sober Atrus—and enjoyed themselves far more than any of them had anticipated.

"That was just *so* clever," Oma said, leaning heavily against his friend Esel. "That one about the bird and the lock with the silver pick. How they think them up I'll never know!"

He grinned and looked about him, then, seeing Hadre at the prow, put his hand to his mouth, acknowledging his gaffe, but the young man seemed not to mind.

"We play riddles from our earliest days," Hadre said. "As I said before, we love the things of the mind. Mental games and memory tests—we delight in all such challenges. They keep one sharp and alert."

"Then you are to be applauded for it," Oma said, making a pretend toast in the air. "For myself, I would surely die of indolence, living as you do."

"I am sure that is not so," Hadre said, sounding more sober than any of them. "I saw you at the library, Oma. I saw how you drank in the sight of all those books. If you want, you can take one or two of them to read on the journey to the capital."

Oma, overwhelmed by the offer, stood and bowed at the waist, bringing ripples of laughter from the others, but Hadre merely returned the bow.

"You are . . ."

". . . *most welcome!*" the five youngsters answered as one, then laughed; a laughter that Hadre joined in with after a moment. A laughter that filled the warm night air as the boat glided slowly, silently beneath the waning moon, toward the distant, shimmering whiteness of Ro'Jethhe.

THEY MET AGAIN THE NEXT MORNING, IN THE GREAT BOOK-
lined study belonging to Ro'Jethhe. The governor was to leave within the
hour and had asked to see Atrus again before he departed.

"Forgive me for summoning you so early," Horen Ro'Jadre said, coming
across to take Atrus's hands as he entered the room, "but I wished to speak
with you informally before this evening."

Atrus smiled. "Then speak. I am listening."

Ro'Jadre nodded, then, releasing Atrus's hands, said, "I enjoyed your
company greatly last night, Atrus, and I know you will make a great impression at court, but I felt I should warn you of one thing."

"Warn me? Of what?"

"Of saying too much of who and what you are. Of D'ni and the like."

Atrus narrowed his eyes. "Why so?"

"Because it is not our place to ask such things of you. You understand?"

"I'm afraid I do not. You *are* governor here, are you not?"

"Governor, yes, but not king."

"And it is for the king alone to ask such questions?"

Horen Ro'Jadre beamed. "There. I told Ro'Jethhe you would understand."

"But . . ." Atrus fell silent, then. "It is your way, I take it?"

"Exactly. The moment the king agreed to see you, it was decided. It
would be wrong for any one of us to know more than he."

"I see."

"Then we shall meet again this evening. Until then . . ."

He stepped forward, embracing Atrus briefly, then was gone.

Atrus stared after him a moment, then turned back, looking to Ro'-
Jethhe, as if for explanation, but all the elder said was, "The king has agreed
to see you, Atrus. It is an immense honor."

"Yes," Atrus said. Then, understanding that Ro'Jethhe wished him nothing but good, he smiled. "I shall not forget your kindness, Jethhe Ro'Jethhe."

The old man beamed. "Look after my son, Atrus. And return here when
you can. And remember, my door is always open to you, so long as you are
in Terahnee."

"INTERESTING," CATHERINE SAID LATER, WHEN HE TOLD HER about the meeting with the governor.

"All peoples have their customs," Atrus said, buckling the strap on his knapsack. "Now . . . where has young Irras got to?"

"I'm here, Master Atrus," Irras said, coming into the room.

"You know what you have to say to Master Tamon?"

Irras nodded. "I have it by heart."

"Then go at once. And return here once the message has been delivered. Jethhe Ro'Jethhe will not mind if you stay until we return from the capital."

Irras bowed his head, then, with a curt, "Take care," he turned on his heel and vanished.

Atrus looked to Catherine, a query in his eyes.

"I think, perhaps, he's disappointed about not coming to the capital with us," she said.

"But that decision was not in my hands."

"It makes it no easier for him, Atrus. Irras was excited at the thought of seeing the great city, and now he must be content to be a runner between here and the plateau. It must have been a great blow to him."

"And yet he says nothing."

Catherine smiled. "So you have taught them Atrus."

Atrus frowned. "Yes, but we ought to make it up to him. I could ask the king if Irras could come on after us."

"You'll ask the king?"

"Of course," Atrus said, unaware of the smile on Catherine's lips. But she did not pursue the matter.

"Are you ready?" Atrus asked, looking about him, checking for the last time that he had everything he wished to take with him.

"Ready," she said.

"Good. Then let us go down and meet with Eedrah. It is time we got under way."

THE YOUNGSTERS HAD PACKED ALREADY AND, WHILE ATRUS AND Catherine went to see Ro'Jethhe and the governor, they decided to explore the grounds.

A narrow, elegant footbridge led over the stream by which they had entered the house, opening out onto a path of colored stone that meandered across a neatly swept lawn to disappear among the rocks of a grotto.

They followed the path, through the rocks and up, emerging on the far side on a ledge overlooking a series of long, barnlike buildings with low, red-tiled roofs.

Several of the cloaked servants were down there, talking among themselves, but noticing the young people up on the ledge, they fell silent and dispersed, one of them heading directly toward them.

He stopped at the foot of the steps that led down from the ledge. "Can I help you, Masters?"

"Thank you, but no," Carrad said. "We shall be leaving soon, and we merely wished to look around before we left."

The man bowed. "Then let me be your guide. I am Tyluu."

"And what do you do, Tyluu?" Esel asked, beginning to descend the steps.

The man kept his head bowed the slightest fraction as he answered. "I coordinate the harvest." He paused. "Would you like to see the grain stores?"

They went down and, with Tyluu as their guide, walked through the great storehouses, impressed by what they saw—especially the two young Averonese, who, coming from a farming world themselves, appreciated just how much work must have gone into this. The great barns themselves were deceptive, for they went down into the earth some way. They had glimpses of great stone stairways that snaked down into the depths, and Tyluu explained that much, apart from grain, was stored in the lower levels.

They walked on, out into great pens where herds of strangely docile beasts milled quietly, their moist dark eyes following the four young guests as they passed by.

All was neat and orderly. Not a fence was broken, not a farming implement out of place. Oma commented on this, and Tyluu bowed, as if some great compliment had been made, and answered, "It is our way."

Here and there, Marrim noticed, there were what looked like wells. Deep, square holes in the ground with borders of finished stone. She glanced down one as she passed and thought she saw some small animal scuttle by beneath.

And then it was time to return. Oma thanked Tyluu, but Tyluu merely bowed and backed away, merging with the shadows.

Carrad frowned.

"It is their way," Marrim said, grinning at him. Then, "Come on, let's get back."

AS THEY JOURNEYED NORTH OF RO'JETHHE THE GROUND BEGAN to rise, the canal winding its way through small, undulating foothills. Once more the countryside was beautiful and there were endless wonders to be seen to either side of the boat. Then, after an hour, they came to the first of a series of locks—huge, elaborately decorated marble halls into which the boat sailed, the end doors closing behind them.

Lamps in the ceiling cast a dazzling light over them as, beneath the flattened hull of the boat, the water suddenly rose, lifting them up onto another level of the "hill," into which they quietly sailed, the daylight up ahead of them once more.

And then out, into a landscape transformed—the hills to all sides of them covered in a thousand different kinds of flowers, while directly ahead lay a strange, emerald-colored structure that seemed almost to explode from the earth.

At first they thought this was the house to which they were heading, but Eedrah quickly set them right.

"That is an antilogy."

"An antilogy?" Atrus queried. "A contradiction in terms?"

"Precisely," Eedrah said.

Moment by moment the boat sailed closer to the strange building, their path leading them slowly around the structure, revealing more aspects of it at every moment.

Eedrah smiled. "What is more dynamic than the moment in which a raindrop hits the surface of a lake, and what more thrilling than to freeze that moment and capture it forever; to transform something that was brief and transient into an eternal statement?"

"And is that what it is?" Esel asked. "A raindrop hitting the surface of a lake?"

"Can you not see it?" Eedrah asked.

And indeed, now that they knew what to look for, they could. They could see the rounded shape of it, the depression at the center, the way the edges of the water drop exploded outward, almost like flames, obeying eternal laws of physics.

Eedrah's smile broadened. "Every district boasts three or four of them. And it is said the king owns a great park containing some of the finest in the land."

Esel, who had been staring at the structure, wide-eyed, now looked back at Eedrah. "Perhaps we shall be fortunate enough to see them."

"Perhaps . . . but look, through the gap in the hills there . . . that is where we are headed. *That* is Ro'Jadre."

A GREAT HILL OF MARBLE FACED THEM, TIER UPON TIER climbing through the hills like the steps of giants. And set into the lowest of those steps, a great ring of blood-red stone that seemed to flicker, as if flames burned within its cool outer casing.

That ring surrounded a tunnel. They headed directly toward it now, across a long, high viaduct that stretched out, its attenuated arches elegantly spanning a gaping chasm.

Inside the tunnel, the door boomed shut behind them and once more the water rose with a great rush, lifting them up and up and up, through a series of locks until they emerged at the top of that great hill of marble, in a massive square pool, huge, tiered walls surrounding them on every side, one side of which glowed in the sun's rays.

And there, standing on a great balcony in the sunlight, was Horen Ro'-Jadre himself, wearing a pale cream flowing gown. He stood out, a tall, proud figure, his dark hair combed back severely from his head. Raising his arm he smiled down at them.

"Atrus! Catherine! Welcome to Ro'Jadre!"

THE HOUSE OF RO'JETHHE HAD BEEN IMPRESSIVE, BUT Ro'Jadre's house was simply astonishing. The entrance hall alone, with its sweeping stairways and magnificent windows, was enough to take the breath, and the party from D'ni stood there, as Ro'Jadre came down to greet them, quite in awe of their surroundings.

Marrim watched Horen Ro'Jadre embrace Atrus, conscious of a change in him since the previous evening. Then the governor had seemed stern and distant even when he smiled or laughed, but today he seemed more at ease, much more relaxed in his own home.

If one could call something this palatial "home."

"I am so pleased to see you all once more," Ro'Jadre said, looking about him, including them all in his smile of welcome. Nearby stood two servants, in attendance, their heads inclined, their distinctive look—wine-red cloaks and wire-fine silver hair—familiar now.

"You must be hungry," Ro'Jadre went on. "There are some light refreshments in the lower gallery. If you would come with me."

They followed him through, into a long, low room, the light of which was completely different from outside, a faint, roseate glow that seemed to be frozen perpetually in that first, hopeful moment of the dawn. Marrim looked about her, trying to see how this was done—by lamps, or filters at the windows—but try as she might, she could not discern the source of it.

Miracles, she thought, taking a couch. Terahnee was indeed a land of miracles.

The journey had not been long, but the air here seemed to feed the appetite, such that Marrim ate voraciously, surprised to find herself so hungry. Ro'Jadre's "light refreshment" would on any other world have seemed a feast, but Marrim, along with the others, was beginning to get used to this level of casual opulence.

As for Horen Ro'Jadre, he watched them silently, picking at this and that, letting his guests eat and drink their fill. Only then, when he saw that most were satisfied, did he look to Atrus, and, smiling, say:

"I understand you are fond of books, Atrus."

"Very fond. They are the lifeblood of a culture."

"Indeed," Ro'Jadre said, nodding gravely. "I also understand that you wish to know more about this land of ours."

Atrus glanced at Eedrah, who was looking down. "That is so. I hoped to learn something of its history and development."

"Its history . . ." There was a strange movement in Ro'Jadre's face. "You mean, you wish to know the names of its kings?"

"I . . ." Atrus paused, then. "Surely things have not always been like this?"

Ro'Jadre smiled genially. "I am sure that is the case."

"Then there will be books, perhaps, that talk of how things once were."

"Maybe," Ro'Jadre said, with an uncharacteristic vagueness. He turned and snapped his fingers. At once one of the servants turned and vanished through the doorway.

Atrus, sensing some kind of awkwardness concerning the matter, let it drop. "Tell me, Governor," he said, "how long will it take us to reach the capital?"

"Three days," Ro'Jadre answered, reaching across to pluck a small black, oval fruit from one of the bowls. "But tonight you will stay here, as my guests. Before then, however, let me show you my house."

He stood. "You asked me about history, Atrus. Well, this house has stood here, much as it is now, for close on four thousand years. And before then there was another house, and before that . . ." Ro'Jadre shrugged.

Four thousand years . . . Catherine looked about her at the effortless elegance of the room. Unlike D'ni, which *felt* ancient, the very stones worn down beneath one's tread, this place seemed newly built. Not a speck of dust met the eye, not a single sign of aging.

Frozen in time, she thought, as she swung round and put her feet down onto the floor. Yet looking at these people, they seemed unaffected by that. There was nothing jaded about them; nothing to suggest that they lived their lives unchangingly. And as Atrus himself had commented, they were as agile of mind as the most learned Guildsman.

"Come," Ro'Jadre said, leading them between the dark blue pillars and out into a high-ceilinged atrium, "let me show you where I work."

ESEL AND OMA STOOD TOGETHER AT THE CENTER OF THE GREAT workroom and slowly shook their heads in amazement. They had never seen a room like this—never guessed that such a room could even possibly exist, but here it was. Ro'Jadre called it his "laboratory," yet, with its various balconies and levels, its side-chambers and raised sections, accessible by narrow stairways, it was more like a whole Guild House in itself. Great racks of chemicals filled one wall, while another had endless cupboards of equipment. And there were books, endless books, everywhere one looked, not to talk of the workbenches and the scientific apparatus, much of which the two D'ni did not recognize.

And everything gleamed, as if newly polished. Even the air seemed clean.

"Astonishing," Esel said quietly, while beside him Oma simply stared.

"You are welcome to use it whenever you wish," Ro'Jadre said, with that same open hospitality they had come to believe was universal in Terahnee. "What is mine is yours."

Atrus gave a little bow. Then, curious, he asked, "What are your own interests, Governor Ro'Jadre?"

"My interests?"

"Scientifically speaking . . ."

"Ah . . ." Ro'Jadre walked across and, reaching over one of the benches, took down a massive-looking ledger and opened it, turning it so that Atrus, who had followed him across, could see.

"I'm afraid . . ." Atrus began, but Ro'Jadre understood at once.

"The script . . . of course. It differs from your own, I understand. Well, what you see are my experiment notes." He flicked back a few pages and indicated several diagrams, beside which were columns of figures and, on the page facing it, three beautifully drawn graphs. "I have been experimenting on inks. Following up an idea I had."

Atrus stared at the pages, clearly fascinated, despite the difficulty of reading the Terahnee script. It was not *so* different when one concentrated.

"But enough of that," Ro'Jadre said, leaving the book where it lay. "Come, let me show you the long gallery. There are things there from the Ages—grotesque and beautiful things—you will not have seen before."

Oma and Esel stood there a moment, reluctant to move on, a look that was almost longing in their eyes. Then, glancing about them as they went, they followed Ro'Jadre out through the marble doorway.

IT WAS ANOTHER HOUR BEFORE ONE OF THE STEWARDS SHOWED them to their suite of rooms, high up on the east side of the great house. As Atrus stepped into the spacious apartment, it was to be met by the sight of four beautiful old books, their covers a deep, burnished yellow trimmed with black, laid out on the massive desk that filled one corner of the main room.

Atrus walked across and opened the first of the volumes. As yet he could not read the strange variant script, but he knew, without having to ask, that these were the books of Terahnee history Ro'Jadre had promised him.

The evening had been wonderful. There had been music and dancing, and games—associative and rhyming—and any number of other clever things; things that they had never imagined. His mind reeled when he thought of all the things they had witnessed. The sounds, the tastes, the sights . . .

"Do you still think these people are not D'ni?" Catherine asked, coming alongside him. "After all you've seen? They speak a dialect very close to D'ni. And they write Ages, exactly like the D'ni."

Atrus smiled. "I concede that the likelihood of them being related to the D'ni is great. But I am certain that the truth is here, in these pages. I shall have Oma and Esel begin work on them at once."

Catherine was quiet a moment, then she asked, "Does it not make you wonder, Atrus?"

"Wonder?"

"Oh, it's just that I keep thinking about what Master Tergahn said. About the reason why this Age was linked to D'ni. For all this to exist and for the D'ni to know nothing of it . . . that seems . . ."

"Incredible?"

"Yes. And yet the Books were left there to be a link between the Ages. Why should that be?"

"Different paths," Atrus mused.

"Yes, but why?"

Atrus smiled and gently tapped the open page. "The answer's here, I warrant." Then, closing the book, he went over to the door and threw it open. "Oma! Esel! Come! I have a task for you!"

EEDRAH CALLED FOR THEM BEFORE THE ENTERTAINMENT THAT evening.

"We can call for the others on our way," he began, as he stepped into the room, then stopped dead, seeing Oma and Esel seated at the great desk in the corner, Marrim and Irras talking with them animatedly.

"The histories," Atrus explained. "We have been busy learning something of your world."

"Something and nothing," Eedrah said, then, smiling, went on, "As the prophecies say, 'Through such tiny cracks the past seeps through to the present.'"

Catherine stared at Eedrah, surprised. "You've *heard* of the prophecies here in Terahnee?"

"Rumors and old wives' tales, mainly. But there are those in the city who have spent a lifetime studying such things. Great scholars who fill their lives searching through ancient books to find some snippet here, some snippet there."

Catherine looked to Atrus, but Atrus seemed uninterested. He had wandered over to the desk again, where Oma was quietly but insistently making a point about a line of text he had translated. For a moment she hesitated, then asked, "Would it be possible to arrange a meeting with one of these . . . scholars?"

Eedrah shrugged. "I guess so. I don't see the harm in asking. And it's said these scholars love to talk of what they know."

Catherine smiled. "You seem a race of scholars, Eedrah."

"And so we are. But come . . . the governor awaits us. I understand he has arranged a very special entertainment in your honor."

Atrus turned back at this news. "Then we shall leave the books for now. Come, Oma, Esel. There will be time for that on our journey. Our host awaits us."

THE GOVERNOR STOOD BEFORE THE DOOR, A FAINTLY AMUSED smile on his face. It was, even by normal standards, a small door, barely large enough for a young child to pass through.

"Who will be first?" Ro'Jadre asked, looking from one to another of his guests. "You, Atrus? Or maybe you, young Marrim?"

Marrim glanced at Atrus, then nodded. "You say that once inside I must choose within thirty seconds or all of the doors close?"

"That is correct," Ro'Jadre answered. "Sometimes there are two choices, sometimes three. Sometimes you will have to climb, sometimes you will need to descend, but always . . . *always* you have only thirty seconds to do so."

"And at the end of it?" Catherine asked.

"You will see. So, Marrim, are you ready?"

"I am."

"Then go through. We shall see you again . . . sooner or later."

Marrim did not quite like the sound of that, but she was committed now. Putting her hand against the door, she pushed, then stepped inside, into a room that was no bigger than a cell. As the door closed behind her, she noted the doors to her left and right, but she had already decided. She would go straight as far as she could go. Two paces took her to the second door. She pushed it open and stepped through.

This room was longer, thinner, the ceiling higher. There was a door in the ceiling but no doorway to her right. Yet even as she took a step toward the facing door, the floor beneath her seemed to move—to turn, though how it could turn she did not know. There were faint noises in the walls. Feeling slightly dizzy, she made her way across to the door facing her. Or was it the left hand door now? She double-checked, the counting in her head warning her that fifteen seconds had already passed.

Straight ahead, she told herself, pushing the door open. But what if the room *had* turned? Was she still heading in a straight line?

This room—the third room—was circular. Not two but five different doors led off. And there, in the center of the floor, was an opening. A chute of some kind? She went across and stared straight down. Dare she go down there?

An entertainment, she told herself, reminding herself of what Horen Ro'-Jadre had said. *It's only an entertainment.*

Marrim eased herself over the lip and slid, down, down into darkness, then felt the chute turn and straighten.

How far had she descended? Twenty feet? More? She got to her feet and walked forward, her hand outstretched before her.

Her hand met the flat, smooth surface of a door. She pushed.

And stepped out into daylight.

No, she thought, *impossible*. For now she seemed to be at the top of the building, the sunlight coming down through a clear glass roof.

Two doors and thirty seconds to choose. Left or right? For there was no door facing her in this room.

Besides, that plan had been abandoned. So what now? What alternate strategy did she use to get herself through this maze of rooms?

Guesswork . . .

She went left, into what seemed to be a corridor, a single door at the end of it, another exit—a square hole without a covering hatch—in the center of the ceiling. Yet even as she walked toward the door at the far end, the room seemed to turn yet again beneath her.

And this time, she knew she was not imagining it. The rooms were moving all the while. Or maybe not all the while, but sometimes—perhaps when she made a certain choice.

But there was no more time to think. Reaching up with both hands, Marrim pulled herself up into the dark.

Or almost darkness, for there was light—a big square patch of light—some way ahead of her, yes, and another just behind.

Another choice.

She turned 180 degrees, and as she did she began to mentally retrace her steps, for in that instant she had understood. It was not necessarily the choice you made, it was the remembering. Her first instinct had been correct—she was certain of it now. The quickest way was to go straight ahead.

For a time there was nothing but rooms—fifty, maybe eighty rooms on who knew how many levels—and then, stepping through a door, Marrim came out into a huge, sunlit dome, beneath the transparent roof of which was a massive water garden, with streams and islands and bridges and, at the very center of all, a huge pagodalike structure in what looked like pearl, beneath the sloping roofs of which was a circle of chairs, most of which were filled by guests.

Seeing her, Ro'Jadre stood and came to the rail, looking across to where she stood. "Well done, young Marrim," he called. "That was quick indeed. Why, I have known guests lost in there for days on end."

Marrim blinked, wondering if she was being ribbed, then asked, "And what would happen to them?"

"Oh, we would send someone in to bring them out. Eventually. But do not fear, Marrim, we would not have let you languish in there too long. Nor any of your party." He smiled, gesturing for her to come across the bridge. "But tell me, how did you manage to work it out?"

ATRUS, WHO HAD BEEN LAST TO ENTER THE MAZE, WAS THE second to emerge, less than five minutes after Marrim.

Stepping into the first room, he had had no real expectations of the experience. A maze was, after all, only a maze. Yet as the rooms had begun to turn and he had got deeper in, he had begun to enjoy it, until, at the last, he had found a real delight in working out the puzzle.

It had been like tunneling through the rock, and after a moment all manner of memories had come flooding back and he had seen his father's face clearly for the first time in many years.

A maze of moving rooms. *Ingenious* . . .

He had said the word aloud, unaware that he had done so.

"I am glad you think so," Ro'Jadre said, coming across the bridge toward him. "I was telling Marrim. It is never the same twice. For each traveler, the maze is entirely different."

Atrus frowned. "How, then, is it done?"

"Oh, the rules of manipulation were set centuries ago. We but perfect an ancient art. But, sad to say, the days of the great maze-makers are long past. There has not been an original new maze for many years. At least, none I have heard of."

"And those rules . . . they determine which rooms move and which do not?"

"That is so. Though not all the rooms *can* move. Like any building, the maze must have structural integrity. But within that rigid framework there is a great deal of flexibility. More than you can possibly imagine. If it were not so, then the maze would soon lose its power to fascinate."

"Do you ever play the maze yourself, Ro'Jadre?"

Ro'Jadre smiled. "Very seldom these days. I am not as sprightly as I was. But the young people are very fond of it, particularly when the choosing time is shortened."

"Shortened?"

"To ten, sometimes even five seconds."

Atrus nodded, imagining it. To have to negotiate the maze under such circumstances—to have to run and clamber and slide like a hunted animal, afraid of being trapped—that would be a game of considerable skill, especially when one also had to attempt to keep the ever-changing map of the maze in one's mind at all times.

It was ten minutes before Catherine emerged. Another fifteen and Esel stumbled from the door, looking flustered, his dark eyebrows formed into a heavy frown. Last to appear, almost two hours after Marrim had first emerged, was Oma, who had a dazed and slightly startled look about him.

"Everything was fine until the rooms started moving," he said as he took the last vacant chair. "After that . . ." He shook his head.

"And yet none of you were trapped, and none took more than two and a half hours," Ro'Jadre said. "That *is* impressive, particularly when none of you had ever played the game before."

Marrim leaned across, whispering something to Atrus. Atrus considered a moment, then nodded.

"Ro'Jadre," he said. "My young companion would like to run the maze again."

"Again?"

"Yes, but this time with a ten-second choosing time."

Ro'Jadre laughed. "Why, certainly. But why not add some spice to the entertainment? Why not make the game a race this time? Young Marrim against one of our young people."

The governor turned, looking about him, his eyes falling on the lounging figure of Eedrah.

"Eedrah Ro'Jethhe . . . will you not take up the challenge?"

Eedrah, who had until that moment been picking at a bowl of fruit in a desultory fashion, now looked up, startled by Ro'Jadre's words. He looked about him, as if trying to figure out some way of escaping the invitation, then, somewhat reluctantly, he nodded.

"Good," Ro'Jadre said, a satisfied smile lighting his lips. "If the two young people would prepare themselves."

As Eedrah and Marrim stood, Eedrah glanced across at her—a strangely awkward look. "Governor Ro'Jadre," he said, "can we not make it fifteen seconds? I fear our guest might find it . . . overstrenuous."

Ro'Jadre looked to Marrim and raised an eyebrow, but Marrim said nothing.

"Twelve seconds," Ro'Jadre said decisively. He clapped his hands and at once two stewards appeared at his side. "Tuure," he said, addressing one of them, "escort the young people to the maze."

Then, turning back, he looked to Atrus and smiled. "And afterward I shall talk to you of the king, and of what you might expect when you reach the capital."

TWICE SHE STEPPED INTO A ROOM TO FIND EEDRAH THERE already. Twice he stared back at her, startled, then moved on.

Relentlessly, Marrim moved from room to room, as floors turned and the great maze fitted itself into new configurations. And all the while, in her head, she counted. Counted the seconds. Counted how many forward or back, up or down she was. For the secret, she understood now, was mathematical—was pluses and minuses. It was no good thinking in terms of direction. One had to strip that away and think pure number, otherwise you were lost.

What she hadn't expected, however, were the pure physical demands of that twelve-second limit. It gave you barely enough time to look about a room and choose, let alone climb up—if climbing up was what you wished to do. But suddenly, almost before she expected it, she was outside again, standing there in the great dome, the water gardens all about her.

"Well done . . ."

She turned, to find Eedrah there behind her. "Oh," she said. "I didn't see you."

"That's because I wasn't there. Until now."

"Then I won?"

Eedrah nodded, but there was a strange sorrow in his face that she did not understand.

"Well done!" Ro'Jadre boomed out from where he stood at the rail, Atrus beside him. "You have a real talent for it, Marrim!"

Marrim inclined her head, accepting the governor's praise, but she was more concerned with Eedrah.

"Eedrah?" she asked quietly. But Eedrah simply walked away, hurrying across the bridge.

"THERE, ATRUS," RO'JADRE SAID, HANDING ATRUS THE HEAD-and-shoulders portrait. "That is Ro'Eh Ro'Dan, king of Terahnee."

Atrus studied the painting, conscious of Catherine standing at his shoulder, then nodded.

Ro'Eh Ro'Dan was a young, immensely handsome man with refined facial features and pleasant, intelligent eyes. Looking at that face, staring into those clear, trustworthy eyes, Atrus found himself convinced that he should link his own people's fate with the fate of these people.

He looked up, his eyes taking in the luxuriousness of his surroundings. Beside this, D'ni was as nothing. All of his schemes to rebuild D'ni seemed futile now that he had seen Terahnee.

Yet as he handed back the portrait, Atrus kept his thoughts much to himself. "He looks a fine man," he said.

"And young," Ro'Jadre said, taking his turn to stare at the painting. "He is not yet one hundred, but strong, and a good writer, so it is said."

"A writer?" Yet that fact did not surprise Atrus. He looked to Catherine and saw at once that she was watching him, an understanding in her eyes. "Then we shall have much to talk about."

Ro'Jadre smiled, then set the portrait down. "Oh, of that I have no doubt. No doubt at all."

PART FIVE

DISCORDANT TIME.

    THE SMALLEST OF ENEMIES UN-MANS THEM ALL.

HIDDEN WITHIN THE HIDDEN.

    A BREATH AND THEN DARKNESS.

                    —FROM THE KUROKH JIMAII. VV. 4302-3

FROM WHERE HE SAT IN THE STERN OF THE GOVERNOR'S boat, Atrus looked out across a land of unending luxury; of glades and winding streams, of magical conceits and beautiful falls of floral color. And greenness. Everywhere one looked, the lush green perfection of growing things.

The silken awning above him rustled gently in the breeze, and for a moment he found himself almost dozing in the warm, late afternoon air. A bird called across the meadows, a piping call, while the boat glided on as in a dream.

It was the end of their third day in Terahnee, and the city now dominated the skyline ahead of them, the sun slowly setting behind its towering walls. In an hour or less they would stop for the night, at the house of another landowner—this one a friend of Ro'Jethhe's named Tanaren Ro'Tanaren.

For this once there would be no feast, no entertainment, and Atrus for one was pleased at that. They had stopped earlier, in a glade, to eat and drink—a pleasant wine that even Atrus had sampled. Which was why now he felt so relaxed.

And happy.

The thought made him stir and wake. He looked about him at the little group in the boat and realized that each of them, like he, was smiling, each one in his or her own little reverie, relaxed after being tense for so long.

And with that thought came another. That they had worked so hard, so long that they deserved this tiny break from their labors; deserved this drifting, effortless journey with its unceasing delights. Things had been hard back in D'ni, there was no mistaking that. But this . . .

He had not even dared to dream that anything like this existed.

Catherine, sensing his sudden wakefulness, turned her head to him and quietly spoke. "Atrus?"

But there was nothing that he wished to say. Not now. Last night he had slept the sleep of children—that deep, untroubled sleep that rarely comes when one is older. And this morning he had awakened refreshed in spirit and confirmed in what he had decided the night before—to petition the king of Terahnee and bring his people through, to settle here in this wonderful place.

This place of eternal summers.

Catherine reached out and took his hand, holding it lightly as she looked out across the beauty of the surrounding land.

No, he did not even have to ask her. He could see it in her face. In all their faces. Why have D'ni when they could have this? And surely there must be space for them here in this endless, rolling landscape?

He sighed, content to let the thought drift from him, like a leaf on a stream.

Simply to be here was enough. And, yawning, Atrus stretched, his body totally relaxed for the first time in so long he could not recall when he had last felt like this.

TANAREN RO'TANAREN TURNED OUT TO BE A GENIAL, PLEASANT man. As they stepped down from the boat he greeted them warmly, embracing each of them in turn before leading them inside.

Imposing as it was, Ro'Tanaren's house had a totally different feel to it than those they had previously visited. It was somehow brighter, airier, such that even as the evening descended, the soft lighting in the house made it seem that day lingered slightly longer there.

As ever, Ro'Tanaren was the very model of a host, and after a brief exchange about their journey, they were ushered to their rooms to rest.

"We can talk later," Ro'Tanaren said, smiling. "Now rest. You have traveled far today."

Alone in their rooms, Atrus wondered if he should broach the subject of bringing the survivors over from D'ni with Catherine, but it was she who spoke first. She was standing by the open window, looking out across the stepped lawns.

"Have you noticed," she said, "how in all our time here we have never seen a kitchen? Never seen a single plate brought or cleared away. It's as if the stewards supervise the air."

Atrus laughed quietly. "To be perfectly honest, Catherine, I hadn't really thought about it. But no. I guess it is their way."

"Etiquette, you mean?"

He nodded, then went across to her. "I wanted to ask you something."

She turned, meeting his eyes, then smiled. "You want to bring the D'ni here, right?"

"And those from Averone."

That surprised her. She thought for a moment, then gave a little nod. "I see. You want to close the link."

"Exactly."

Catherine took a long, slow breath. "I agree."

"We cannot let what happened to D'ni happen here," he went on. "You've seen this place. To think of it suffering the same fate. No. We must throw in our lot with these people. I will petition Ro'Eh Ro'Dan when I see him."

"And if the Averonese do not wish to come?"

"Then they can stay. But the Book must be destroyed, the Temple sealed."

THEY JOURNEYED ON INTO THE HEART OF TERAHNEE, AND EVERY day the city grew, the sheer scale of that gargantuan edifice finally imposing itself upon Atrus's imagination, making him understand that what he had glimpsed from the plateau was not, after all, the capital, but merely one of

its outlying districts, for beyond that great wall of buildings another larger
wall seemed to climb to the heavens, such that the whole of D'ni could have
been placed in a tiny hole in its side. It was like a mountain, only this mountain had been built, stone upon stone, so Eedrah said. And the histories,
which gave clue to little else, at least confirmed that much. A thousand years
of building had produced that magnificent pile.

The nearer they came to it, the grander everything seemed to be. The
locks that raised them up or lowered them down were bigger, the canal itself much broader. Fields gave way to parks. Great houses lay on every side
of them now, some so impressive that they seemed the palaces of kings. Yet
these were ordinary citizens. Boats were moored alongside the canal now,
and sometimes partying groups of people would hail them and call out
greetings.

Finally, in the midst of that great sprawl of wondrous buildings, they
came to a junction of several waterways and entered a massive curving channel—the King's Cut, they were told it was called—which carved its deep
blue furrow through broad avenues of beautiful mansions lined with the
most extraordinary trees they had yet seen in all of Terahnee, the night-black
scented leaves drifting down on them as they passed, while ahead of them
the city climbed to the sky.

Atrus stared wide-eyed, his neck craned back, and still it seemed he could
not see the top. He turned, looking to Eedrah and asked, "How do we get
up there? Or is that the way we are going?"

"That is indeed our way," Eedrah said, "and the boat will take us there."
He grinned. "Have patience, Atrus, and you will see."

The walls of the channel grew slowly higher and higher on both sides,
with here and there a massive wooden gate set deep into the smooth-carved
stone.

Coming around the next turn, Atrus noticed a faint rippling up ahead,
a sharp line of turbulence drawn straight across the placid watercourse, like
a weir. As they passed over it, Atrus turned to look, even as a wall pushed
up out of the water behind them, closing off the channel.

At once they were lifted up on a great tide of water, the boat's pace accelerating with the rush of the incoming water, then slowing as the walls began to grow once more to either side.

Time and again this happened. Time and again they were lifted and the boat rushed forward. And then, suddenly, the walls dropped away and they were out in the open, high up on a massive aqueduct, the avenues of the capital spread out below them like a map, while directly ahead, across an artificial chasm at least a mile wide, was the king's palace, its towering ramparts piercing the blue sky.

Seeing it, Atrus felt in awe of the power that had built this place; in awe of the men who had planned and carried out such a mighty scheme. Nor was it the sheer bulk of the edifice that took the breath, it was the delicate working of the stone, the careful balance between size and elegance. It had a natural, flowing look, yet nothing in nature could have made so beautiful a structure.

Atrus glanced across and saw that Eedrah, too, was awed—saw by his parted lips, his astonished eyes, that this son of Terahnee had never, until that moment, guessed at the splendor at the center of it all.

Slowly they drifted toward that massive work of stone, then passed into its shadow, the towering entrance arch swallowing up their tiny craft.

They passed inside, into a cavernous hall, the floor a single sapphire pool, the ceiling echoing high above them, not a single pillar supporting that huge mass of stone. But Atrus barely had time to consider that a wonder when, coming to the center of that hall, the boat was lifted on a column of water toward the ceiling.

There was a moment's shock and fear as they sped toward it, and then the stone parted with a silent rush and they were through, into a great vertical shaft, the walls studded with lamps, the great column of water falling away into the dark beneath.

Up and up they went, and then, even as the wonder of it began to fade, they burst through into a chamber even larger than that from which they had come, tier after tier of benches reaching up on every side, those benches filled with thousands of lavishly dressed men and women. And there, facing them, on a massive throne of cut emerald, a flight of fifty golden steps leading up to him, sat the young king, Ro'Eh Ro'Dan.

He stood up and stepped out onto the top step, smiling broadly, his deep, rich voice filling that chamber.

"Welcome, Atrus of D'ni. I hope your journey was a pleasant one."

CATHERINE WATCHED FROM THE FOOT OF THE STEPS AS ATRUS climbed to meet the king, greeting Ro'Eh Ro'Dan, who had come precisely halfway down that golden flight, the two men grasping each other's hands warmly.

The portrait had not lied. Ro'Eh Ro'Dan was a handsome man with sparkling blue eyes and an air of immeasurable authority. Even so, he seemed genuinely pleased to meet with Atrus and greeted him as one might greet a long-lost brother or the son of a favorite uncle. There was no coldness in that greeting, no distance, and that more than anything reassured her.

"Well, Atrus," the king said, standing back a little, his voice raised so that all in that great chamber might hear, "do you like our land of Terahnee?"

"It is a land of wonders," Atrus answered, smiling at the other man. "And your people have been most kind. We could not have asked for better treatment."

Ro'Eh Ro'Dan grinned broadly. "That is good. But we must show you the full richness of Terahnee hospitality. Tonight you will be our special guests at a grand feast, and you will tell me then of D'ni."

"You have heard of D'ni, then, King Ro'Eh Ro'Dan?"

"Not before four days ago. But now I feel I know it well. Or as well as any scholar in my land."

"Then it is known to you in your books?"

Ro'Eh Ro'Dan laughed. "Mentions of your land are rare, Atrus. It was some while ago, it seems, since last our lands had congress. But I have had my scholars scour the great libraries of the capital and they have discovered several references to D'ni."

"Then there *is* a link?"

"Do you mean, are we cousins?" Ro'Eh Ro'Dan grinned once again. "It would certainly seem so. The language, the fact that we both write Books. Both facts speak eloquently for a distant split between your people and mine, Atrus. For what reason, who knows—we cannot fathom it from the ancient books—but now that breach is healed. Those who were parted now have come together. And I am glad it is so. Most glad indeed."

IT WAS LATE WHEN THEY FINALLY RETIRED. OF ALL THE FEASTS they had attended in Terahnee, this had been the most sumptuous, each course a feast in itself, such that after a time they had not eaten so much as tasted the food before complimenting their host. Not that Ro'Eh Ro'Dan had seemed to mind. He had been far more interested in what Atrus had to say of the D'ni Guilds and the Common Book Rooms and all of those many other things that were, it seemed, quite alien to Terahnee life. In particular, he had been fascinated by the mention of the Maintainers, and had questioned Atrus a full hour and a half about their practices.

"Astonishing!" he had said finally.

"Why so?" Atrus had asked. "If anything, the absence of such a body is what I find most incredible about your land, Ro'Eh Ro'Dan."

"You think so? Why, I would find it strange indeed if, in a land where everyone has all they wish for, anyone should want what another has enough to take it. And as for quarrels, they happen, yet if a society is *civilized* enough, and the people distant enough from each other not to let it bother them, then violence cannot take seed. Still, I suppose it is all a question of what one is used to."

"That is so," Atrus had agreed. "Yet it is still quite astonishing to find that in an orchard so vast and varied as Terahnee, one does not find a single rotten apple."

Ro'Eh Ro'Dan had inclined his head at that. "It has all to do with good horticulture, Atrus. True breeding brings the best results, wouldn't you say?"

But there the conversation had ended, as the great gong sounded and the entertainer—a scholar, versed in the ancient prophesies—had stepped up to begin his recitation.

Now, three hours later, Atrus sat down on the edge of the massive bed and began to pull off his boots.

"I think he will be receptive to the idea, Catherine."

Catherine was standing before the mirror. Looking up, she met Atrus's eyes in the glass.

"He seems a kind and cultured man."

"Indeed. A man after our own minds. Yet having spoken to him one thing troubles me."

"What thing is that?"

"What he said about his people. About their breeding. It made me consider our own people."

"They are good people, Atrus."

"Oh, I know that. Yet can we vouch for every single one of them? D'ni and Averone and all? What if one bad apple among them spreads contagion? This is a land without contention. I would be loathe to introduce it to them."

Catherine smiled and turned to face him. "I think you worry too much, Atrus. You know our people. They are the best. They will fit in easily here. So put your proposition to him, then burn the Books and seal the Temple up."

"And Chroma'Agana?"

"Oh, I shall miss it, but it's a small price to pay."

"Are you happy here, Catherine?"

She came across and took his hands, smiling down at him. "Very. Now put your doubts aside. This is what you wanted. So reach for it. Heal the breach and bring the D'ni home to Terahnee."

He smiled and squeezed her hands. "It shall be so."

IN THE DAWN'S FIRST LIGHT THE PINNACLE OF THE KING'S high chamber, a slender tower separate from the rest of that great stone pile, jutted from the great bowl of darkness beneath, its whiteness touched with gold. A narrow bridge of stone linked it to the rest; a curving line of white etched delicately on the black.

Looking across at the king's tower from the recessed doorway in which he stood, Atrus hesitated, thinking of the meeting to come, then stepped out onto the bridge, his booted footsteps echoing in the silence, his cloak flowing behind him in the cold morning air.

He had woken while it was still dark and, dressing quietly so as not to wake Catherine, had ventured out. It was not that he had expected to see the king so early—indeed, he was surprised to learn from the steward that Ro'Eh Ro'Dan was already in his rooms—merely that he felt he needed to walk and consider precisely what it was he was to say to the king that morning.

Yet here he was, before the sun was fully risen, stepping out across the dark to meet with him.

Halfway across, he stopped and, grasping the balustrade, leaned out, staring down into the shadowed depths. Down there—a mile or more below where he stood on that narrow parapet—the city slept, oblivious of him. He took in the pattern of the parks and buildings, the endless bridges and canals, pleased by what he saw, then raised his eyes, looking to the distance, to rolling hills and wondrous mansions stretching from horizon to horizon.

It truly was a land without equal.

He took a long breath, then let it out, giving a single nod, as if in that moment he had confirmed some fact that until then had not been certain.

"Atrus?"

He turned. Ro'Eh Ro'Dan was standing at the far end of the bridge, his head bare, his dark blue cloak wrapped tightly about him.

"Come . . . there's breakfast if you want it."

The very informality of the words and the casual gesture that accompanied them reassured Atrus. The friendly intimacy of the previous evening was still there between them, and as Atrus stepped up to Ro'Eh Ro'Dan, the other took his arm and, with a smile, led him inside.

Inside was a large circular chamber, at the center of which was a massive desk. Five elegantly robed ancients stood about, several of whom Atrus had met the night before. As Atrus and the king entered, they lowered their heads respectfully. It was a cozy room, its luxuries surprisingly simple ones. The stone walls to either side of the doorway were bare, while, on the far side, a twist of stairs followed the curve of the wall, leading up to a recessed wooden door.

After the magnificence of the audience chamber, this was unexpectedly low-key, yet Atrus, looking about him, found himself more impressed by this than the grandeur he had seen elsewhere, for this spoke of the more human side of Terahnee.

"Gentlemen . . . we can continue later."

Smiling at Atrus, the ancients departed, leaving him alone with Ro'Eh Ro'Dan. The king turned, facing him.

"Did you sleep well, Atrus?"

"Wonderfully."

"Good." He smiled. "You know, I am glad to have the chance to speak with you alone. But come. We can talk while we eat."

Atrus followed the king up the twist of stairs and out into daylight. Five narrow steps led up onto a platform. Stepping out onto it, Atrus stared in real delight, for it had been laid out as a tiny formal garden, at the center of which was a low table and two long chairs.

A breakfast meal had been laid out on the table, but it was not that which caught Atrus's attention; it was the beauty of the delicate flowers that lay on every side, their tiny blooms cascading over the edges of the platform.

Atrus went over to the edge and stood there, looking out. There were no walls. If he stepped out now he would fall a mile or more, and it was that— that absence of any barrier between this and what lay beneath—that gave this place its unearthly beauty. All around him was the world, and here this tiny perfect garden.

"It's beautiful," he said, turning back.

"I am glad you think so." Ro'Eh Ro'Dan gestured toward the seat. "Won't you join me, Atrus?"

Atrus took a seat, conscious that beneath him was a mile of empty air. A cool breeze blew, ruffling his hair. He let his eyes wander over the perfection of the garden, then looked to Ro'Eh Ro'Dan once more.

Ro'Eh Ro'Dan was watching him attentively, his deep blue eyes trying to fathom something. And then he seemed to relax. Once more he smiled.

"You seem surprised," he said brightly.

"Everything here surprises me."

"Has D'ni not its wonders?"

"Compared to this?" Atrus shook his head. "No. Not even at its height."

"I see." Ro'Eh Ro'Dan looked down, frowning. "You speak almost as though your land were in decline."

"Decline? No, that is no word for it. The truth is D'ni fell. It is no more. Unless you count its ruins."

Ro'Eh Ro'Dan sat back, clearly shocked. "But I thought . . ."

"There are survivors," Atrus went on, "and I have been trying to rebuild. Even so . . ." He met the young king's eyes. "I wish to ask you something, Ro'Eh Ro'Dan."

The king seemed stunned; even so he nodded. "Ask."

"I would like to bring my people here from D'ni, to settle permanently in Terahnee."

"Of course. There's room for everyone." Yet the king seemed distracted now. "D'ni fallen . . ." He shook his head once more, then stood. "You must tell me all that happened, Atrus. Everything . . . right from the beginning."

"It is done!" he said joyously. "Ro'Eh Ro'Dan has agreed to have us here. Space will be found for all our people."

Catherine stood. "That's wonderful!"

"We spent a long time talking, discussing D'ni, our people, and the tragedy that befell us. And it was strange, Catherine, for I sensed that whilst he was shocked and sad for us, another part of him reacted differently. I don't know what it was, for by no sign or word was he unkind, yet . . ."

He stopped, conscious suddenly that Eedrah was in the doorway.

"Forgive me my intrusion," Eedrah began, "but I think I can explain. Not many know of these things, but the king most certainly would."

"Know?" Atrus asked. "Know of what?"

"Of the ancient prophecy. That Terahnee would fall. That a great cloud of darkness would descend and destroy it with its poisoned breath."

Both Atrus and Catherine now stared at Eedrah.

"So you see," Eedrah went on, "your tragedy might prove our joy. At least, that is one interpretation. Since our earliest times we have dreaded this calamity and now you come and tell us it has already happened, and that we, here in Terahnee, have come through it totally unscathed. You can be sure right now that Ro'Eh Ro'Dan is meeting with his close advisers and telling them this news."

Eedrah smiled. "It will do your people no harm, Atrus. No harm at all."

"Maybe not, yet if I had known this beforehand I might have broached the matter differently."

"My husband does not believe in prophecies," Catherine explained. "He thinks them unscientific."

"As they are. But Eedrah is right. And what's done is done. Our task now is to unify our peoples and to bring them here to their new home in Terahnee. Nothing else must distract us. The king has given his permission. Space will be made."

"He knows how many are to come?"

"I said five thousand."

Eedrah looked surprised. "Is that *all* of you that remain?"

"On D'ni and on Averone, yes. And fortunately so, perhaps, for how would even a great land like this take on any bigger number?"

"With ease," Eedrah said, a strangeness in his voice. He looked away a moment, then looked back. "Did the king say he wished to meet with you again?"

"He did. But not today. He has given his permission for us to return at once to Ro'Jethhe, there to organize the linking through of all the D'ni."

"Then I shall see to things," Eedrah said, and, turning, hastened from the room.

Atrus looked to Catherine. "All will be for the best."

"Yes." But she seemed distracted, too. "Forgive me, Atrus, but I wish to speak with Eedrah a moment. Something he said . . ."

"Of course. I shall pack, then see the others. There is not a moment to be wasted."

"No." She smiled. "I shall not be long." Then, turning from him, she hurried after Eedrah, anxious to catch up with him.

EEDRAH WAS SILENT ON THE JOURNEY HOME, WITHDRAWN, AND when Catherine asked him what it was he would not say, preferring to look away from her rather than answer her question.

Atrus, however, was full of plans, and spent much of the journey back discussing with Catherine and the rest how best to transfer all their people through.

Marrim, when she first heard of Atrus's plan, had fallen silent, and for almost half a day had said nothing. It was only when she understood that Atrus meant to include those from Averone that she perked up again. But even then she had reservations. These she resolved to keep to herself until she had a chance to speak privately with Atrus.

That chance occurred the first night of their journey back.

"Atrus?" she asked, closing the door quietly behind her.

Atrus looked up from where he was writing in his notebook, then gestured for her to come across. She was silent while he finished.

"Well?" he asked, closing the book.

"What if they will not come?"

"Your people, you mean?"

She nodded. "It is their home, after all." She hesitated, then, "Could you not write a Book, from here to there?"

"No, Marrim."

She looked down.

"It will be all right," Atrus said. "They will be happy here. There must be seas on this world. We'll ask Ro'Eh Ro'Dan to find a place for them beside one. So do not let it trouble you any more. There's a great deal of work to be done, arranging the move. Let that fill your mind over the coming days."

She looked up and smiled.

Atrus returned her smile. "Eedrah tells me we are to start early and travel direct to Ro'Jethhe tomorrow. It will be a long journey, so get what rest you can."

Marrim laughed. "You speak almost as if we shall be walking back, not sailing in a boat!"

In answer Atrus handed her the notebook. "Take this. I want you to read the last ten pages. And then, tomorrow, I want you to consider the best way of persuading your people that this move is in their best interests."

Marrim bowed her head, giving a single nod.

"Good. Then go now. Tomorrow will be a long day."

JETHHE RO'JETHHE HUGGED ATRUS TO HIM, THEN STEPPED
back, looking about him at the others. It was late evening now, and the lamps
that hung from the flower-strewn balconies threw a pearled light over the
pool and the silken awnings of the boat.

"I hear that everything went well!" Ro'Jethhe said. "Indeed, I hear that
your people are to join us here in Terahnee."

Atrus smiled broadly. "That is so, Ro'Jethhe. It is a good day for both
our peoples."

"An excellent day. And we must celebrate." Ro'Jethhe clapped his hands.
At once a door opened in the wall behind them and a ramp descended. As
Atrus turned, he saw that two ledges of stone had extended from the sides
of the pool to cover all except the boat, which lay completely enclosed at
the center. "Come," Ro'Jethhe said, leading them across, "I have invited a
few friends."

He turned to Atrus, smiling as he walked on. "Oh, you are quite famous
now, Atrus. There are many who wish to see you. Why, there would not be
room, even in the governor's halls, for so many. But I have asked one or two
whom you might find interesting." He raised a hand quickly. "Oh, and I
know you have traveled far today, but we shall not keep you up all evening.
Besides, I did not wish the moment to pass when we might toast the joint
future of our peoples."

Atrus smiled. "Nor I." And with that he let Ro'Jethhe lead his party up
the ramp and into the great hall where a good number of Ro'Jethhe's friends
awaited them.

THE EVENING HAD GONE WELL, BUT NOW IT WAS LATE. IRRAS had been dispatched to the plateau once again to warn Master Tamon of their imminent return, and Atrus would have followed would it not have offended their host. And so he sat on, doing what he so rarely did—socializing late into the night.

Talking to the local landowners, it was clear that none of them felt threatened by the proposed influx from D'ni. It was just as the king had said—when everyone had so much why should they begrudge others sharing their good fortune?—and that, as much as anything, had convinced Atrus finally that everything would work out for the best.

Catherine, looking across at Atrus, smiled, for she had rarely seen him in such good humor. Now that the king had been informed, he was free to talk of D'ni and its ways, and was enjoying doing so. Just now the talk had turned to the art of writing and to the kind of Ages the D'ni wrote. Ro'Jethhe's friends plied Atrus with question after question, fascinated by the whole notion of Guilds and particularly the Guild of Maintainers, though they clearly found it hard to comprehend just why such a Guild should exist in the first place.

"But *why?*" one of them insisted for perhaps the dozenth time. "Why do you need such a highly specialized Guild?"

"To restrain the weaker-minded," Atrus answered patiently, "to protect against faulty Ages, and to ensure there is no abuse of the Ages."

Another of the locals laughed. A drunken laughter. "But civilized people control themselves, so they can be seen!"

Atrus laughed awkwardly, not understanding the statement.

The local continued. "We write, we live, we control ourselves, we are seen." Pounding his chest with each *we.*

" I beg pardon," Atrus said, still smiling and looking for a clue to what was being said.

"Self-restraint and the ability to write. They distinguish us from the beasts, wouldn't you say, Atrus? They make us what we are. Men, and not unseen beasts."

"Of course we are not beasts," Atrus replied awkwardly. "But what is seen? What beasts are unseen?"

"You have much to learn." The local laughed. "Perhaps your lenses can help you see the beasts that we cannot."

Laughter broke out among the guests.

Atrus enjoyed riddles, but now he was the focus of the entertainment, without having a clue of what was being discussed. It unsettled him. But he gathered his wits and began to consider the information he had been given. Seen, unseen, control, writing, beasts . . . the choice of that particular D'ni word, bahro, was an odd one. It was a derivative of the root word for beast, bah, easily recognized, but the suffix ro had been added. It had to be a key to the riddle. The Terahnee would often prefix a name with ro in order to represent a people group, household, or family. Now he wondered what those combined words could imply. Beast families or households, unseen, what was unseen? Perhaps it referred to farms where unseen beasts were raised for food. No, he'd heard them use the word for beast without ro when referring to livestock. Wild animals—families or packs of unseen wild animals, out of control, in the far reaches of this Age, perhaps dangerous. That had to be it.

"Are we in danger when traveling beyond the civilized lands? Are there beasts that might be hostile?" Atrus tossed out the question looking for some confirmation of his conclusion.

Laughter again filled the room.

Atrus once again had to smile. He was not on the right trail.

"The beasts are neither civilized, nor distant, nor hostile, nor seen." The local was truly enjoying this impromptu contest of wits. In fact, everyone in the entire gathering was smiling, watching.

Except Eedrah. Atrus noted that he was hanging on every word of the exchange, but intensely—deeply staring at Atrus, without a hint of a smile on his face. It was enough of a contrast to the others as to cause Atrus to lose his train of thought. He stared back at Eedrah.

The riddler continued. "The civilized control the civilized *and* the uncivilized. The civilized see the civilized *but* the uncivilized see all."

Cheers arose from around the room.

Atrus glanced back at the speaker, the last clue simply adding to his confusion. He smiled and raised his hands upward, signaling surrender. The guests erupted in applause as the riddler took a bow.

Ro'Jethhe stepped in. "Atrus, it is not so difficult. You will be surprised at the answer." He was smiling broadly. "Writers and nonwriters, it is merely a riddle of words. Bahro, or beast-people, and ahrotahntee, nonwriters, otherworlders. Clever, yes?"

Atrus let the words sink in—still not grasping what the connection was. "Beast people?"

"Why, yes," Ro'Jethhe replied, reaching across to take a fresh cup of wine. "It is, after all, only we of Terahnee and D'ni who can write. The ahrotahntee have no such talent. It is why things are as they are. Surely it is so in D'ni, Atrus?"

Ahrotahntee. Catherine, grasping the riddle, felt herself go cold. She had not heard the term since Atrus's father, Gehn, had used it. *Outsiders,* it meant. *Book-worlders.* Those who were not of D'ni blood. Or Terahnee . . .

Atrus sat up straight. "With great respect, you are mistaken, Ro'Jethhe. The ahrotahntee *can* write. You have only to teach them."

There was a shocked silence. All eyes were on Atrus now, as if he had spoken something obscene.

Ro'Jethhe looked aside, clearly embarrassed. "You jest with us, Atrus, surely?"

Atrus looked about him, his eyes going from face to face, not understanding what was going on. "But Catherine writes, and *she* is ahrotahntee!"

There was a universal gasp. A look of utter shock had come to Jethhe Ro'Jethhe's face, while all about the chamber men glared at Atrus and his party with open hostility, while their wives and daughters blushed and looked down. Even several of the stewards, who were not known to react, had glanced up at Atrus's words and were looking to one another, as if asking what to do.

"Take care what you say," Ro'Jethhe said, wiping his mouth.

"But it is true," Atrus said, ignoring Catherine's hand on his arm. "Indeed, my grandmother and my mother were both ahrotahntee!"

There was sudden uproar. Ro'Jethhe stood, looking to the stewards, who immediately went to the doors and, taking keys from the belts about their waists, proceeded to lock them. Ro'Jethhe watched them, then, his face hard and angry, turned back, facing Atrus.

"Even were such things true," he said, "they should not be uttered. The unseen . . ."

"The unseen?" Atrus said, standing and taking a step toward his host. "What is this riddle?"

Atrus stopped, listening suddenly. There were noises in the walls surrounding them. A bumping and then a distinct thud, followed by a curse. Then, suddenly, a door opened in the wall where, but a split second before, there had been no door. Atrus knew that because he had been staring at the spot the very instant it had opened. And through that door, like ghosts, came six pale, silent figures, their shaven heads like ivory, their black, tight-fitting clothes making them seem more like cyphers than men. For they were men, despite their bowed, obedient heads, their averted eyes, their palpable fear of the steward who, with a snarling face, drove them silently across the floor between the Terahnee and out through a second door that opened as though by magic.

Atrus looked about him, wondering for that brief instant why they were not all as shocked as he was shocked, but all he saw were statues—faces that stared but did not see; eyes that, for that moment, were blank as stone. And as he saw them he understood, and that understanding sank into him, deeper and deeper, like a smooth, dark rock tumbling slowly to the ocean floor.

Slaves. The relyimah—the "unseen"—were slaves. And this whole place . . .

Atrus's mind reeled. Looking about him now, he saw not a world of splendor, but a world built to his father's dark design; a world where the false notion of blood had so blinded its natives that they saw their fellow men as beasts—that was, when they deigned to see them at all.

The thought of it staggered him.

Atrus turned, looking to Jethhe Ro'Jethhe, seeing the man suddenly transformed. But his host, this seemingly genial man he had thought so kind, was glaring at him now.

"I spoke but the truth," Atrus said.

Ro'Jethhe's answering words were curt, acidic. "You have said enough. Nor will you repeat what you have said. Do you understand me, Atrus of D'ni?"

"Oh, I see now," Atrus answered, a coldness shaping his words. "I see and understand."

"Make sure you do." Ro'Jethhe turned, gesturing to his senior steward. "Kaaru!"

At once the steward was at his side.

"See Master Atrus and his party to their rooms. And make sure they stay there."

"What is this, Ro'Jethhe?" Atrus protested.

"It appears we cannot trust your lying tongue. That being so, you will be confined to your rooms until I get word from the king." And with that he turned his back and hurried from the room. Within a minute all the rest of the Terahnee had likewise gone.

Atrus turned, looking to his tiny party, then looked across at the steward. The man had never seemed handsome, but now, studying his features, Atrus thought he could detect something brutish, something almost bestial about him. The steward, however, merely bowed.

"If you would come with me . . ."

BACK IN THEIR ROOM THEY HELD A CRISIS MEETING. CATHERINE, Marrim, Carrad, Oma, and Esel sat in chairs while Atrus paced the floor like a caged animal.

"We cannot stay," Catherine said.

"I agree," Esel said. "We should leave here immediately."

Oma nodded. "Yes, and destroy the Books *and* seal the Great King's Temple once again."

Atrus shook his head. "The king gave his word."

"Yes," Catherine said, "but that was when he thought we were D'ni. Now we are ahrotahntee." She laughed bitterly. "Why, it's a wonder they can still *see* us!"

Atrus turned, facing her. "I do not like this any more than you, Catherine. But Ro'Eh Ro'Dan is a decent man. I believe he will keep his word."

"You want to stay?"

"Perhaps we should. We might use our influence to change things here."

"*Change* things?" Catherine looked away. "All right," she said. "Do what you must. But send Carrad back to tell Master Tamon what we know."

"And what *do* we know?"

"That this is a slave society. What more do we *need* to know?"

"How they treat their slaves, perhaps?" Atrus said.

"But what *can* we do?" Oma asked. "You heard Eedrah. There are two hundred million of them."

"We wait. But first we send Carrad back to the plateau." Atrus paused, then shook his head, clearly distressed. "There has been a misunderstanding, on *both* our parts, but the Terahnee never lied to us."

"Only because we never asked the right questions!"

Atrus looked to Catherine. "That's true. We let what we saw seduce us; we mistook the surface for the substance. But that was our fault, not theirs! As I say, they never lied."

"But this whole world is a lie!"

"Maybe so, but we cannot blame Ro'Jethhe and his like for that. They know nothing else."

"And that is what I most fear," Catherine said. "You want to give them eyes, Atrus, but what if they do not want to see? What if we cannot *make* them see? Conditioning is a powerful thing. To break it in an individual is difficult enough, but when that conditioning is social . . ."

"You forget one thing, Catherine. We have the ear of the king."

"His ear, yes, but not his eyes." She stared back at him, then, quieter. "I think you're wrong, Atrus. I don't believe they *can* be changed."

ATRUS WOKE IN THE NIGHT FROM A FITFUL SLEEP—A SLEEP plagued by dreams of doors opening and closing before and behind, in rooms that turned and twisted in an unending maze—and turned, expecting to find Catherine there beside him in the bed. But she was gone.

He sat up, then saw her, there on the far side of the room, at the desk, a lamp beside her as she wrote in her journal.

"Catherine?"

She half-turned toward him. "I couldn't sleep. So I began to reread what I'd written since we came here."

"And?" He stood, then went across, taking a chair beside her.

"Kitchens. There were no kitchens. That alone should have alerted me. All that food awaiting us wherever we went, and no sign of it ever having been prepared. It was like everything. Magical, it seemed. And we accepted that."

"We had no reason not to."

"No. And then there was what Hadre said to us when he first met us. Do you remember? He said, "Can I see you?" And his eyes—I remember it now—they seemed to look straight through us. Until you mentioned D'ni. And then it was like a connection was made. He *saw* us."

"And Eedrah, too . . ." Atrus shook his head. "I'd come to like him. "But how can I trust him now? He might have told us. Indeed, he *should* have told us."

"Maybe he thought we knew."

There was a knock. Atrus looked to Catherine, then stood and walked over to the door.

"Who is it?" he asked quietly.

"It is I. Eedrah. I need to talk with you."

Atrus opened the door a fraction. Eedrah was standing there in the half-dark, alone.

"All right," Atrus said, opening the door more fully.

Eedrah hesitated, then stepped through. As the door closed behind him, he glanced about him nervously. "There's something I must show you."

SILENTLY THEY FOLLOWED, DOWN TO THE END OF THAT LONG, shadowed corridor and left into a narrow gallery. There, a mere two or three paces in, Eedrah stopped and, leaning into the wall, pushed.

A door opened where a door had not been.

They followed, down three narrow steps and into a dark passage that ran *within* the walls. Atrus reached out and touched the smooth, worn stone. No wonder the walls had seemed so thick.

Two steps in and the door closed silently, depriving them of light. Several seconds passed and then a glow grew in the darkness close by, illuminating first the hand that held the lamp, and then the face, the chest, the walls surrounding them.

Eedrah put a finger to his lips, then turned and walked on.

On, through branching corridors and down a long, straight flight of steps, the stone worn by four thousand years of use. And as they went, Atrus saw it in his mind. Saw the endless silent figures who had passed this way, fetching and carrying, never a word or sound betraying their presence to their masters behind the walls.

The relyimah—the Unseen.

Now and then they would pass a row of niches set into the wall, in which were all manner of things for cleaning and repairs. Elsewhere were built-in storage cupboards, and everywhere doors and tunnels branched off. Here, too, at this lower level, were well-stocked kitchens with long, marble-topped tables and huge stone shelves, and massive pantries, every surface spotlessly clean.

All was revealed in the pale white glow of the lamp, appearing from nothing and vanishing behind them in the dark.

A whole world beneath the world.

Beyond the kitchens the tunnel broadened and four long, broad rails of glistening silver were set into the floor, running parallel into the darkness ahead. They walked between those rails, beneath a high, curved ceiling. A hundred paces they went and then the tunnel opened out into a broad chamber, along both sides of which, on spurs that jutted from the central lines, rested the empty wagons that ran upon the rails. Huge wagons of some dull, rocklike material, thick ropes hanging limply from the great eyelike hooks that studded their sides.

On they went, into a smaller tunnel that turned then briefly climbed. Above them now the ceiling was breached every so often by big circular vents. Glancing up, Atrus had a glimpse of stars—a tight circle of brightly glimmering stars as at the bottom of a deep, deep well.

And on, through a strange gallery that ran away into the darkness on either side. Here, to their right as they passed, a dozen thick ropes stretched down diagonally from a long gash high up on the wall to the far side, where they were tethered about a dozen big, studlike protuberances, that seemed to swell like mushrooms from the surface of the floor.

Like the taut strings of a huge musical instrument, Atrus thought, not understanding what he saw.

And then, suddenly they were standing before a massive studded door, into which was set a grill. Eedrah turned to them, then lightly rapped upon the door.

No noise. No sounds of hurrying feet. Only that same dead silence. So silent, that Atrus did not at first notice that the grill had opened. A face stared out at them for an instant and then the grill snapped shut.

Slowly the door swung back. Eedrah looked to them again, his eyes imploring them to understand, then he turned back, leading them through, into a dimly lit chamber.

The ceiling of the chamber was high above them and the walls were crudely cut. Long, twisting flights of steps led up those walls to doors set deep into the stone. Twenty, maybe thirty doors, giving access to six separate levels that all led off this chamber.

Atrus turned back, to see that the man who had admitted them was still standing there, his head bowed, his eyes averted, his every aspect menial and subservient. By his shaven head and his jet-black tight-fitting clothes Atrus knew at once that he was relyimah.

"Come," Eedrah said quietly, speaking for the first time since they had entered that great warren. "There is someone you must meet."

AS EEDRAH AND ATRUS STEPPED INTO THE ROOM, THE OLD MAN glanced up from his book, then quickly stood, his head lowered, his eyes averted. The room was small and cramped, the old man's desk filling a good half of it, but the surface of the desk was piled high with Books. That in itself was wholly unexpected.

"Welcome Atrus," the old man said, keeping his head lowered. "I am Hersha."

Atrus looked to Eedrah queryingly, then gave a tiny bow. "I am pleased to meet you, Hersha."

"He is leader here," Eedrah said.

"Leader?"

"Of the relyimah. Hersha is their great secret. Not even the stewards know he is here."

"I am astonished," Atrus said.

Eedrah looked to him, a sudden seriousness in his eyes. "I thought you knew. D'ni . . ."

". . . is not like this. We have no slaves. No relyimah. Nor did we ever permit them in our worlds."

"Yes . . . I see that now." Eedrah looked down. "There have been misunderstandings. I thought you other than you are. And you, Atrus . . . you doubtlessly think me other than I am."

"You are their friend?"

Hersha answered for him. "Eedrah does what he can to help. But he is a rarity. Not one in ten thousand is like him."

Atrus looked back at Eedrah, seeing him in a new light. "You *see* them, whereas your father does not, is that right?"

"Yes."

"And you, Hersha, what do you see?"

"The waste of it," Hersha answered, daring to meet Atrus's eyes once again. "The ruinous waste."

WHILE THE THREE MEN TALKED, CATHERINE TOURED THE SILENT maze of rooms at the heart of the slave quarters, horrified by what she saw. After the casual luxuries of the world above, the primitive conditions down here were quite appalling. Young men slept forty to a tiny space, five to each of the narrow alcoves that had been cut from the rock—more catacombs than beds; the coldness of the stone covered only by the thinnest layer of sackcloth. Their washrooms were basic, more cattle troughs than bathrooms, and their kitchens were tiny and inadequate.

As she walked among them, those few that were awake turned from her, afraid to meet her eyes, shying from her inquisitive gaze as though from a blowtorch. Yet she could not help but see how badly they had been treated. Their pale limbs were covered with ugly, purple weals, while a few sported

scars, fresh and long-healed, their severity clear evidence of far harsher brutalities.

"Who did this?" she asked, turning to face Atrus as he joined her.

"The P'aarli," Atrus answered. "The stewards. It seems they regularly beat the relyimah, to make sure they are obedient . . . and silent."

Catherine made to speak, then saw the old man who stood just behind Atrus, next to Eedrah.

"This is Hersha," Eedrah said. "He is the leader of the slaves."

"They have a leader?"

"Yes, and a religion, too." Atrus took a slender volume from his pocket and handed it to her.

Catherine studied it a moment, then looked up at him wide-eyed. "These are the ancient prophecies." She frowned. "But why is it *their* book?"

Eedrah answered her. "Because of four lines in one of the oldest prophecies—four lines that speak of the freeing of the slaves."

"I see."

"With respect, I am not sure you do," Hersha said, almost hunching into himself as he spoke.

"What do you mean?" Eedrah asked.

"I mean that those lines are not in isolation. And with things being as they are . . ."

This was all too cryptic for Atrus. He interrupted. "What *do* you mean, things being as they are?"

Eedrah looked down. "Things are happening, Atrus. There is a sickness . . ."

"A sickness?" Catherine stepped closer.

Eedrah nodded. "It is a recent thing. Over the last few days a number of the relyimah took to their beds with stomach cramps. It was thought at first that they had eaten something bad, but their condition has worsened and many of them are now running a fever."

"Can I see them?"

Hersha led them down a corridor and through another of the hidden

doors into a long, low chamber, at the far end of which, on makeshift pallets, a dozen or more relyimah lay, several of their fellows in attendance.

Going over to them, Catherine knelt and began to examine one of the
sick. She was silent a moment as she felt the glands at the man's neck, peered
into his pale, unconscious eyes, and felt his pulse. She looked up at Atrus,
concerned. "We need to help these men—we need equipment and medical
supplies."

"Whatever you need," Eedrah said. "I shall have it brought at once."

BACK IN THEIR ROOM IN THE GREAT HOUSE, CATHERINE AND
Atrus sat across from Eedrah as he talked.

"It was my fifteenth season when I first saw one of the Slave Ages. As a
child, of course, you have to be taught not to see the slaves. Trained not to
speak to them or even notice them. Not that you would see them all that
often, for the stewards keep them out of sight as much as possible. But by
fifteen your eyes have learned not to see, your brain not to make the connection. It isn't difficult. But I guess my illness made me different."

"Your illness?" Atrus asked.

"A simple fever. But I almost died. A harvesting slave found me in the
orchards outside and carried me into the house."

"And was rewarded, I hope," Catherine said.

Eedrah swallowed and looked down. "He was killed. Executed by the
stewards for the impertinence of touching a master."

Atrus and Catherine both stared at him, shocked.

"So it is here. Remember the entertainer? The gymnast who fell?"

"Ah, yes," Catherine said. "I wondered how he was."

"He was severely punished for his mistake."

Catherine shook her head. "No . . ."

"It *is* our way. Mistakes are not tolerated. You saw how he did not even make a noise though he was in pain. Had he done so, the stewards would have killed him without hesitation."

Atrus sighed. "I did not know."

"Nor I," Eedrah said. "Not until that first visit. Then I saw how the young boys were recruited. Not orphans, as I'd speculated, but ordinary children like myself, only boys of four and five, taken from their parents and relocated in Training Ages where, in circumstances of the most extreme cruelty, they were prepared for service in Terahnee. Those Training Ages are the bleakest places I have ever seen, and the children are taught in the crudest manner to obey or die."

"Does Ro'Eh Ro'Dan know of this?"

For a moment Eedrah stared at Atrus in disbelief. "Do you not see it yet, Atrus? Ro'Eh Ro'Dan *authorizes* it. He is in charge of this terrible system. He and his ministers set the quotas. They say how many boys are to be taken from their families and trained."

Atrus stared and stared.

"I know," Eedrah said quietly. "It is hard to believe."

"But he was so kind to us. You were all so kind, so hospitable."

"It is a kindness that is confined to our own kind. While my people believed you to be exactly as themselves, they accorded you the same rights and benefits. But now . . ."

Catherine had been looking down into her lap, now she looked up again. "Why did you say nothing of this before now?"

"Because I did not know whether I could trust you."

"And when did you know?"

"Last evening. When you were puzzled by the riddle. And I saw your faces when those slaves were led away."

"Were they beaten?" Atrus asked, a hollowness in his voice.

"No, Atrus. They were killed. You see, it could not be allowed for them to repeat what you said in that room."

"Then we must do something."

Eedrah grimaced. "There is nothing you *can* do, can't you see that? You heard Hersha. There is not one in ten thousand of my people think as I think. And you saw how my father treated you the moment he heard that you were not pure D'ni. And so will the king treat you when he hears. You would be best to flee while you can!"

Atrus shook his head. "No. I will *not* run away. Besides, the king *will* keep his word. Terahnee he might be, but he is also a man."

Eedrah stood, exasperated now. "Don't you understand, Atrus? They will kill you. As surely as they killed those slaves. Indeed, you would all be dead right now but for the fact that you are still under the king's protection."

Seeing that Atrus would not be budged, Eedrah said. "All right. I'll do what I can to help you, but I must return now and help Hersha with the sickness, before the P'aarli come back on duty."

"Are you not afraid for yourself, Eedrah?" Catherine asked.

Eedrah turned back. "For myself, no. But there are times when I fear for my own people. There is something missing in them. A depth. I don't know what you'd call it. A void, perhaps. And they fill it with cleverness and all manner of distractions. Like the rooms."

"I did not know," Atrus said once more, anguish in his face.

"You are not to blame," Eedrah said.

"Yes, but . . ." He looked to Eedrah suddenly, frowning. "You thought we knew. You thought we condoned it."

Eedrah nodded. "Yes. But now I *see* you."

PART SIX

THE CREAK OF CART WHEELS

IN THE SILENT DARK.

DEAD MEN FALL BETWEEN THE WORLDS.

A TIME OF GREAT SORROWING.

—FROM THE URAKH'NIDAR, VV. 87–89.

ATRUS WOKE, STRANGELY REFRESHED, THE SUNLIT PEACE-fulness of the room making the events of the previous evening seem strangely dreamlike. Beside him, Catherine slept on.

Slowly it all came back, and as it did the sunlight seemed to fade until there was a darkness underneath all things.

Even the birdsong seemed transformed.

Careful not to wake her, Atrus rose and pulled on his robe. He did not know what time it was, but from the way the shadows fell in the room, the sun was high, the day well advanced. That, too, was strange.

He began to cross the room, then stopped. There, on the desk where Catherine had been writing, was her equipment box. It had not been there when they had gone to sleep, but now it was. And beside it was a note.

Atrus went across. The note was addressed to him. He slit it open and unfolded the single sheet:

> Atrus,
> Eedrah has told me everything. It is hard to believe but I do not think
> he lies. He warns us to prepare for a hurried departure and that I have
> done. At a word from you the Books will be destroyed and the link between
> the Ages closed for good, but I shall not do this unless I must. I send
> both Irras and Carrad back to you with this, as well as medical supplies
> and equipment. Our thoughts are with you all.
> Master Tamon

So Eedrah had gone himself to the plateau. Folding the note, Atrus slipped it into his pocket, then stepped outside, conscious now of the secret the massively thick walls held.

The corridor was empty, silent. No steward waited to do his bidding or anticipate his need.

Strange.

He walked from room to room, but it was as if the great house had been abandoned. There was no sound or sign of anyone. And then there came a shout, from the gardens outside. Going to a window, he threw it open and looked out. Marrim was down there. She seemed distressed. Seeing him, she waved furiously, then beckoned him to come.

"Wait there!" he called.

Marrim met him at the gate.

"What is it?" he asked, trying to calm her.

"It's one of them. One of the slaves we saw. He's just lying there. He won't move. And his eyes . . ."

"Where, Marrim?"

She led him across an ornamental bridge and into a formal garden. There, on the other side of a small wall, not ten paces from what looked like a well, lay the slave.

Atrus crouched down beside him, feeling at the neck for a pulse. "He's alive," he said, looking up at Marrim. "Go ahead and warn Catherine. I'll bring him up to our room."

Marrim nodded then hurried off.

Atrus turned back. This one was but a boy—seven or eight years old at most—yet like the others he was scarred and bruised, and his anonymity was emphasized by the tight-fitting black clothes he wore and his closely shaven head.

Swallowing back the sudden anger he felt, Atrus put his arms beneath the child and lifted him up. It was not difficult, for the boy barely weighed a thing.

Cradling the child against his chest, Atrus walked back to the house, determined not to be stopped by any steward. But no one stopped him. The corridors and stairs of the house were empty, and when he reached his rooms, only Catherine and Marrim were there to greet him.

"But he's only a boy," Catherine said, astonished by how young this one was.

"You heard what Eedrah said," Atrus answered, laying him carefully down on top of the covers. "They take them at four and five."

Catherine sighed. Sitting on the bed beside the child, she opened her case and prepared some supplies. "Marrim," she said. "I understand Irras and Carrad are back. Go fetch them. They can accompany me back to D'ni."

Selecting a tool from within the case, she looked up at Atrus. "We need to know what this is. Perhaps we can find a cure." Writing out a label, she fixed it to the side of a glass tube, then, taking a needle, took a sample of the boy's blood from his arm.

"Do you think he's dying?"

She did not answer, but that look said quite enough.

"We must do something," he said. "We must bring back all of those who have medical skill. Oma will know who they are. Or ask for volunteers."

Catherine nodded. Atrus stared at her a moment; only then did he realize that something was wrong.

"Are you all right, Catherine?"

She placed the sample tube into the slot in the case then closed the lid. Looking up at Atrus she shrugged. "It's nothing physical. It's just . . ."

"I know," he said, not wanting her to say it. "But let us do what we can. Let us take each moment as it comes."

NOTHING PHYSICAL . . .

Catherine gazed at the sleeping child, then turned, looking about her at the room.

Strange that I didn't see it before . . .

Atrus had gone back to see Eedrah and the relyimah, leaving her to conduct her tests, but the tests were the last thing on her mind. For a moment earlier she had felt an abyss open beneath her—a vertiginous crack in reality that had threatened briefly to engulf her.

Words, she told herself; *they were only words.* But for that brief, ridiculous moment they had seemed the most meaningful, the most *real,* thing in the room, and yet they were only echoes in her head: the memory of two lines she had read in Gehn's notebook, months ago, lines that were strangely duplicated in the *Korokh Jimah,* the Great Book of Prophecies used by the relyimah.

Discordant time. The smallest of enemies un-mans them all.
Hidden within the hidden. A breath and then darkness.

For a moment she had felt the way she used to feel when she was writing—in a fugue unrelated to her rational self. Atrus had taught her to focus that part of her through her conscious mind, but for a moment back there, shocked by all that had happened, she had felt herself let go . . . and the connection had been made.

She had felt herself link to something deeper than the physical world. Something that lay *beneath* appearances.

Catherine turned back, looking at the child. But now she seemed to see beyond the flesh and bone, beyond the sickness that ravaged him.

There is a purpose to all this, she thought, and knew, even as the thought was framed, that it was true.

"AH, ATRUS, I WONDERED WHEN YOU'D COME."

Eedrah looked drained. Beside him, on the bare swept floor of the slave infirmary, the number of pallet beds had risen to more than a hundred, and on at least six of those the sheet had been pulled up over the occupant's head.

"Yes," Eedrah said, answering the unspoken query. "Whatever it is, it's killing them one by one."

"Then we, too, are in danger."

Eedrah smiled bleakly. "I have heard it has spread to other estates. And the stewards . . . they, too, have been struck down by it."

"I wondered where they had got to."

"Some of them fled, I'm told. Afraid. And Catherine?"

"She is returning to D'ni. She's taking a sample with her to analyze."

"Good." Eedrah yawned. "I must get some rest, else I shall be no good for anything."

"I agree. But before you go, tell me this, Eedrah. Has there ever been anything like this before? There must surely have been epidemics."

"Long, long ago, perhaps, but most of those have been eradicated. They inoculate all of the relyimah on the Training Ages. Diseased slaves are poor slaves, after all. So what this is, heaven alone knows. All we do know is that they don't seem to have any natural defenses against it."

"Then let us hope that Catherine can come up with an answer."

Eedrah nodded somberly. "Let us hope so, Atrus, before we all find ourselves grinning like the Lord of the Dead."

JETHHE RO'JETHHE HAD NOT SLEPT WELL AFTER THE EVENTS OF the previous evening; he had tossed and turned, wondering whether he had been right to hold his hand and await word from the king, or whether he should have followed instinct and had the book-worlders slaughtered to the last man—and woman!—for their great heresy. After all, these were special circumstances, and the king had clearly not meant to extend his protection to any who were ahrotahntee. Against which was the possibility that he might be thought to have acted beyond his authority as a common citizen. After all, to act so precipitately might be thought a snub to the king himself, and that was unthinkable. Yet what if they slipped away? What if, when the king's word finally came, he could not carry out those high instructions?

And so it went on in his head, hour after hour into the night, until, exhausted, he had fallen into the deepest of sleeps and had overslept, so that now, at midday, he emerged from his room in a rage, bemused, not to say furious that Duura had not woken him earlier.

"Duura! *Duu-ra!*"

He was not properly dressed, and his hair was in a dreadful state, uncombed and tousled from sleep. Normally, it would all have been done long ago, and without him having to stand in an empty corridor and bellow.

Ro'Jethhe turned and went back into his suite of rooms, walking through to the great bathroom with its enormous sunken pool. On the far side of the empty pool, beyond the bathing chair—the great arm of which extended through a long slot in the wall—was his dressing room. He went there now, standing there and staring into the empty air, at a loss as to what to do. His eyes looked about the empty room, not seeing the young female slave who was slumped in one corner, his ears not registering her rasping breath.

"Where *is* the man?" he hissed. Then, hurrying from the room, he went out into the corridor again, bellowing down the echoing hallway.

"Duura! Du-u-uura!"

THE MAIN CAVERN OF D'NI WAS DARK AND SILENT AS THE BOAT slid into the great harbor and tied up beneath the ancient steps. In the glow of the lamps that lined the harbor's edge, Catherine stepped from the boat and quickly mounted the steps, Carrad following a moment later.

As Catherine came up over the lip of the harbor, a figure—stooped and ancient—made its way across to her. She did not notice him until he hailed her.

"Catherine . . . I am surprised to see you back."

She turned and gave a tiny bow. "Master Tergahn . . . it's rather late for you to be up, isn't it?"

Tergahn stepped closer, his heavily lined face coming into the light. "Not at all. The older you are, the less sleep you need. Until . . ." Tergahn blinked, owl-like, then gestured toward the case she was carrying. "Is that it?"

"The sample? Yes. I suppose you know what's happening."

"I know."

She waited, but Tergahn said nothing more.

"Forgive me, Master Tergahn. I must press on. We need answers and we need them quickly."

"Then let me not keep you any longer."

Later, alone at the bench in the special sealed-and-sterile workroom, she watched the ancient centrifuge whirl round and round, separating the elements in the tube for examination by the Guild Healers who had been summoned. Catherine found herself wondering why the old man had bothered to make himself known to her. He had advised them strongly against setting off on this venture, certainly, and now that he'd been proved "right" he might be justified in crowing, in saying "I told you so," but there had been no sign of that in his rheumy eyes. Indeed, if she had seen anything there, it had been concern.

In a rack to the Healer's left were nine similar tubes, in two groups of four and five—tested and untested. To his right stood the great brass-and-stone viewing lens. The results so far were inconclusive. The sample seemed relatively harmless—normal, one might say. As the centrifuge slowed, he took the tube and, spilling a little into the transparent dish, placed it beneath the viewing plate and put his eye to the lens.

The Healer studied it a while, watching the strange microscopic dance of the living cells, fascinated by it. But this sample too seemed normal. His notebook was open on the bench beside him. Moving his eye away, he picked up his pen and began to write. The results made little sense as yet, but there were still a number of tests to make.

The Healer worked on, silent and methodical, content to wait patiently for the answer he knew must come. It was simply a matter of exhausting all the probabilities.

The centrifuge slowed. He took another tube from its grip and spilled a little of the precious liquid into the dish.

This time, the Healer's response was different as his eye reviewed the magnified specimen. He spoke briefly with Catherine and she quickly walked over to the air lock. Outside, Carrad operated the locks and she stepped through, into the isolation chamber.

Catherine felt the air flow over her arms and face as the filters switched on. A moment later the outer door opened with a hiss.

She stepped out. Carrad was standing there, his eyes expectant. "Have you . . . ?"

She walked past him, her face closed. "Come," she said simply. "We must get back."

RO'JETHHE STOOD AT THE TOP OF THE GREAT SWEEP OF STEPS, his right hand slickly gripping the rail. Beneath him, the whole stairway seemed to be pulsing; growing and then shrinking again, while the walls flickered grainily on every side.

He shook his head, but it didn't help. Sweat dripped from his forehead and ran down the side of his nose.

Something was wrong.

"Guu-reh . . ." he slurred. "Guh . . ."

He staggered, then turned, his back slamming against the wall. For a moment he stayed there, as if pinned to the wall, his eyes closed, the blackness pulsating madly about him. Then the fit passed and his eyes popped open once more.

The library. Duura would be in the library. Of course.

He pushed himself away, unsteady now, each step like a drunkard's, his legs far away from him suddenly. Crossing the enormous hallway, he lurched into the room, then swayed back, steadying himself against the massively thick doorway, his neck moving up and back in an exaggerated motion as he tried to focus on the room.

"My eyes," he said, with a quiet puzzlement. "Something's wrong with my eyes . . ."

Duura was at his desk on the far side of the room. For a moment Ro'-Jethhe wondered what was wrong; wondered why the man had not come across the instant he had appeared in the doorway.

The arch of the door seemed to hold his hand like a sticky web. Ro'-Jethhe turned his head, staring past his own shoulder at his hand, then forced it—*commanded* it—to push him out, away from the door.

He staggered slowly across the room, the pulsing at his temples and just behind his eyes making it seem as though the room were expanding and contracting. He was sheened in sweat now, and each breath was a shuddering effort, but the desk was not far away now. He was almost there.

"Duura," he said, straightening up, his voice at least sounding clear. "Duura!"

But the steward was ignoring him.

Ro'Jethhe blinked. There was a book open in front of the man and he seemed to be reading it intently. Lurching over to him, Ro'Jethhe grabbed the man's arms and shook him.

"Duura!"

He let go. Slowly the body toppled back, then slumped and slid, clattering to the floor in an ungainly heap, the chair beneath it.

Ro'Jethhe stepped back, horrified. Dead. Even he could see that Duura was dead.

"Eedrah . . ." he said softly. Then, turning, he began to shout. "Eedrah! Eedrah, where are you?"

EEDRAH SAT BACK, AWAY FROM THE DYING SLAVE, THEN WIPED his forearm across his brow. He wasn't feeling well. He had tried to persuade himself that it was only tiredness, but he knew now—he, too, had the disease.

Across the now-crowded room, Atrus was tending to one of the recently stricken. He wondered briefly if he should call to him and tell him what he suspected, then let the idea drop. Atrus had enough on his hands.

He felt a hand on his shoulder and looked up, to find Marrim crouching over him. "Eedrah? Are you all right?"

The concern in her eyes warmed him. "I'm not sure. I think . . . well, I think I'm coming down with it."

Marrim nodded. "I've been watching you."

"Watching me?"

"Yes, I didn't think you looked well. I think you should go and rest now."

He made to get up. "There isn't time to rest." But Marrim's hand kept him down. He stared up at her again, surprised.

"Maybe you should return to the house," she said.

"To lie down?" Eedrah shook his head. "No, here will do. If I must share their fate I will share their circumstances."

She smiled fondly. "Did you hear they found several of the stewards . . . the P'aarli as you call them."

"Dead?"

Marrim nodded.

"It's as I said," Eedrah went on. "The relyimah were all inoculated. I don't know whether that was so for the P'aarli. Maybe not."

"And the Terahnee?"

Eedrah closed his eyes. "I keep seeing it, Marrim. Two hundred million dead. Not to speak of the relyimah. What is it? What in the Maker's name is this cursed thing?"

At the far end of the infirmary a door opened and two figures stepped inside.

"Catherine!" Eedrah sat forward, even as Marrim straightened up and went across, threading her way between the pallets that now covered the entire floor.

Atrus, too, had straightened and, turning, had seen Catherine and had begun to make his way across to her. They met close by the doorway.

She stared at Atrus, a strange expression in her eyes. "I think we had better talk."

"Then talk."

"Not here."

Atrus blinked, surprised, then nodded. "Okay. We'll speak in Hersha's room."

"THIS ISN'T A DISEASE." SHE SAID. "AT LEAST, NOT IN ITS natural form."

"Catherine?"

"Harmless bacteria," she said. "That's what's doing this. They live in our stomachs."

"I don't follow you. . . . Harmless? Then why . . ."

Atrus's voice dropped away. There was a tiny motion of understanding in his face. When he spoke again, the words were almost a whisper. "D'ni bacteria, you mean. Harmless to *us* as we've become immune to it over the years."

"But not to the relyimah."

"Nor the P'aarli, it seems."

"They have it, too?"

Atrus nodded, yet it was clear he was in shock. He shook his head. "*We* brought this thing here. *We* released it. The Maker help us!"

"Brought what?" Eedrah asked. He had come in silently.

Catherine turned, a slightly guilty look on her face, but Atrus faced the matter squarely.

"The sickness. It came from D'ni."

Eedrah stared, shocked.

"It's a stomach bacteria," Catherine explained. "Harmless to us, harmful to the relyimah."

"And to the Terahnee," Eedrah said.

"The Terahnee?" Atrus sat forward. "Is your father ill?"

"And my brother . . ." Eedrah stopped and looked down, for the first time close to tears. Taking control of himself again, he looked back at Catherine. But there was no sign of hope in Catherine's face.

"We cannot cure this, Eedrah."

"Then we all must suffer."

"We shall do what we can," Atrus said. "We shall bring in help from D'ni to tend and nurse the sick. Some will die"

"Yes," Eedrah said, a flicker of bitterness in his face. Then that was gone. "Yes," he said, more clearly.

Catherine, noting suddenly how drawn and pale Eedrah looked, reached out and gently held his arms. "Let us get you to a bed. I shall have Marrim come and nurse you."

Eedrah smiled gratefully, yet there was a bleakness in his eyes—the bleakness of realization.

Atrus sighed. He seemed, in those moments, to have aged a hundred years. "I am so sorry, Eedrah. If I had known . . ."

But Catherine shook her head. "You were not to know, Atrus. You made your choice on reasonable grounds."

"I do not believe that. I made a choice and my choice was wrong. Now millions must suffer."

"But Atrus . . ."

"No," he said, standing and walking round the desk, his face like stone.

"*Atrus!*" Catherine called after him. "Atrus!" But Atrus was gone; vanished into the darkness of the tunnels.

THE GREAT BOAT GLIDED SLOWLY AROUND THE CURVE OF THE river, then slid beneath the bridge, Ro'Jethhe's house directly ahead of it.

In tunnels that ran parallel to the waterway, beneath and to either side of it, two teams of slaves pulled on the great ropes, four to a rope, dragging

the boat along, the occasional spillage of water cascading down over them from the partially sealed slot above their heads.

Silently they strained, maintaining the even walking pace that kept the boat in motion, while behind each team a single steward jogged along, carried in a sturdy four-man palanquin.

Up above, the boat eased its way beneath the massive walls of Jethhe Ro'Jethhe's house and into the central space. As it did, the slaves abruptly reversed direction, moving with practiced ease. For an instant the great ropes were slack, and then they took the strain once more, slowing the boat smoothly to a standstill.

Exhausted, most of the slaves fell silently to the floor even as a number of them secured the ropes.

Up above, four men, wearing official cloaks and pendants of office, stepped out onto the unswept marble, surprised to find no one there to greet them.

"Ro'Jethhe?" one of them called, looking to his companions and frowning. "Jethhe Ro'Jethhe?"

A door opened on the far side of the concourse and a figure stumbled out; a scarecrow of a man, wearing stained and ragged clothing, his hair unkempt. Slowly it came toward them, limping and hopping by turns.

Closer, they saw that it was indeed a man.

"*Ro'Jethhe?*" the first messenger queried, astonished by the sight that met his eyes.

But the disheveled-looking figure did not answer. Instead, he turned and looked about him squintingly, as though he could not understand who he was or what he was doing there. His face was smeared with dirt and with what looked like tears and his hair hung in clumps.

"Ro'Jethhe? What has happened here? Have you been attacked?"

The scarecrow laughed and hopped, its eyes flickering from side to side in a manic, feverish fashion.

"Ro'Jethhe," it said, parrotlike. "I *am* Ro'Jethhe."

Again the chief messenger glanced to his companions, then he took a long silver tube from within his cloak and offered it to the scarecrow.

"If you *are* Jethhe Ro'Jethhe, then I am commanded by the king, Ro'Eh Ro'Dan, to place this official edict in your hands."

Ro'Jethhe took the tube and stared at it, blinking and squinting, incomprehension in his eyes. "Ro," he said quietly. Then, enjoying the game: "Ro! Ro! Ro-ro!"

"Gentlemen!"

The four men turned as one, to face another, younger man; pallid and clearly ill, yet neatly dressed, his hair combed back, his manner apparently quite normal.

"Forgive my father," the young man said, approaching them, "but he is not himself. There is a sickness . . ."

The four men looked to each other, concerned.

"A plague, it seems," Eedrah went on, enjoying the discomfort of the king's men. "There is no defense against it. Already many here have died."

At that the four men blanched. Quickly they went into a huddle, discussing the matter in a low urgent murmur. There were nods of agreement and then their spokesman turned to Eedrah once again.

"Our task here is fulfilled, Ro'Jethhe's son. The king's message has been safely and properly delivered, therefore there is no need for us to stay. We are certain your father will obey the king's instructions to the fullest."

Eedrah looked beyond them to where his father stood, as if frozen, staring at the silver tube in his hand as if his eyes had been glued to the sight.

"It will find you," Eedrah said solemnly, wiping the perspiration from his brow, "*wherever* you run to!"

"It is the prophecy!" one of them said in a harsh whisper, but the others quickly hushed him, even as the first of them stepped back on board the boat. Quickly the others followed.

The chief messenger stared at Eedrah, then raised his hands and clapped them together.

There was a moment's delay—an awkward moment—and then the boat began to move.

Eedrah watched them leave, then, walking round the central pool, stepped up to his father and took the tube from his hand.

For a moment he stood there, feeling the sunlight on his face and arms, and wondered whether he would ever experience that again, then he cracked open the tube and took the sealed message from within.

It was as he'd feared. The king had ordered that all of the D'ni, including the ahrotahntee, be chained up and brought back to the capital to be tried in secret for their heresies.

Rolling the scroll up again, Eedrah slipped it back in the tube, capped it, then, smiling bleakly, tossed it into the water.

So much for kings and edicts. So much for heresies. They were all equal now, masters and servants, Terahnee and relyimah. Death would come for them all, whatever cloak they wore or did not wear, whatever their eyes could see or not see.

He looked to his father, saddened. His brother Hadre was already dead, taken in his bed, and now Jethhe Ro'Jethhe had gone, leaving in his place this fool in his disheveled clothes—this babbling madman with his staring eyes and sickly flesh.

He reached out, taking his father's hand, then slowly led him back across the square and through the door, inside, to where his deathbed waited.

THE LONG DAY PASSED, AND AS THE SUN BEGAN TO SET, ATRUS climbed the steps up out of the darkness of the slaves' quarters and, his D'ni lenses pulled down to protect his eyes, crossed the sunlit lawn and up into the silent house.

After the meeting with Catherine and Eedrah he had walked for some while, eaten up by the thought that this was all *his* fault; this whole tragedy had been caused by *his* impetuosity. He kept seeing old Tergahn's face, telling him to burn the Books and seal up the chambers again. But he had known better.

He walked and walked; then, after a time, feeling much calmer and know-

ing that there was nothing else for him to do, he had returned to the infirmary and carried on his work tending to the sick. There Catherine had come
to him and, holding him briefly, had told him of Ro'Jethhe's death. Eedrah,
meanwhile, slept, a milder form of the fever settled on him.

Now, as he climbed the long, curving steps to the room he shared with
Catherine, Atrus wondered what was left for him to do here. Exhausted as
he was, he saw it clearly. This world was dying, and there was nothing they
could do now but alleviate the discomfort of some of these poor wretches
in their final hours.

So much for his great plan of unifying D'ni and Terahnee. It was as
Eedrah had said, what happens happens, and what are a man's petty plans
in the face of that?

For the first time in his life he almost believed in fate. Yet still a small
part of him argued against it. Life surely had no meaning unless a man was
free to *choose* his fate, to mold it and fashion it according to his nature.

"I am too tired," he said aloud as he stepped into his room. "Too tired
and befuddled."

He peeled off his shirt and threw it down, then turned, hearing a noise
behind him in the room.

"Marrim?"

His young helper was slumped over the bed. The sight made him start.
Then he remembered. They were not affected.

Yes, but she is not D'ni . . .

He hurried across, worried now. What if she *was* ill of the sickness? But
her soft snoring made him understand. She was not ill, she was asleep.

Atrus smiled and made to turn away, then stopped, a strange little ripple going up his spine. The slave-child Marrim had been tending was
awake, his dark eyes staring straight at Atrus. They blinked, then looked
away.

"Child?"

At once the boy slipped under the covers, hiding himself.

"It's all right," Atrus said, walking round to the head of the bed. "I won't
harm you, child. I promise."

But the child would not emerge again. He trembled beneath the sheets like a trapped young animal.

Hersha, Atrus decided. *I shall bring Hersha. He will know what to do.* Then, turning, he hurried from the room, hope mounting in him for the first time in all that long, dark day.

WHILE HERSHA TALKED QUIETLY TO THE CHILD, DISTRACTING him, Catherine took the sample from his arm.

It was not that the child fought to evade the needle, it was just that he was trembling so much that it was hard for Catherine to keep the needle still. Marrim had to help her keep that emaciated limb from shaking itself apart.

Then it was done and, while Catherine put the sample into her case and clicked it shut, Marrim reached out and clasped the slave-child to her, hugging him tightly.

Slowly the trembling ceased. Slowly the child calmed down again.

Marrim smiled and looked to Hersha, who was staring at her in astonishment. "What is his name?" she asked.

"His name?"

"Yes. He has one, surely? Or did the Terahnee simply number them all?"

"No . . . His name is Uta."

"Uta . . ." Marrim moved back a little, trying to look into the boy's face, but however she moved, he would position his face so it could not be properly seen.

"Even in one so young the conditioning is strong," Catherine said, seeing what was going on. "It will take some while to change that."

"But at least now it *can* be changed," Atrus said. "At least the relyimah have some hope."

"And the others?" Marrim asked.

"We shall know soon," Catherine answered. "I have taken a sample of

Ro'Jethhe's blood, and of Eedrah's, too. If we can discover what it is that allows some to survive this and makes others succumb, then perhaps I might find something that will help."

"Then go at once," Atrus said.

As Catherine hurried from the room, Marrim turned back to the child. "Well, young Uta. You give us all hope."

But the child said nothing. As he had done all his infant life, Uta looked away, his body hunched into itself as he tried not to be seen.

HOREN RO'JADRE LAY IN HIS GREAT BATH, ON HIS BACK, WHERE death had found him, his mouth open in an "Oh" of surprise. His P'aarli stewards had fled that afternoon, when news had first come of the sickness that was sweeping the south. But they ran in vain, for they had long ago been caught by the strange bacteria that now crawled and multiplied unseen inside them all.

Yet death, for now, moved at a walking pace—or, to be more accurate, at the pace of a slowly gliding boat. Eight days was the gestation period for this sickness. Eight days before a mild disorder became fierce cramps and then, with a suddenness that often killed, something much worse.

Master and slave succumbed. And the P'aarli, first to flee, were taken in the fields, or in some well-trimmed field of exotic blooms, their groans alone distinguishing them from the silent acquiescence of those they had once beaten and killed.

Across the whole land the sickness was spreading now. News of it had come to the capital, where Ro'Eh Ro'Dan, uncertain yet how serious it was, took advice from ancients who had known no illness in their long and worthless lives.

"If slaves are dying," the old men counseled, "then bring in more from the Ages. Replace their numbers."

It seemed a simple and effective policy. But the new slaves were not trained. Could they be counted on to be obedient?

"No matter," the old men said. "Slaves are slaves. They will obey."

But some did not. And as word of the sickness spread among the relyimah, so one or two among their number took it upon themselves to exact swift vengeance on those who had afflicted them with years of misery.

One such was a slave named Ymur. As his overseer raised his whip to beat Ymur, the slave grabbed the P'aarli's wrist and, twisting it, snapped the bone.

There was a cry of pain, silenced in an instant. And as the others stared at the fallen corpse of their tormentor, so Ymur looked about him, allowing his eyes to see what they had never properly focused on before.

"Come," he said, gesturing to them. And, obedient as slaves, they followed.

MANY MORE DAYS PASSED, AND SLOWLY THE PATTERN BECAME clearer. Many of the relyimah were dying, but only those who were too weak to survive the first full shock of the sickness. The majority survived and, within weeks, were on their feet again. Among the Terahnee and the P'aarli, however, the death rate was higher. Some, like Eedrah, survived, but a great number succumbed. Thus it was that Eedrah had buried his father, mother, and three of his sisters.

He was sitting alone in the great library, writing, when Hersha came to him.

At first Hersha had found it uncomfortable—one might even say frightening—coming into the main house. Old he was, and well read, yet he was still relyimah, and from childhood had been taught to be invisible. Now he had a new fate.

"Eedrah . . ."

Eedrah looked up, a slightly glazed expression in his eyes. At Atrus's suggestion he had begun to write down his feelings, hoping thus to purge them, or at least to understand what he was undergoing.

"Yes, Hersha?"

"Forgive me for disturbing you, but important news has come. There is to be a meeting."

"A meeting?"

"Of the relyimah. At least, of their leaders. I have been asked to attend. It is to be held at the great mound, in Gehallah district."

Eedrah stared at the old man, then set his pen aside. There was something strange about Hersha's manner.

"Hersha? What is it you're not telling me?"

The old man looked down. "You see right through me, Renyaloth."

That use of his nickname among the relyimah—"the sickly one"—told him he had been right. Whatever this was, Hersha was finding it difficult telling him. Eedrah knew he would have to coax it from him.

"So what is the purpose of this meeting?"

Hersha's ancient head tucked itself even deeper into his chest, old reflexes taking control. "They mean to overthrow the Masters."

"Ah . . ." It ought not to have been a shock. After all, what was there to overthrow now that many of them were dead or dying? But for the relyimah to think like this was unheard of, and Eedrah found himself not surprised but actually astonished by the news.

"Is this a warning, Hersha? Are you telling me that I should leave Terahnee? Go back with Atrus, possibly?"

Hersha's eyes flicked up briefly before he averted them again. Eedrah saw how he steeled himself to speak again, and when he did it was another shock.

"I want you to come with me," Hersha said quietly. "To speak to them. persuade them not to act too rashly."

"*Speak* to them?"

Eedrah sat there, astonished. *And say what?* he thought. *That we treated you abominably, but not to punish us for that?*

He sighed. "Let me consider it, Hersha. And let me speak with Atrus. Then I shall tell you whether I will come with you or not."

Hersha gave a little bow. "As you wish, Renyaloth." And, without another word, the old man turned and scuttled away, hunched into himself, his eyes glancing from side to side as if he expected at any moment to be waylaid by stewards for his impertinence.

"ANY LUCK?" ATRUS ASKED, LOOKING OVER CATHERINE'S shoulder at the page she was writing.

"None at all," she answered, finishing the sentence she had been writing, then looking up at him. "Not that it matters now. If what Hersha has heard is true, then there is not a corner of this land that has not been ravaged by the sickness."

Atrus nodded somberly. "It seems almost like a judgment."

Catherine hesitated, as if about to say something, then nodded. "Eedrah certainly thinks so." She looked past Atrus to where Uta sat in the corner chair, hunched in to himself, trying not to be noticed. "I just wonder how the relyimah will cope. There's food for now, but when that runs out, what then?"

"They grew it," Atrus said.

"Yes, but that was when there was someone there to organize them. You've seen them, Atrus. Without someone to tell them what to do, they're lost. They're not mindless, I know that, but they sometimes act as if they are. Our problem is getting round that conditioning before they starve. We need to get them to make decisions for themselves."

Atrus nodded, but both of them knew that it was easier said than done. How did one change not just a lifetime's habits but long millennia of custom? Yet there must be one or two of these relyimah who could be used—molded—to shape the new society that must emerge from this disaster. But where would they be found?

Eedrah, it seemed, had the answer. "Atrus," he said, coming into the room. "I have a problem. The slave leaders are to have a great meeting, it seems. Tonight, at sunset, at the great mound in Gehallah."

"Is that far from here?"

"Two hours' walk, at most."

"And what is to be discussed at this meeting?"

"The overthrow of the Masters." Eedrah smiled bleakly. "By which I take it they mean the wholesale slaughter of survivors."

"You think they'd do that?" Atrus asked, surprised.

Eedrah nodded. "Some have already done so, killing P'aarli and Masters both. They did not wait, it seems, for the sickness to descend."

"And is Hersha to attend this meeting?"

"Yes, and he has asked me to go with him and speak to them."

"So will you go?"

"If you will come with me, Atrus. I know them, true, but I am no speaker. Not as you are."

"And you think I can convince them to act decently?"

"If anyone can."

Atrus considered a moment. "All right. I shall come with you. But first I must return to D'ni. There is something there I need."

"Will you be long, Atrus?"

Atrus smiled. "No, not long. Three hours, maybe four at most." He turned, looking to the boy. "Uta! Come, my little shadow!"

The boy jerked, then, burying his head into his neck, he stood.

"Until then," Eedrah said.

"Until then."

RO'EH RO'DAN STOOD AT THE EDGE OF THE HIGH PLATFORM AND looked outward. Beneath him the land of Terahnee stretched away into the distance, swathed in the late afternoon mist. From this height it seemed eternal and unchanged, but he knew better. There was not a household down there that had not been touched.

"*The bricks alone will stand on that day, / And the blind shall be given eyes.*"

He said the words softly, almost in a whisper. Ro'Addarren, his chief adviser, had read them to him only that morning from the ancient book, and now the old man was dead.

"So they were true, after all," he said, and almost laughed, remembering how excited they all had been when they had heard of the tragedy that had struck D'ni, and how they had thought that *that* was what had been prophesied. Well, now they knew.

But knowing did not help them any.

From far below there came a hammering. He turned, staring down into the depths, and saw the great host at the Valley Gate and knew, without needing to be told, that this was the rabble of new slaves they had brought in from the Ages.

"So be it," he said, no longer caring about his own personal fate. What did it matter if he died? He was king of nothing now.

But others would not let him succumb to fate. As he stood there, two of his ancient counselors ventured out onto the platform, clearly afraid of the great drop. Their eyes went from Ro'Eh Ro'Dan to the platform's edge constantly, while they themselves stayed close to the top of the steps.

"You must come, my lord," one of them said, beckoning to him as if to a child.

"Your boat is awaiting you," the other added. "If we leave now . . ."

He sighed, then walked across to them. It was no use arguing. Besides, maybe he was wrong. Maybe once this rabble was dispersed they could rebuild. From what he'd heard many of the slaves were still alive, and they, certainly, would need organizing.

"All right," he said, letting them usher him down the steps and through his room, out onto the narrow bridge. He was halfway across when some instinct told him to stop and turn, and as he looked back, he saw himself, in memory, greeting the stranger.

I liked him, he realized. *I really rather liked him.*

"Master!" the old men said, trying to hurry him along. "Master, we must be gone from here!"

He shook his head, trying to clear it of the memory, but still he could see them both, cloaked against the coolness of the early morning, and smiled. It made no sense to like the man after all that had happened, and yet he did.

I see you, Atrus. Then, conscious of the old men fussing all about him, he hurried on toward the waiting boat.

ATRUS STEPPED FROM THE RUINS, THE HEAVY PACK ON HIS back, and, adjusting his lenses, turned to look as Oma and Esel stepped out behind him. They, too, carried the big-framed backpacks. Behind them came the slave-child, Uta, and finally Master Tergahn.

As Atrus turned back, Tamon hurried up. "Atrus! Something's happening! There are great plumes of smoke in the distance!"

They hurried across to the chairlift. From its upper platform a clear view of Terahnee could be had.

Atrus scanned the distance, then looked back. Tergahn was watching him. "You must listen to me, Atrus," the old man said. "You did not before and look what happened. We must pull our people out and destroy the Books. Yes, and seal up the Temple, too, for if the relyimah find the Temple they will link through and destroy us all."

Atrus nodded. "I hear you, Master Tergahn. But I must take this one chance to make amends." He looked to Tamon. "Master Tamon, if you do not hear from us in two days, you will do as Master Tergahn says. You will dismantle the chairlift and return to D'ni, destroying the Linking Books. Then you will seal the Great Temple."

"But Atrus . . ."

"No arguments, Master Tamon. Tergahn is right. We do not know how the relyimah will act, and we cannot risk our people. Two days is sufficient to do what I must do. If I fail, I shall have failed by then, and D'ni will be in danger. Indeed, it might be well to post lookouts."

Tamon frowned, clearly dismayed by this turn of events. Even so, he bowed his head obediently. "I shall do as you say."

"Good." Atrus reached out, taking his old friend's hands. "I hope it will not come to that."

"And I," Tamon said. "Good luck, Atrus, and hurry back."

Atrus smiled. "I shall do my best, Master Tamon." Then, signaling to Esel and Oma and young Uta to join him on the chair, he climbed aboard, his eyes going outward to the tall dark plumes that climbed the distant sky.

PART SEVEN

DESCENDING THE GREAT LADDER OF TIME, WE SEE FOUR FACES.

THE FACES OF FOUR WOMEN.

AGED AND DEAD THE FIRST TWO ARE.

THE THIRD, A DREAMER. THE LAST, A TEACHER.

—FROM THE VISIONS OF JO'IRIMAH, CANTO 157

THE SUN WAS JUST SETTING AS HERSHA AND HIS PARTY made their way up the long, sloping ramp and onto the great mound of Gehallah.

There the relyimah were gathered, over twenty thousand strong, the uniformity of their dress and their shaven heads emphasized by the utter silence in which they stood.

A canopy of golden silk had been placed at the center of that massive amphitheater, and in the last rays of the sun four banners—purest black—hung limply. Beneath that canopy a smaller group was gathered. It was toward them that Hersha now headed, Eedrah and Atrus behind him, the others—Oma, Esel, Uta, and two other relyimah—several paces back.

"Hersha," one of them said, as the old man stepped up onto the platform, a greeting that was quickly taken up by the others there.

"Friends," Hersha said. "I have come at your summons."

"And brought others with you, I see," another of them said, stepping out from where he had been standing at the back.

Hersha looked about him for clarification, clearly not recognizing the man who had spoken.

"I am Ymur," the man said, hesitantly yet at the same time belligerently. "I am leader of the relyimah of Ro'Tanak."

Hersha frowned. "I thought Rafis was their leader."

"He was," Ymur said humorlessly. "And now I am."

Atrus, looking on from just beneath the platform, saw how all but Hersha found it hard to meet each other's eyes. It was as Catherine had said; it was hard for these men, even the boldest among them, to throw off their conditioning. They could not change overnight. Yet they might break altogether under the strains of the new demands on them, and if they did, then there would almost certainly be bloodshed.

"Who are these *strangers*?" Ymur asked.

Hersha turned to one of the others, an old slave, and asked, "Have I to answer to this newcomer, Baddu?"

Baddu looked uncomfortable. "It might be best, Hersha. Eedrah we know, of course, and welcome as a friend, but the others . . ."

"Are friends also," Hersha said. "They are ahrotahntee."

There were looks of surprise at that, for all there had taken Atrus and his fellows for Masters. But Ymur was not convinced.

"Are these not the ones who went to see the Terahnee king?"

"That is so," Hersha answered.

"Then they have no place here at this gathering." Ymur looked about him threateningly, then raised his voice. At the sound of it many of those closest to him cowered. "Hear me, brother relyimah. No friend of the Terahnee can be a friend of ours."

"That is not so," Hersha began, but Ymur spoke over him.

"It is said that they made a pact."

"That is untrue," Hersha said.

Ymur stepped forward, confronting Hersha. "Are you calling me a liar, old man?"

Hersha dropped his gaze. "You heard wrong, that is all. No pact was made. These *are* our friends."

"So they would have you believe!" Ymur said disdainfully. He turned his back on Hersha. "Myself, I will not hear them."

"Just as others would not *see* you, Ymur?"

The speaker stepped from the darkness at the back of the platform, his thin cloak rustling about him.

"*Gat!*" The whispered name rippled through the thousands gathered in the growing darkness. "*Gat!*"

The ancient stopped amid those gathered at the center. He was older even than Hersha and his hair was white and long. Hersha had mentioned his name reverently many times, but Atrus had always assumed that the man was legend, buried long ago. Yet here he was, as large as life; a strong, vigorous-looking old man.

"Well, Ymur?"

And as Gat turned to face the younger man, Atrus realized with a shock that he was blind.

Ymur had hunched into himself, his head tucked down, like a beaten dog. "But they are not relyimah," he grumbled.

"Maybe so," the ancient said, "yet we would do well to listen to what they have to say."

From Ymur's expression he clearly did not like this, but he was not going to argue with Gat. He gave a grudging nod.

"Good, then light the lamps and let's begin. There is much to be said this night."

IN THE GLARE OF THE FLICKERING LAMPS—REAL LAMPS, burning in cressets—Gat stepped to the front of the platform and began to speak.

"I remember my father and my mother, and I can recall quite vividly the day that I was taken from them. Blind as I am, I can still see the pain in their eyes. Terahnee did that. Terahnee and the servants of Terahnee. And I vowed that day that I would never forgive them for what they did. That I would fight them to the last—here *inside* me."

Gat tapped his chest, then paused, his blind eyes searching about him. "Like you I have pretended to be nothing. To bleed and suffer and be silent. To exist for work and yet not to exist at all. To live without love or recognition. All this I did, not choosing to do so, but because I had no choice and found that the force of life in me was stronger than the desire for death. It is that which makes a slave. That choice, when all other choices are denied, to carry on."

Gat leaned toward them, lowering his voice slightly, as if speaking personally to each one of them. "But now the Masters are gone, it seems. Swept away. And we are free."

He smiled blindly. "Look about you. *Dare* to look about you. See those who have suffered with you. Meet their eyes and see the pain there that all here have endured."

Atrus, looking about him, saw how some of the relyimah risked tiny glances at their fellows; but most looked down, ashamed, still locked in the prison of habit.

Gat, blind as he was, seemed to comprehend this, and now his voice softened. "Oh, it is hard, brothers. Perhaps the hardest thing we have ever had to do; to shake off our bonds and be ourselves, not some other man's *thing*. But we must learn to use our eyes anew. To see each other and thus *cease* to be relyimah. It will take time. Perhaps even a long time. But we must make that journey to seeing. To *being* seen. And while we do, we must be patient. Patient, because it would be unwise to act rashly and hot-bloodedly. That path can bring us only more grief, more injustice. The past is past. We must let go of the hatred and bitterness we feel. And so I counsel you, my brothers. To look and see and be calm."

And with that Gat turned away, stepping back into the darkness.

Next to speak was Ymur. He came to the front of the platform, self-conscious and ill at ease now that he must address the multitude.

"Brothers," he began. "Gat speaks wisely. Like us, he has suffered. Like us, he has known what it is to be nothing. I say that no man who has not suffered that can speak of it."

As he said the words, Ymur turned, looking pointedly at Atrus and Eedrah and their party.

"And so we listen to Gat. As now you listen to Ymur, who suffered and was nothing. Who, like you, is relyimah. And I say that I, too, remember the day I was taken from my home. I remember how my father fought the P'aarli and was killed for his pains. And I, too, took a vow that day."

Ymur paused. As he spoke, his voice had grown louder and more confident. Now he seemed to swell with every word, a burning anger behind his every utterance—an anger, Atrus saw, that touched many in that great crowd.

"Gat says the past is past. But is that really so? Are all the Masters dead? No. Some live. And while they live, will they not be tempted to return to how things were? Will they not bring men from other Ages to subdue us once again? Who here would dare to say no?"

He paused, a snarl on his features now. "The truth is this. We *know* what the Terahnee are. The scars on our bodies tell us. So, too, the chains in our heads. Gat speaks of learning to use our eyes. He is right. But first we must see the threat the Terahnee still pose. Gat says we are free, but we are not free. Not until the last Terahnee child is dead."

There was a murmur from the gathering at that—both shocked surprise and vehement agreement. And Atrus, hearing it and looking about him, understood at once. Whatever Gat had said about learning to be themselves, *this* was the single issue that divided the relyimah.

Ymur spoke on, a cold vehemence in his words now; their former anger transformed into a chilling certainty.

"If any of you still doubt, look back. Remember what was done to you. Not once or twice, but every day for all your lives. Unseen we were. Well, I for one will pluck their eyes from their heads!"

And with that he turned and strode into the darkness, leaving behind him a crowd that now seethed and murmured, like a great soup that had been brought almost to the boil.

"May I speak?"

Baddu had stepped forward, meaning to address the gathering. Now he turned, looking to the speaker. It was Eedrah.

"Eedrah?" Baddu said, surprised and perhaps embarrassed after what had just been said.

"Let him speak," Gat said from the darkness. "Unless Ymur wishes to pluck out the eyes of one who is our friend."

There was fierce murmuring at that. Baddu looked down, then nodded.

"Thank you," Eedrah said, stepping to the front of the platform. He looked about him, clearly nervous, then began, his eyes pleading for the relyimah to listen.

"Ymur is right. My people do not deserve to live. They were cruel and self-obsessed. No words of mine can wash away the shame I feel." He turned, looking to Gat. "Indeed, I would give my own eyes were it to help."

He turned back. "And Ymur is right about one other thing. Were enough Terahnee to survive, they would surely try to make things as they were. For they know no different, and even this great tragedy, this *judgment* as it seems, will not make them see. Which is to say, I understand you, Ymur. I cannot feel precisely what you feel, for I have not suffered as you have suffered, yet I can *imagine* how it feels. And, imagining it, I can understand the desire for vengeance that burns in you."

Eedrah paused. "I understand it, yet part of me holds out against that path. We have had enough of violence. Enough of kill or be killed. Our way must lie in another direction. Besides, there are more important issues to be debated. How, for instance, are we to feed the relyimah? And how should we direct their energies now that Terahnee has fallen?"

This was too much for Ymur. Stepping out into the center of the platform, he began to harangue Eedrah.

"What has that to do with you, Terahnee? We shall feed ourselves, yes, and choose our own leaders. You think to control us with clever words, no doubt, but I for one am not fooled."

"A fool is never fooled," Gat said, walking across to Eedrah's side. "Or so he claims. But you, Ymur, speak ill of one who has often proved his worth. Eedrah is right. We must think of more than killing. We must consider how our freedom should be used, not just now but in the future also."

Ymur bristled. "I say once more. Destroy the Terahnee. Then we can go home."

"*Home?*" Gat shook his head sadly. "Do you not understand, Ymur? This *is* our home. The question is, what are we to make of it?"

"You have a plan?" Ymur sneered.

"Not I," Gat answered him, "but I understand there is one here who might offer us a way to follow." Gat turned, looking in Atrus's direction. "Atrus of D'ni. Would you step forward now and speak to the relyimah?"

Atrus stepped up, conscious of the watchful yet unwatching crowd surrounding him. Silent they were, like a great army of the dead.

"What has happened here is a great tragedy," he began. "Many of your people have died, and many more will die before this scourge has passed. So it was in my own Age of D'ni. Yet no two things are ever quite alike, and D'ni was not Terahnee. This world, which so bewitched me at first sight, I see now was corrupt and wicked. Corrupted to the core by those given the responsibility to lead. As Eedrah said, its makers deserved their fate. But that was not so for D'ni. My world—or I should rightly say, my *grandfather's* world—was a world of order and fairness, as unlike to this as the rock is to the air. It was a world of fixed and certain laws, where every man was treated with the respect and dignity he deserved. We had no slaves, no stewards. There were no beatings in our world, no deaths—unless by accident or natural cause. Each man was seen for what he was, and given recognition for his talents."

"So you say," Ymur said, interrupting him. "But I say you made a pact with the Terahnee. I say you meant to bring your people here and settle in Terahnee."

Atrus shrugged. "That is true, but . . ."

"There!" Ymur said. "What did I say!" Turning away, he went to the edge of the platform. "Well, brothers? Are we to swap one set of masters for another?"

"This is not mastery!" Atrus exclaimed. "Unless you call it mastery of oneself. I do not wish to rule you, Ymur, just give you guidance."

"So you say. But I say that we relyimah will find our own way now. For too long have we listened to others and done what they have told us to do. Now it is *our* time, and we shall not be bound by masters' ways."

"It is not so!"

Ymur turned back, his face scornful. "Why should we listen to you, Atrus of D'ni?"

"Because I have your interests at heart!"

"*Our* interests, or *yours?*"

Atrus stared at Ymur, understanding suddenly that whatever he said he would not convince this one. Ymur was set against him, set against reason itself. And sadly, Ymur was not the only one, for his fiery words had once more ignited the dark mass of humanity gathered there before them.

He was about to turn and walk away, to take the books of law he had brought with him from D'ni and go home, when a figure moved past him to stand between himself and Ymur.

Ymur half-turned, sensing the presence of someone close beside him, then frowned. "Boy?"

Atrus took a step toward the child then stopped. Uta was trembling, yet there was something about his stance that warned Atrus not to interfere. The child had steeled himself to do this. He was hunched into himself, his head tucked tightly against his chest, yet his voice sounded clearly in the sudden silence.

"Y-you are . . . wr-wrong."

"*Wrong?*" Ymur twitched his head back, as if someone had flicked him in the face. And then, unexpectedly, he laughed. "Go away, child. Let the elders speak."

"You are wrong," Uta repeated, no stammer this time. "Atrus *is* a friend. He found me when I was ill and nursed me. He carried me, not fearing for himself."

But Ymur simply sneered. "Only because he knew he could not catch it."

"Not then," Hersha said. "Uta is right. Atrus acted as a brother, not fearing for himself. And his people helped tend our ill."

Uta looked up into the old man's face. Then, in a strange incantatory tone, he said:

> "*What ails the sickly child?*
> *What stranger comes?*
> *What words will follow him,*
> *Spoken by sleeping tongues?*"

Utter silence followed the words.

Atrus turned, sensing that something was happening in the crowd and saw, to his astonishment, that many now were looking at the platform, staring in awe at the child—yes, and at himself, too.

"What is it?" Atrus asked, looking at Eedrah. "What is going on?" But even Eedrah, it seemed, did not know.

One by one the relyimah were dropping to their knees, an awed whisper spreading across the great arena.

Up on the platform, Gat stepped past Atrus and raised his arms. Silence fell.

"We have heard enough," he said, his voice trembling with a strange, inexplicable emotion. "It is decided. We shall learn this new law and embrace new ways. Ymur, is it not so?"

Atrus looked to Ymur, expecting the man to argue, but Ymur's head had dropped in defeat. "It is so."

AS THE RELYIMAH DISPERSED TO THEIR ENCAMPMENTS, THEIR leaders went through the great arch at the back of the amphitheater and into the Chamber of the Moon.

Once water had tumbled in huge illuminated curtains from all sides of the great hall, but now those artificial falls were still, the curved surfaces of marble dull and dry. Behind them, glimpsed through the spaces between the bulky segments, twelve huge revolving "scoops"—six massive troughs of stone between two equally massive wheels; troughs that were designed to lift the water from the reservoirs below—sat idle now. The thick ropes trailing from the wheels lay slack, the leather harnesses empty.

Overhead the moon, a huge shield made of glittering crystal, rested where its last journey across those illusory heavens had brought it, the fierce blue-white light of a powerful lamp shining through it onto the floor a hundred feet below.

But Atrus barely noticed anything of this. As the great doors closed on them, he turned, looking to the child.

"Uta . . . what were those words you spoke just now?"

Uta, startled by Atrus's request, glanced at Gat, then tucked his head into his chest.

"Gat?" Atrus asked, turning to the old man.

"Those were lines from the *Korokh Jimah.*"

"The Book of Prophecies?"

"So it is sometimes known."

"Your people seemed to attribute some significance to the words."

"Words spoken by sleeping tongues." Gat smiled. "The D'ni books of law seem to fit that description well, would you not say, Atrus? Not to speak of the ailing child."

"Most anything would fit." Atrus shook his head. "Well, let us move on to more important matters." He stopped, looking about him at the small group who were gathered there. "Where is Ymur?"

"Gone," Hersha said. "I saw him leave."

"Ymur is quite hotheaded," Atrus said. "It might be best to have him watched."

"You think him a danger?" Hersha asked.

"His is a single voice," Gat answered. "He might be angry, but he will not challenge the word of the relyimah council."

"Maybe so, but you need to find a task for him. Something to harness all that anger."

"You could be right, Atrus. We shall consider the matter. But tell me . . . these laws of yours . . . they can be adapted for the relyimah?"

Atrus smiled. "I have no doubt of it. Indeed, I shall begin the task at once. But I shall need help copying out the resultant passages. Are there any among the relyimah who could help us in the task?"

Gat laughed. "Thousands. You think those lazy good-for-nothings, the

Terahnee, would lower themselves to undertake such hard and difficult work?"

"Then I shall have my companions, Oma and Esel, help me make a suitable translation of the laws, to be copied and disseminated."

"And we shall appoint those among us who seem suitable to act as teachers of these new laws." Gat paused. "But there are other, far more pressing problems."

"Food," Hersha said.

"Food? But food is plentiful."

"Now it is. But unless the fields are harvested, the fruit picked from the trees, and the animals tended to, then we shall very quickly have a problem. Since the sickness came, almost nothing has been done."

"I see." Atrus considered a moment. "And the problem is getting them to work again?"

"Not at all," Baddu said. "There is a will among the relyimah to work. But many have died, and without the stewards . . ."

"Our people feel lost," Gat said. "Without direction. Oh, they hated and despised their masters, yes, and their masters' servants, but now that they are gone they find they also needed them."

"I understand," Atrus said, looking to Eedrah, who was strangely silent. "But that need will pass. They must be their own masters now. And we shall help them in that task." He paused. "Each man knows his work, does he not?"

"They do."

"Then that is what each will do."

Gat frowned. "But who will arrange it all?"

"The relyimah. Eventually. But first they must return to their routines." Atrus smiled. "I know what you are saying, Gat. They need someone to tell them what to do. But it is not true. Not entirely. They have only to act as if the stewards were still there—but unseen."

There was surprise, then laughter at that.

"You mean, pretend?" Gat asked.

"Until a better system is devised. Until *real* changes can be made. But you are right . . . these basic tasks must be continued, for without them nothing will work."

"Then so it will be," Gat said, a beaming smile lighting his blind face. "But what of the women?"

"Women?" There was a look of consternation on Atrus's face. "There are *female* relyimah?"

"Of course. Who do you think did most of the work in the great houses?"

"The men, I thought . . ."

He looked to Hersha, who shrugged. "I thought you knew, Atrus. They have their own quarters, far from the men's quarters."

"Segregated, you mean?"

But the word meant nothing to Hersha.

Atrus looked about him, seeing things anew. "And the two never meet?"

"Never," Gat answered.

"And now?"

Gat looked away, embarrassed. "It is . . . difficult. More difficult than seeing and being seen. To even look at one was an offense for which a male relyimah might die."

Atrus grimaced. "I didn't . . ."

"*See?*" Eedrah said, breaking his long silence. "Oh, it was the worst of it, Atrus. Beside that, all other cruelties were bearable. But to break *that* bond." He shuddered. "For that alone I agree with Ymur. If I were relyimah I would hunt my people down until the last of us was dead."

"Yourself included, Eedrah?"

Gat was staring blindly at Eedrah, astonished by the depth of bitterness he had displayed.

"I was but barely better than my fellows. I did nothing to persuade them they were wrong."

"You helped us, Eedrah," Hersha said, reaching out and actually touching the Terahnee.

Eedrah stared a moment at the place where Hersha's hand rested on his arm, then looked about him. Not a face condemned him. He closed his eyes, the pain he was feeling at that moment overwhelming him. "To live such a lie . . . some days it was unbearable."

"I understand," Gat said. "But now that all is done with, and you, my brother, you must help us find a better way."

Eedrah looked at the blind man, then bowed his head. "As you wish . . . my brother."

BACK AT THE GREAT HOUSE IN RO'JETHHE, ATRUS SAT DOWN with Catherine, quickly confiding to her all that had happened at the assembly.

"There are *female* relyimah?" she asked, astonished.

"So they tell me. But Hersha says they are kept separate. Segregated. Apparently they were not even allowed to look at each other. On pain of death. And they are neutered—male and female both—just in case any should escape and hide away."

Catherine stared at him, horrified. "This changes everything."

"How so?"

"It's very simple. You wish to make a proper world of this, a real society, with good laws and fair treatment for all. But how can you create any kind of society when there are no children and no possibility of children?"

"Then we shall bring them in, from other Ages. Oh, not as the Terahnee brought them in, as slaves, but with their families."

"Do you think that will work?"

"I do not know. Yet we must try." Atrus sat back, kneading his neck with one hand, tired now after the long day. "One thing I do know: This is an undertaking far larger than the rebuilding of D'ni ever was. But if the will is here—and I think it is—then we can make it work. And maybe we might settle here, after all. Be part of this."

She smiled. "Maybe. But first you ought to send a messenger to Master Tamon, to tell him all is well."

"I shall. At once."

He stood and turned to go, but Catherine called him back. "Atrus? One other thing. Have you noticed . . ."

"Noticed?"

"Marrim and Eedrah. Have you noticed how they spend time with each other?"

MARRIM POKED HER HEAD AROUND THE DOOR.

"So there you are. I've been looking for you everywhere."

Eedrah sat at the desk on the far side of the library, a journal open in front of him. At the sound of her voice he had set his pen down. Now, as Marrim walked across, he sanded the page and closed the journal.

"Something you don't want me to see?" she teased, coming up to the desk.

He looked back at her sullenly, then pushed the journal across the desk to her. "Look, if you want."

"No," she said, realizing she had hurt his feelings. "Are you all right?"

He looked to one side of her, then shook his head. "No, not really. I feel . . ." He looked straight at her. "I feel like I oughtn't to have lived."

"It's what half the D'ni suffer from," she said brightly. "So Catherine says." Then, she spoke more seriously. "You don't really feel like that, do you? I mean, I thought you wanted to help the relyimah."

"I do." Eedrah frowned, then stood up, walking halfway across that massive floor before he turned to look back at her. "Things were said tonight, at the assembly. There was this one relyimah called Ymur. A disagreeable type, yet what he said brought it home to me. How evil it all was. And I felt that I'd permitted it somehow."

"You had no choice."

"Didn't I? You see, that's just it, Marrim. I used to argue that way, but now that it's all gone I can see clearly. It was *my* silence, the silence of people *like* me, that permitted it to continue. To carry on unchallenged. It was up to us, who *saw*, to *do* something. But we didn't. For thousands of years we just accepted it."

"But you didn't create Terahnee, Eedrah."

"No. That's true. I merely used it, like everyone else."

"I think you're being too hard on yourself."

He laughed bitterly. "Hard? I'm dying inside."

Eedrah looked down. "Do you remember the maze, Marrim, at Horen Ro'Jadre's house?"

"I remember beating you."

"Has Atrus told you how that worked?"

"No. Some kind of clever machinery, I suppose."

"You *suppose!*" He huffed out a breath. "Slaves did that, Marrim! Relyimah! Hundreds of them harnessed to great cogs and pulleys, straining to lift and turn those massive rooms. And if one fell, or slipped, he would be trampled by his fellows, because there was no time to stop. The rooms had to be turned. Twelve seconds they had, *remember*? Twelve seconds!"

Marrim was staring at him in shock.

"How does that make you feel, Marrim, knowing that your sport probably killed several young men?"

She stared, horrified.

"Yes, well, imagine feeling that each and every day of your life! Or worse. Imagine *numbing* yourself so that you could no longer feel!"

IN THE DAYS THAT FOLLOWED, THEY BEGAN TO UNDERSTAND THE scale of the problems facing them. Before the sickness Terahnee had been a land of two hundred million souls, not including the P'aarli and the silent relyimah—uncounted, naturally. Now the native population had plummeted to less than a hundred thousand—ironically, those who, like Eedrah, had been sickliest among them. But now the slaves, that great unseen mass, had emerged into the sunlight, and even after their own losses, they numbered in excess of two billion souls.

It was a huge logistical problem, and one that not even Gat had properly understood. The old man busied himself, going from gathering to gathering, speaking to the local relyimah and talking of the "way ahead," but the practical details he left to Atrus and Eedrah.

Their first task was to organize a team of "scribes"—relyimah who could write and had experience of various nonmenial tasks. Word went out among the local estates, and very quickly they began to come, in twos and threes and just occasionally alone, making their way to the great house at Ro'Jethhe.

Master Tamon was given the job of bringing the D'ni survivors through and settling them in Terahnee, where they might aid Atrus and the others in the task of building the new social order.

Catherine, meanwhile, dedicated herself to the task of bringing together all of the slaves, both male and female. It could not be done hurriedly, not unless they wished to court disaster, for they were conscious that, as in so many spheres, the relyimah did not know how to behave socially. It was not something they had been taught; indeed, they had been positively discouraged from thinking of themselves as human beings with human emotions and human needs. But now they must, and the transition was not going to be easy. And so, for the while, a form of segregation was maintained.

And there was one other, perhaps more pressing, problem. The Terahnee Ages. It was like D'ni again, only this time the problem was increased a thousandfold. How many Books were there? And who was in them?

Atrus's first instinct was to gather all the Books in, but was that really the answer? There were not enough of his own people to undertake the task, and he was not certain he could trust the relyimah to do it for him. Indeed, he wasn't even certain that they *knew* the difference between an ordinary book and one that linked with another Age. Besides, he had seen with his own eyes how large the Terahnee libraries were, and the thought of trying to bring back and then store what might possibly be several million Books was a daunting one. And that was not to speak of searching them. Busy himself, he asked his young helpers, Carrad and Irras, to come up with a scheme.

Yet even as the problems mounted, there were successes. Atrus's plan to send the relyimah back to their individual tasks worked well. Most seemed happy to have something to do again and the need for supervision proved less pressing than might have been thought. But all knew that the situation could not be maintained forever. Changes would have to be made, and soon.

But Atrus's priority in those first few days was to give the relyimah laws, and, with Oma's and Esel's help, he worked late into the night, reading and making notes from the six great volumes they had brought back from D'ni, ignoring what was specific to D'ni while attempting to frame a code of behavior, based on the core code of D'ni, that might serve the relyimah in the difficult times to come.

One problem Atrus was glad not to have to deal with was the aftermath of the sickness—the burning of the dead. That the relyimah took charge of, and for days the sky was filled, on every side, with great plumes of dark smoke. Under that pall, it might have been easy to despair, but there was hope, too. Hope that this greater freedom might prove permanent. Yet they must work hard if that was to be so.

On the fourth day after the gathering at Gehallah, Atrus called on Hersha and presented him with a Code of Law—a list of forty basic rights and responsibilities that could be understood by all and acted on at once. More detailed law would follow, Atrus said, but this was the essence of it. This was how the relyimah would henceforth govern themselves.

That very morning Oma and Esel began to organize the teams of rely-imah scribes, setting up benches in the great library of Ro'Jethhe. By evening the first batch of a thousand copies were ready for distribution among the people. It was an enormous achievement and there was a general sense of euphoria.

Then word came that the body of the king had been found, and an hour later, even as night fell, Gat arrived to see Atrus, the torches of his guards lighting the way before him as he came up the ramp.

They embraced.

As Gat stood back his blank eyes flickered in the gusting flames of the lamps as if alive with vision.

"I want you to come with me, Atrus, to the capital. To bury the last king of Terahnee."

"I will come."

"Then let us go at once."

Atrus turned, embracing Catherine briefly, then followed Gat back down the ramp toward the waiting boat.

AS THE FIRST LIGHT OF MORNING TINTED THE HORIZON, ATRUS woke. Gat sat beside him in the boat, silent and, so it seemed, watchful.

Behind them the rowers—twelve young relyimah; volunteers, honored to serve the legendary Gat—kept their steady rhythm, drawing the long craft through the water. The sound was reassuring.

"You needed that," Gat said, sensing that Atrus was awake. "Hersha says that you push yourself to the limit."

"Hersha exaggerates. I like to work."

"Yes, and we are grateful for it." Gat turned his head and smiled. "But you must rest now. Besides, we need to talk, Atrus, and what better oppor-tunity than this."

Atrus sat up. "Are you uneasy, Gat?"

"A little. Oh, we are making real progress, but our greatest problems lie ahead of us, I fear. Your laws will help, yet it seems to me that simple habit is our greatest enemy."

"Habit?"

"The habit of obedience and silence. The habit of not-being." Gat turned his inert gaze fully on Atrus. "My people are like newborns. They do not know how to behave. But newborns are small and helpless and can be chastized by their parents. So it was among the Terahnee. But my newborns are large and muscular and—right now, at least—confused by the emotions they are feeling. Emotions they have always before held back, for fear of punishment or worse. Put simply, Atrus, they must learn how to live, and in doing so they will need all the guidance we can give them."

"I agree. And the D'ni and their friends will help."

Gat smiled again. "I know. Your friendship is most valued, Atrus. But think. Think just how many of us there are. Two thousand million. How do we set about teaching so many? How can we possibly keep such a host in check?"

"It worries you, Gat?"

"To be sure it worries me. Time is against us, Atrus. Right now they are obedient, with the learned obedience of their kind. But the more we give them of themselves, the more they will want, and the worse, perhaps, they'll be."

"Do you think so?"

"Were not the Terahnee men? Oh, they may have acted like uncaring monsters, but given other circumstances they, like Eedrah, could have been different. Kinder, certainly. And so with a host of newborns. My relyimah. When they learn to be seen, then their problems will really begin, for some will like what they see and some will not. Some, like Ymur, will be angry at the waste of their former lives, while others, thinking back on it, will sink into a despair so deep they will never emerge from it."

Atrus sighed. "I had not thought . . ."

The old man reached out and held his shoulder. "You have been busy, Atrus. Nor can you think of everything."

"Then what are we to do?"

"Reduce the numbers, maybe. You spoke to Hersha of the Books—the Ages the Terahnee wrote. Perhaps we might use some of them, for resettling our people."

"It's possible."

"Then we should investigate that possibility. It has been in my mind that maybe we should send the women there."

Atrus turned to him, surprised.

"Oh, I have been thinking long and hard about it, Atrus. Wondering if there might not be a peaceful way of dealing with the matter. Of bringing together those who have so long been apart."

"And?"

Gat let out a long, slow breath. "I believe it would not work. Catherine, I know, is looking at this problem, and I will wait to hear what she has to say before we act, but my feeling is that there is no solution to this most singular problem. Not for this generation, anyway. To introduce them to each other now might be to tear the fabric of our new society apart before it has had a chance to grow and prosper."

"But a society of men . . ."

"And families, and children."

Atrus frowned and looked down. "I do not like it, Gat. It would be too much like keeping things as they were. It would be . . . well, like denying the relyimah any kind of real normality."

"You think they *can* be normal, Atrus, after all they have suffered?"

"I believe that they should be given the chance to try, even if it ends in failure. Life isn't life without that risk."

Gat looked away a moment, then he nodded. "Sometimes I feel you are much wiser than you appear, Atrus."

Atrus laughed. "And how do I appear to you, my friend?"

"Like the voice of blind certainty itself."

AS THE SUN ROSE HIGHER AND THE LANDSCAPE ABOUT THEM
was revealed, they saw just how much damage the relyimah had wreaked
upon it. Statues were smashed and many visual conceits destroyed entirely.
This surprised Atrus, who had heard nothing of such activities. At the same
time, he noted how most living things—the trees and flowers—were untouched, and this, as much as any other thing he'd seen, gave him hope.

Yet now that he knew what he was seeing, this landscape, which had
seemed so wonderful when first he'd viewed it, so constantly surprising, now
seemed merely desolate: a fragile artifice that had been shattered in an instant.

Like the Ages my father wrote . . .

"We should remove all this," he said, speaking to Gat for the first time
in hours.

"Their playthings, you mean?"

"Yes, and their houses, too. All signs of what they were."

Gat smiled. "It would take forever."

"Yet we could make a start."

"Maybe." The old man sat forward, gesturing toward the city, which now
lay directly ahead of them. It had grown constantly these past few hours,
dominating the skyline, more like a mountain than anything mere men had
made. "But what of that? How would you begin to take *that* down?"

Atrus smiled. Sometimes it was almost as if the old man actually saw
what he was looking at.

"Little by little."

Gat's laughter was gentle. "I can think of better things to do, can't you?"

"You cannot live in the ruins of the past."

"And yet you tried, Atrus."

"Then maybe I was wrong." And for the first time he saw clearly that he
had been wrong to try to build his new D'ni in the ruins of the old.

"And maybe we have no option but to try," Gat said, a defensiveness in
his voice; then, softening, "Yet your idea has merit, Atrus. We should destroy their toys, at the very least. All of their hideous distractions. But the
houses . . . we could use them, perhaps. Partition the rooms. Use them to
treat the sick, or as centers of local government."

Atrus nodded distractedly, yet he found himself appalled by the idea, if only because of those tunnels in the walls. Each Terahnee house that stood was a monument to the Great Lie in which they had all once lived; a reminder of the relyimah's imperative *not* to be seen.

Yet not everything could be achieved at once. Some things would have to wait, and maybe this was one of them. He looked to Gat once more and saw how troubled the old man was. It was an unexpected insight.

"Everything will be for the best," he said reassuringly. Yet even as he spoke, he recalled what Gat had said of his "blind certainty." And, sure enough, the old man's face changed, a smile coming to those strong yet ancient features.

"Yes, Atrus. I am sure it will be so."

THAT AFTERNOON IT RAINED: THE FIRST RAIN ATRUS HAD known since coming into Terahnee.

Gat had wanted to pull the canopy across, not for himself, but to protect Atrus from the downpour, but Atrus had refused and had stood there instead, enjoying the feel of the rain beating down on him. It felt refreshing after the heat of the last few days, *cleansing*.

The storm passed and he sat again, the rhythm of the oars dipping and rising from the water lulling him, his clothes, which were stuck to him, slowly drying in the sunlight.

He woke to find Gat tapping his arm. "Come, Atrus, we must walk a while."

Atrus looked about him, then stretched and got up, climbing from the boat. Ahead of them the canal disappeared into the side of a great hill of marble. From his previous journey Atrus recognized it as the beginning of the great system of locks that ended in Ro'Jadre's house.

None of those locks worked now, for Gat had forbidden any of his people to place themselves in harness and lift the great weights that moved the water from one level to the next. And so they made their way on foot, climbing the long flights of steps that led up the side of the hill, and out onto a great ledge of stone overlooking Ro'Jadre.

Beyond the house another boat awaited them, fresh rowers already in place. And beyond that the city.

Standing there, Atrus found himself overwhelmed suddenly by a strange ambivalence. The house, the view itself, was truly magnificent. No understanding of the evil that lay behind it could take that from it. Yet how could such beauty, such a sure instinct for what was beautiful, coexist with such inhumanity?

He followed Gat across, surprised as ever that the old man knew his way without his eyes. And as he climbed into the boat behind Gat, he found his earlier doubts washed from him.

It would work. They would make it work.

And as Ro'Jadre receded beyond the surrounding hills, Atrus found himself looking outward again, embracing the whole of that vast world in which he found himself involved, his mind beginning to formulate new plans for the relyimah, new schemes for them to carry out.

THE CAPITAL WAS SILENT, EERILY EMPTY. AS THEY MADE THEIR way up the great channel at its heart, the young rowers pulling slowly, staring about them as they went, Atrus came to understand just how completely Terahnee was undone.

Here nothing had survived. At the first appearance of the sickness, the relyimah had fled, leaving their masters to their fate. Weeds grew between the slabs of stone, encouraged by the recent rain.

Already it looked unkempt, abandoned, the evidence of many fires—accidental or deliberately set, it was hard to say—blackening its once-pristine whiteness.

Baddu and several of the other relyimah leaders met them at the foot of the great pile that was the royal palace, greeting them warmly in that place without warmth.

"Are they all dead?" Atrus asked, for it was like being in a giant mausoleum.

"Those that are not mad or long fled," Baddu answered him with a hint of dry humor. "We saw one earlier, wandering the streets and mumbling to himself."

"And he saw you?"

"Mad or otherwise, he was Terahnee."

Atrus nodded, yet he was pained by the thought that even after all they had suffered, the Terahnee still could not *see*. "So," he said finally, "where is Ro'Eh Ro'Dan?"

"Come," Baddu said, turning toward an arch on the far side of that marbled jetty. "It is some climb, but worth it just to see."

BADDU HAD NOT BEEN JOKING. A THOUSAND STEPS OR MORE they climbed, and still the stairway twisted through the rock. Up and up they went, until, suddenly, they came out into a dimly lit chamber, the size of which was difficult to gauge, for it seemed like a great cavern in the rock.

For a moment Atrus thought he was back in D'ni, so reminiscent was it. But then he recognized where he was. This was the king's audience chamber, where thousands upon thousands of Terahnee notables had sat to witness his arrival. And there, somewhere in the darkness on the far side of the great chamber, was the king's emerald throne.

"Is he here?" he asked, his voice echoing in that silent space.

In answer Baddu clapped his hands, mimicking perfectly how a Terahnee master might once have commanded his servants. At once lamps were lit on all sides of the chamber, and there, at the very center, in a boat of delicate stone, lay the great king himself, Ro'Eh Ro'Dan.

Atrus went down the steps until he stood less than ten paces from the boat. Ro'Eh Ro'Dan lay on his back on a bed of golden sheets, a narrow band of gold about his ice-pale brow. Dead he was, yet still he exuded power, so that even Baddu, who had seemed so dismissive earlier, approached the boat with awe.

"The book . . ." Atrus began, gesturing toward the tiny, leather-bound volume that was clasped against the dead man's chest. "What is the book?"

The relyimah looked to each other. None there dared to touch the king, dead or otherwise. Why, even to look on him was hard for many of them.

Seeing that he was going to get no answer, Atrus walked across and, grasping the stern of the boat firmly, climbed aboard. It swayed gently, rocking the corpse that lay at the center of the deck.

From this close, Atrus could smell the sickly sweet embalming fluid, could see where the embalmer's art had worked its magic on that bloodless flesh.

He turned, looking back at Baddu. "Who prepared the body?"

"Relyimah," Baddu answered. "His body servants. They came and found him here."

Carefully, he stepped across and, leaning over the corpse, prised the book from its rigid grip.

It was a history. A history of the earliest days of Terahnee. He opened the cover and read the inscription there, then felt himself go cold.

It was for him! Ro'Eh Ro'Dan had dedicated the book to him!

"What is it, Atrus?" Gat asked, coming across and standing by the stern.

"A history," he answered, his surprise becoming wonder at the thought that Ro'Eh Ro'Dan had thought of him before the end. "A history of how Terahnee came to be."

Catherine will treasure this, he thought. *Yes, and Oma and Esel, too.*

Atrus looked down, studying the king's pale yet handsome features. To what extent had Ro'Eh Ro'Dan been a prisoner of Terahnee and its customs? Or had he been the willing embodiment of its excesses, its utter lack of virtue? It was hard to say. Though he had been king of this evil land, Atrus could not shake from his mind his personal impression of the man.

I liked you, Ro'Eh Ro'Dan, and in other circumstances we might even have been friends.

Instead he had come and killed him, just as effectively as if he'd plunged a knife straight through his heart.

And so D'ni had erased Terahnee. Removed it like a footnote from a book. The page turned and it was gone.

Atrus turned away. It was time to bury Ro'Eh Ro'Dan. Time to say farewell to the past and get on with the future.

THEY CARRIED RO'EH RO'DAN ON A BIER OF CAMPHOR WOOD and bronze, down through the levels of his mighty palace, where a hundred kings had ruled before him, and out into the great square at the heart of the capital. There, before the statue of the Nameless King, founder of Terahnee, the relyimah set him down, bowing before him in death as they had not been permitted to in life.

Just beyond the statue they had piled a big stack of wood. Having shown the king respect, they carried him across and placed the bier on top. There was a moment's silence, then Gat stepped forward and, his voice heavy with emotion, began to speak

"The chains that bound us now are broken, and we celebrate their passing, just as we honor the passing of the last king of Terahnee." He paused, then proclaimed, "Let no man henceforth be our master."

And with that he lowered his arm, and as he did several relyimah set torches to the huge pile. There was a moment's panic and then the flames rushed up, catching with a roar, a sudden brightness. The eyes of the Unseen went to that, drawn to it, seeing how the flames danced about the king's body like servants attending to it, how they stripped it of its finery, as if for sleep.

"Jidar N'ram!"

The cry startled Atrus. Turning, he saw that a small party of relyimah had come. Breathless, they hurried toward Gat, then slowed, seeing how the old man's attention was held by the fire.

"Jidar N'ram!" one of them said, kneeling before the old man. "We have news!"

Atrus narrowed his eyes. He did not recognize the term; yet it was clearly Gat who had been addressed.

"What is it?" Gat said, wrenching his attention away from the burning pyre.

"They are coming!" the messenger said tremblingly, his eyes anxiously skipping here and there, afraid to focus on the old man's face.

"Who?" Gat said, with untypical impatience. "*Who* is coming?"

"The P'aarli! They have brought a great army from their homeworld to subdue us!"

There was a groan from the listening relyimah. Their eyes were round with fear. And then, as one, they seemed to hunch into themselves, as if trying to disappear from sight.

"The P'aarli . . ." Gat said, the words almost an exhalation. All color had fled from the old man's face. Even he seemed deflated by this news.

"You must fight them," Atrus said. "You are many . . ."

"Maybe so. Yet we know nothing of fighting."

"Then summon Ymur. You talked of giving him a task. Well, harness him to this. Let him raise a force to stop the P'aarli. If he is half the man I think he is . . ."

Gat shuddered. For a moment he seemed completely lost. Then, as if waking to himself again, he gave a tiny nod. "All right. We shall summon Ymur and make him the leader of our forces. Yet what if he fails?"

"Then he shall have bought us time." Atrus smiled, then laid his hand firmly on the old man's shoulder. "Come, Gat. Call a meeting of the elders. There are more ways than one to defeat one's enemies."

THE MAN STOOD ON THE SUMMIT OF THE HILL, LOOKING DOWN
the lush sweep of the valley toward the massive house that overlooked
it. There, to the left of the house, at the center of the valley, a host of
black-clothed relyimah were on the move across the fields, the front line cutting the stalks of the massive plants and passing them back to others, who
carried them quickly to the side and deposited them in massive carts. But
this was no harvest. Even from a distance he could see that the crop was un-
ripe, the swathe they were cutting merely a means of making quick passage
across the land. Besides, just beyond that wall of stooping human bodies, a
huge phalanx of P'aarli, their red cloaks marking them out as distinctly as
their silver hair, marched slowly in ranks, a great boatlike carriage at their
rear, carried by forty slaves. There was an ornate golden canopy and, at the
back of the carriage, an extraordinarily large chair. But whoever it was that
sat in that chair was almost totally hidden from view. Only a pair of long,
pale hands showed in the daylight, clutching the arms of a huge green
throne.

The man had been a slave himself, before the sickness, and now, seeing
that great army of P'aarli descend into the valley, he felt a sickening dread.
They had returned. The brief dream of better times was ended. He could
hear the incessant clanking of the chains even from where he stood and
knew that soon his own limbs would feel once more the cold fire of the iron.

As he watched, one of the P'aarli peeled off from the main body and
walked back to the carriage, matching his pace with it as he spoke to whoever was within. There was a moment's pause and then, with a bow, the fellow turned away, hurrying along the edge of the P'aarli ranks, speaking to
this one here and that one there as he went.

Seeing that, the watching man grew still, a faint tremble passing through
him. And then he gasped, as four groups of eight men separated from the
main mass of P'aarli and, in running formation, made their way out from
that great marching host.

He had seen this once before, back on his home Age, when, as a child of
four, the P'aarli had come. He had witnessed the same that day: the march-

ing host in endless ranks, and then the smaller groups—scouting parties—
sent out with nets and knives and hooks to find their prey. The nearest of
the squads was already climbing the slope toward him, moving in a crouching run. With a cry one of them spotted him.

The trembling in him grew, and for a moment he could not move. Then,
with an urgency he had not felt since that day twenty years before, he turned
and ran, his heart hammering in his chest, his breath rasping from him, not
knowing where or if he would find safety.

THE P'AAR'RO, THE GREAT STEWARD, LEADER OF THE P'AARLI,
lounged in his chair, in the cool of the great canopy, lulled by the movement
of the carriage beneath him. The campaign had begun well. Already a huge
number of the relyimah—more than eight hundred thousand in all—had
been taken and penned, and more were being taken by the hour. Those who
resisted were slaughtered, but that was not many, and he was loathe to waste
good slaves. The habit of obedience, deeply instilled in them, had not been
shaken by events, and it was that as much as anything that reassured him.
They were a rabble, after all. Disorganized. Totally without rational thought.
One had only to tell them to submit and they obeyed. Even so, the task was
not inconsiderable, and he had prepared his men for trouble.

He gazed about him indolently. It was some time since he had last been
in Terahnee, and he had forgotten how pleasant a place it was. In recent years
much of his time had been spent in the home Age, supervising the great task
of training new stewards, but the sickness had changed all that. Now their
priorities had changed.

He looked down, past the broad, elaborately decorated gunwales to
where the slaves slowly walked, their eyes averted, the long wooden poles,
cut to resemble a thickly corded rope, resting on their shoulders. Could he
train himself *not* to see them?

The thought amused him. It was like the chair in which he sat; it was a perfect copy of the king's great chair, only jade, not emerald. But why should he put up with copies anymore?

Yes, things had changed, and they must change with them.

They would need stewards for a start.

Well . . . maybe there were some among the relyimah who could be trained to that task. The scribes, perhaps.

The P'aar'Ro grinned, then sat back, letting his eyes close lazily. It was time they took things easy. Time they got someone else to do the dirty work.

YMUR WAS WAITING FOR THEM IN THE ORCHARD. AS THE P'aarli passed between the trees, his men fell on them from above, while others, who had been hiding behind the trunks, rushed at them with nets and knives, using their own tricks on them.

Most of them were killed in that first frenzied minute, but two of the P'aarli survived, pinned down beneath his men. Ymur watched them struggle to get up, listening to their incessant shouting, then stepped up to the nearest of them and slapped his face hard.

The man fell silent. There was blood on his lip and his eyes were wide with shock.

"How many of you are there?" Ymur asked, crouching over the man, meeting his eyes and letting him see he was not afraid of him.

The P'aarli just laughed.

Ymur slapped him again, harder this time, making the man cry out.

There was laughter from the watching relyimah; a cruel, satisfied laughter.

Ymur looked about him, grinning now, then straightened up. "What does it matter?" he said, turning his back on the two. "We'll have them all before we're finished." Then, drawing his long knife, a great butcher's knife used for cutting haunches, he turned back and showed it to them, enjoying the sight as the blood drained from their faces.

YMUR'S MEN PLACED THE BODIES ON STRAW PALLETS, THEN took them out and displayed them around all the local estates, making much of the wounds, and laughing as they told how easy it had been. And then, when that tale was told, they would raise the standard and bid all there to come and join them in the great task of liberating Terahnee.

Many blanched at that and turned away, but many others responded, and so the small rabble with which Ymur had begun became a host, and then an army.

As he went about his camp, arranging things, Ymur nodded to himself. It was strange how it had happened, how the old men had come to him, for it had been in his own mind to raise a force and take on the accursed P'aarli. Better that—better death—than be a slave again. And so he threw himself into the task, cajoling and bullying, attempting to meld that docile host into some kind of fighting force.

He knew it would not be easy. That business in the orchard had been a cheat, in a way. He had known he could get away with it . . . with luck. But fighting a full-fledged battle against a well-disciplined army was another thing. He had seen the P'aarli at work in the Ages, and could not forget how fearsome they had looked. It did not scare *him*, but he knew he was exceptional in that regard. Most of his men would as willingly jump into a raging fire as face that great host. Yet there had to be a way.

Four days he had, if reports of the P'aarli's progress could be believed. Five days at most.

He stopped, then laughed, seeing that the answer had come, unasked, in the very weave of his thoughts. Fire. That was it! He would use fire.

"Uta!" he called, summoning the slave-child who had been one of the first to flock to his banner. "Come, child, I have a message for you to run. To Atrus, back at the capital. It begins . . ."

ATRUS WAS STANDING AT HIS DESK, STUDYING THE MAP OF THE capital that was spread out before him, when Uta stepped into the room.

"Uta!" he cried, pleased to see the boy. "You have news for me?"

Uta came across and, stopping before Atrus, bowed his head low, not looking up as he spoke.

"Ymur bids me hail you his friend, and asks if such a thing as liquid fire can be had. If so, he asks for a thousand barrels of it, to be delivered to him by tomorrow evening latest."

Atrus stared at the boy, astonished. "Liquid fire?" he said quietly, more to himself than in answer. "Yes . . . I will supply it."

He nodded decisively. "Tell our good friend Ymur that he will have what he asks for."

Uta made to turn and leave the room, but Atrus called him back.

"Hold on, Uta! Wait an hour before you return. Catherine, I know, would like to see you before you go."

AFTER THE BOY HAD GONE, ATRUS STOOD THERE A LONG WHILE, wondering to what use Ymur was thinking of putting the liquid fire. Whatever it was, he would have to give him instructions—send Irras, maybe, or Carrad to advise him in its use. Then, shrugging that off, he turned his attention back to the map.

He had already marked which avenues and canals in the eastern city should be cut off, and Hersha and Eedrah were already busy organizing the task. Now he needed to decide which of the remaining thoroughfares was best suited to his plan.

If his guess was right, the P'aarli would want to take the capital. If so, then he would lead them into a maze of sorts. A deadly maze, where things were constantly dropped on them and shot at them.

There would be no battles, not even hand-to-hand, for the relyimah would remain unseen.

Gat, particularly, had liked the plan. But Baddu had been far less convinced by it. "Why should the P'aarli come into our trap? What if they wait outside?"

"Then they wait," Atrus said. "But we make sure they have no means of supporting themselves while they wait. We take away their food and water."

"But how do we do that?" Baddu had asked.

"By burning every field about the east of the capital and blocking up every waterway."

"And if that fails?"

"Then we find another way to fight them. We are many."

"We are many," Gat echoed, liking the phrase, nodding his blind face enthusiastically. "And the P'aarli . . ." He grinned broadly. "The P'aarli are arrogant. They will come into our trap!"

THEY HAD DRAWN THE BIG AWNING BACK, TO REVEAL THE P'aar'Ro, seated in his honorary chair of state. The relyimah had moved back out of sight, and the carriage seemed to rest—to float almost—between the pillars.

The three Terahnee halted, looking about them, not certain quite how to proceed. Then, gaining in confidence, they walked through into the great hall, smiling as they saw the silver hair of the old man, the wine-red cloak. This much, at least, was familiar.

"P'aar'Ro!" one of them called, hailing the Great Steward. "We welcome you to Ro'Derraj! We are the last Terahnee in the district. The governor . . ."

He fell silent, then waited, expecting the P'aar'Ro to stand, perhaps, and come down to greet them, but the chief of the servants merely sat there, as if no one had spoken. Indeed, now that they looked closer, the Terahnee noticed that he was eating!

They turned, looking back at the line of P'aarli who now stood along the line of the great doorway, blocking it, then turned back.

Strange . . .

"When we heard you had returned, we were overjoyed!" The second of them said, then stopped, for the P'aar'Ro had sat forward, as if about to speak. Instead, gesturing to the stewards behind them, he nodded toward the three Terahnee then drew his finger across his throat.

"P'aar'Ro?" one of them queried. "Is the interview over?"

But he had barely finished the sentence when he was grabbed from behind.

The P'aar'Ro considered the half-eaten fruit in his hand, then threw it aside, feigning not to notice the slave who quickly and unobtrusively retrieved it and carried it away.

Practice, he told himself. *All it needs is practice.*

YMUR WENT DOWN THE LINE OF CARTS, INSPECTING EACH ONE'S stock of barrels carefully, then turned, looking to Carrad.

"Excellent!" he said. "But let us hope we shall not have to use them!"

Carrad scratched his bald pate. "You mean to hold them in reserve, Ymur? But surely . . ."

Ymur took the young man's arm and led him across to his tent. Inside, he turned and faced the big fellow.

"I will say this once and not repeat it. Nor will you mention this to anyone, Master Carrad. The fire is not for the P'aarli, it is to be used on our own men, in case they do not have the stomach to fight."

"But . . ."

"No buts. We can defeat the P'aarli. Overrun them by sheer weight of numbers. But not if we are running the wrong way! I mean but to stiffen their resolve."

Carrad nodded, but he was ill at ease suddenly. To be truthful, he had not liked the sound of this little man when Atrus had briefed him about what to expect, and in person he found him even less attractive. Yet Uta, whom he took to be a good judge of character, seemed to idolize the man.

"Tell me who I am to instruct," Carrad said.

"Good," Ymur said. "You will speak to the mutes later . . ."

"Mutes?"

Ymur smiled. "You think I could trust such a thing to men with tongues? Even relyimah talk among themselves!"

He met Ymur's eyes briefly, seeing the cruelty there, alongside the anger he had expected to find, then lowered his head. "As you wish, Ymur."

THERE WERE SO MANY NOW THAT IT WAS BECOMING A PROBLEM to feed and water them, to clothe them properly and find them weapons. But it would not be a problem for long. The P'aarli army was, if his scouts were right, but an hour away, camped in a great hollow on the edge of the local governor's estate.

It was an hour from sunset, and if he took his men directly there they could engage with the P'aarli before dark. Not that it mattered. Ymur was prepared to fight them beneath the moon, if necessary. Indeed, he had considered long and hard whether there would be any advantage to doing so. But sunset seemed right somehow. Men were relaxed at that time of day. Or would be, in a camp. Whereas his own men would be tense from a long forced march.

Half a million men followed his banner now. It was more than a hundred times the number of the P'aarli. But that was no guarantee of success. If the first line faltered and turned, then he could find himself at the head of a retreating herd. They would trample themselves to death.

He stretched his arms as he walked, then looked about him at his chiefs, who walked along beside him—men he had picked from the ranks for their attitude. Men like himself, mainly. And, at the back of the small group, young Uta, who had proved a surprise. He had thought at first that Uta was a plant, an ear in his camp for Atrus and the rest of them, but the child could not hide his enthusiasm. He was as keen as Ymur to rid Terahnee of the Masters and their helpers.

Ymur grinned at the thought, then turned his attention to the runner who had come up over the hill and was heading directly toward him.

"What is it?" he asked, neither stopping nor slowing his pace, letting the man fall in beside him. "Are the P'aarli on the move?"

"No, Ymur," the man answered breathlessly. "Unless you count moving toward their beds as strategy!"

There was laughter among the leading group.

"Then let us hope to find a few of them asleep," Ymur said, and, hastening his pace, drew the long knife from his belt and raised it, as if the P'aarli were already in sight.

THE P'AARLI WERE SEATED ABOUT THEIR FIRES, TALKING AND laughing, discussing the day's "sport." The sun was low now, the shadows long, and the moon was already climbing the sky to the west.

This was a pleasant land—more pleasant than most they ventured into—and the relyimah here were docile and conditioned. Even so, they had set a guard, as they did in more hostile Ages, though more from habit than expectation of attack.

It was thus that they failed to note the sudden darkening of the sky about the upper ridges of the valley. And if any there heard anything they no doubt thought it the sound of distant thunder.

Ymur, looking down on the encampment from the ridge, took in the neat disposition of the tents, the orderliness of the fires, the way the food wagons were placed, and other details, knowing he could learn from them. Then, having looked enough, he raised his arm and, with a whooping cry, threw himself down the slope, yelling at the top of his voice as he ran, his weapon held high, hearing the great thunderous cries of his ragtag army as they threw themselves after him.

He had considered silence and surprise—had thought of stealing into the camp at night and slitting throats—but this was better. He would lose more men, but what of it? No one praised a skulking man, but a bold one, that was different.

As they smashed into the first line of P'aarli, Ymur felt a great wave of elation rise up in him and sweep him away, and for a time he was mind-less, his knife arm rising and falling, cleaving friend and foe without distinction.

And then, even as their defeat seemed certain, the P'aarli rallied. A small group of them formed up at the center of the camp and began to fight their way out toward the great house at the far end of the valley. The relyimah, facing this determined group, buckled and fled, throwing their weapons down in fear, but Ymur, coming to himself again, saw this and, taking sev-eral of his handpicked men, went and intercepted them, taking risks with his own life—showing his men by example what could be done—and in a moment the P'aarli were overrun as more and more relyimah rejoined the fight.

And then, suddenly, it was over, and a strange silence fell over the camp.

Ymur walked out into the center of the camp, seeing, by the light of the campfires, the great piles of dead that had fought here. "Burn it!" he said, looking about him. "Burn it all! Then on to He'Darra. Let us finish with these P'aarli!"

"WHERE ARE YOU GOING IN SUCH A HURRY?"

The P'aar'Ro stopped, then slowly turned. The relyimah he was facing came barely to his chest, and in the flickering lamplight he seemed to have a strange, squinting face.

"Is no one *carrying* you, Great Steward?"

"I . . ." The P'aar'Ro swallowed. The truth was, his slaves had deserted the moment the relyimah had attacked the encampment. He, fortunately, had been in the house at the time and so had had the chance to escape. Or so he'd thought.

"Would you like *us* to carry you, P'aar'Ro?"

The man looked about him. The shadows might be playing tricks, but he had the strong sense that there were no friendly faces here. Were these men part of the slave army, or just stragglers? If so, he might yet intimidate them.

"You have a litter?" he asked, trying to sound more confident than he felt.

"We do," their spokesman answered, and at his gesture four of the relyimah brought up a simple straw pallet, then squatted there, as if about to let him mount.

"*That?*" the P'aar'Ro asked, incredulous now.

"It's what we use," the little man said.

"Use?"

"To carry the bodies . . ."

The P'aar'Ro's mouth went dry. "I . . ."

"Hold him," Ymur said, smiling, almost gentle as he stepped toward the Great Steward. "Hold him tightly while I gouge out his eyes."

ATRUS HEARD THE CHEERING LONG BEFORE THE MESSENGER
arrived. Going out onto the balcony, he was in time to see Hersha hurry
across the courtyard to intercept the man.

There was a moment's brief consultation, and then the old man straightened, letting out a great whoop of joy.

So Ymur had done it. He had crushed the P'aarli army. Atrus took a long
breath, glad in a way that he had not been needed.

"Atrus!" Hersha called, coming across. "The P'aarli have been destroyed, the P'aar'Ro taken! And now Ymur goes on to He'Darra to finish
the job!"

"He'Darra?"

"It is the place where they bring through the slaves. It is an awful, terrible place. Ymur means to destroy it and close the link with the P'aarli homeworld."

Atrus nodded, but he was wondering if Ymur understood what was re-
quired to close the link. "We should stop the construction work," he said,
setting his mind to practical matters.

"I shall see to it," Hersha answered. "But at the same time I shall give
permission to break into the Terahnee wine cellars. We have been sober far
too long, Atrus! It is time to celebrate. And when Ymur returns we shall
throw a great feast in his honor!"

"And Gat . . . does Gat know yet?"

"I know," Gat said, coming up silently behind them. "Can you not hear
it, Atrus? . . . listen. That noise . . . it is the sound of freedom."

THE ENTRANCE TO HE'DARRA WAS A LONG, DARK SLIT IN THE
earth. Broad, black steps descended into that darkness, and as you walked
down them the ground seemed to swallow you up. Down and down those
steps went, as if to the very center of the world.

The place stank. Its foul and fetid odor wafted up from the darkness like
an unseen cloud.

Ymur wrinkled his nose. He had been six when he'd left here. Less than
eight weeks, that was all the time he had spent at He'Darra, and yet those
fifty days had left so deep and dark a scar on him that even now he shivered
at the thought of what lay below where he stood.

He bared his teeth; then, signaling for his men to follow, began the
descent.

Here, nearest the surface, spreading out to either side of the main stairway, were the quarters where the guards—P'aarli, of course—slept and ate,
with spacious kitchens and good beds and huge lamps hanging from the
ceilings of the rooms. Here, too, were the storerooms and weapons rooms.
Ymur stopped at one, going down the line of whips that hung from one
wall and selecting a particularly fierce-looking one. But there were other
things here, too: scourges and chains, cleavers and surgical knives. Things
that the Masters—the Terahnee scum—knew nothing of. For this was the
domain of the P'aarli. Here the stewards were the lords and masters, given
power by the Terahnee to turn compliant captives into true slaves. Here the
long months of subjugation in the Training Ages was given its final polish,
its final shape.

Stepping out onto the great stairway again, he gestured to his men.
"Bring lamps!"

They hurried, returning a moment later in a blaze of light, falling in to
either side of Ymur as he began the descent again.

Ahead lay the great gate. Beyond it were the pens.

It was a huge circle of stone, wedged into the surrounding earth. At the
center of it, twenty feet apart, were two enormous doors made of thick
stone bars, like the doors of a massive cell.

THE BOOK OF D'NI • 289

And so it was. For down here they had kept more than a million rely-imah at a time. Boys, none of them older than seven or eight, and most far younger.

Ymur looked to his left. "You remember this place, Uta?"

Uta hesitated, then nodded, his eyes filled with fear.

"Some shut it out," Ymur said. "It is the only way they can deal with it. But I remember *everything.*"

"Yes," Uta said, his voice small, afraid. "I remember, too."

"Good," Ymur said, then walked on.

The gates were unlocked. Ymur waited as his men pushed the massive things back on their hinges, then went through.

Here the stink became a stench. Farther up, in the P'aarli quarters, there had been ventilation shafts and fans, but here, though there was some ventilation, it was of the most basic kind, and the smell of the millions who had passed through here lingered on.

That stench, more than anything, reminded him. He had seen such cruelty here, such studied brutality, that in retrospect he had found the Training Age almost humane by comparison. Here not a single mistake was tolerated. Floggings and beatings had been the norm. And worse. Even those who complied were sometimes taken. For sport, or simple malice. And the worst of it had been his own impotence to act. What he felt now, he had felt then. That same burning anger, that same hideous sense of injustice.

Well, now he could do something about that. Now he could take an army through, to destroy the P'aarli world and erase all memory of their existence.

He went down, the torches burning in the darkness, revealing, to either side, the great cages—pens, they had called them, as if the relyimah were simple beasts—that had held ten thousand boys at a time. Endless rows of ankle chains littered the floors, deep drainage sluices crisscrossing the cold stone. Here, if a boy died, he was left until he rotted, as a "lesson"—one of many that the P'aarli taught them.

Next, running back into the earth for miles in all directions, were the tunnels where they had learned the art of moving silently; tunnels in which, should a boy forget which exit he should take, he could be lost forever.

Farther down were the chambers where they kept the training weights, the massive iron blocks still on their pulleys, a hundred ropes dangling limply down, the leather harnesses lying empty on the floor.

Once more he bared his teeth at the memory, then turned away. Down he went. Down past more pens, more chambers where they'd learned their hideous tasks. Down finally to the lowest level where, beyond one final gate, the Book Rooms lay.

YMUR WAS SITTING IN THE NIGHT, SILENT, THOUGHTFUL, THE P'aar'Ro's throne beneath him, his army camped in the valley below, their campfires speckling the blackness.

It was there that the messenger found him. Kneeling, the man held out the scroll that had been sent. Ymur took it, then handed it to the scribe who stood there, ever-present, at his side.

The scribe unrolled the paper and quickly read it through, then, raising his voice, he read aloud.

"Good brother, we salute you! Your victory is a victory for all the rely-imah! To celebrate this most happy occasion, there shall be a great feast in the capital when you return. The elders thank you and hold you in great honor!"

Ymur waited, then looked to the man. "Is that all?"

The scribe kept his eyes averted. "That is all . . . Master."

Ymur grabbed the paper from him and tore it up. So that was it, eh? A feast! And then what? Was he their servant, to do *this* for them and *that*? No, it wasn't enough. Not half enough. When he went back the old men would still be in control. And what would he do? Sit on his hands and watch them make a mess of things? No. No, that would not be!

He stood, angry now. Forget the P'aarli. He would deal with this first.

"We *thank* you . . . and *honor* you . . ." he said, a mocking sneer in his voice. Then, turning, he clapped his hands. "Scribe!" he barked. "Bring pen and paper! I have an answer for the old men!"

FALLING TO HIS KNEES, THE MESSENGER HUNG HIS HEAD before old Gat, as if he was ashamed.

"Well, man?" Gat asked. "What is it?"

Not looking up, the man held out the paper that the scribe had written. Eedrah took it and, unfolding it, began to read it aloud for Gat's benefit. Halfway through he slowed.

". . . and so, for the safety and security of all, I, Ymur, will take on the great burden of governing Terahnee . . ."

"He means to make us all his slaves," Gat said.

"Then we must fight him," Hersha said at once.

"No," Atrus said. "I shall meet him. I shall talk with him and persuade him from this course."

Atrus saw how the messenger flinched at that.

"You think he will not meet?"

The messenger's head dropped lower. His voice was barely a whisper. "He might meet with you, brother, but not to talk."

"Then why should he agree to meet?"

"Why, to kill you, brother. He has already sentenced you to death. You and all the other D'ni."

"I see."

There was a brief silence, then Gat spoke again. "It seems we have but two choices now, Atrus. To fight or to submit. Which is it to be?"

Atrus looked to him, a sadness in his eyes. He had hoped it would never come to this. "I have no experience of battle. Nor do I feel that violence will solve this. If we begin that way, then a pattern has been set."

Yet even as he said it, Atrus understood that what Gat had said was true. It was not like fighting the P'aarli. Nor were there any compromise solutions to this. Ymur's actions had changed things totally.

"If you wished to leave, we would understand," Gat said. "This is not, after all, your fight."

"Do you think I would leave you now, brother?"

"Then we must arm ourselves as best we can." Gat looked to Hersha and Baddu, his blind eyes seeming to see first one and then the other of them. "So, brothers, who is it to be?"

THE SPIRAL TOWER TWISTED INTO THE SKY, THE SHATTERED edges of its pearled interior fire-blackened, its delicate glass windows, once a Terahnee child's delight, now dark like blinded eyes.

Within its jagged shadow, at the center of a deep, luxurious lawn, Ymur's great tent had been pitched, its blood-red canvas like a stain. About it the burned-out ruins of the once-great house still smoldered, sending a smudge of black into the cloudless summer sky.

Beneath the mound on which it stood a valley sloped away. Once wooded, it had been cleared and the tents of a great army, half a million strong, now filled it, a vast tide of multicolored canvas stretching out of sight, surrounding the ancient watercourse that wound its way between the folding hills.

It was a warm, windless evening and the ragged golden banners above the great tent hung limp now. Slaves moved back and forth across the green,

going about their tasks, while in a palanquin before the tent sat Ymur himself, his chiefs and servants in attendance.

Right now he was silent, brooding, staring past the valley at the distant
city. It was no more than five days' march away, a massive marker that drew
the eye constantly to it.

Ymur belched noisily, then looked down at the pair of lenses in his
hands. He had not dared to look through them himself, yet it was said
that with these the D'ni could see far into the distance, yes, and even penetrate the darkness with them. They were magical, and he had stolen that
magic.

He had watched Atrus at the gathering; seen that disdainful look on the
liar's face, and though the others might be fooled, *he* was not. The D'ni were
masters, like the Terahnee, and given the chance they would install their mastery once more. They spoke the same language and shared the same blood.
How could they not be masters?

Not that everything about the masters had been wrong. The relyimah
had to be ruled, after all, but all this nonsense about absolute codes and laws
could not do it. It needed a strong man to make strong laws.

Ymur looked about him. Good. All of their eyes were averted. So he had
ordered. They were not to look at him, not even to cast their glance over him
as their eyes traveled elsewhere. Relyimah he was, and so he would remain,
even when all others could be seen.

On the far side of the mound, a path led down into the valley. Along
that path a great line of wagons made their way, a dozen slaves harnessed to
each wagon, straining to pull the heavy loads of food that would feed Ymur's
army, a chosen man seated at the bench of each, whipping on their fellow
slaves.

Old habits could prove useful, Ymur knew, and he would not discour-
age them. Some men were born to be slaves—they had a menial cast of
mind—but others could be raised and used. So he would order *his* society,
so build *his* kingdom from the ruins of the old.

His eyes strayed to the path again, noticing something. A running man, heading up the path, against the stream of wagons. Ymur stood, drawing the big cleaver he had chosen as his preferred weapon.

As the man approached, he relaxed. It was one of his own messengers. Even so, he kept the cleaver at his side. Just in case.

Ten paces from Ymur, the man dropped to his knees and bent double.

"Speak," Ymur said.

"We have had word," the man said. "A rival army has been formed. Old Baddu is leading it."

Ymur laughed. "And how big is this . . . army?"

"Fifty thousand men. Some say eighty."

Ymur grinned and looked about him. Others were smiling now, though none dared to look, each one of them flinching from his gaze. Even if the higher figure were true, his own army was at least six times that size. And better armed, no doubt.

"How far are they from here?"

"Two days' march."

Ymur grinned. "Good." He raised his hands and clapped them together. At once two slaves came scuttling and fell to the earth beneath his feet.

"Bring me food!" he ordered, clipping one of them hard about the ear, just as he had so often been struck, back in those days when *he* had been a slave. "And wine! The best in the cellars!"

Ymur looked about him arrogantly. "Come, brothers, let us celebrate our victory!"

YMUR HAD BURNED ALL OF THE LAND FOR MILES AROUND, THEN had waited at the center of that great circle of darkness, the best part of three hundred thousand men at his back, as Baddu's "army" timidly crossed that black, featureless terrain.

Poor Baddu, Ymur thought, resting his foot on the old man's corpse. He hadn't stood a chance. Not that he'd had more than a hundred of his men with him by the time he'd reached Ymur. The rest had run. Not far, for Ymur's own men were waiting for them, with whips and chains. Now they crouched nearby, chained to each other hand and foot, waiting to see what Ymur would do with them.

"Uta . . ." Ymur said, calling the boy to him, "I have a task for you. I want you to go to the elders and tell them this. If they want to avoid my wrath in battle they must send the D'ni, Atrus, to meet me. If not, I shall kill them all."

Uta, who had averted his eyes, nodded.

"Then hurry, boy. I am impatient for their answer."

THE WIND WAS BLOWING GENTLY AS UTA WALKED UP BETWEEN the trees at the foot of the valley, and passed the guard post. On he went, up that much-trampled path and out onto the hump, from where he could see the great house, nestled into the hills at the far end of the valley.

The house was ruined now, and as he looked he saw the blood-red smudge that was Ymur's tent. Between was a large swathe of makeshift canopies, of silk and sack and canvas, and of as many colors as the eye could imagine.

Two days he'd been away. Only two days, and yet it all had changed. Atrus had begged him to stay, had said he'd send another messenger to give the man his answer, but Uta had refused. He had chosen. He was Ymur's messenger now, and he must live with that.

Uta scratched at the stubble on his head, then scrambled down the well-worn path. A dozen paces and he was among their tents, conscious suddenly of what a ragtag assortment of ill-fed and undisciplined souls they were.

Some lay within their tents, drunk or asleep, others sat outside and nervously picked at their unwashed limbs. Most were silent, however, and subdued, their natural docility unchanged. Dark-eyed like cattle they were, though some were palpably afraid.

Walking among them, he seemed to see their faces for the first time, his gaze, like his presence, unchallenged. Makeshift weapons hung from the poles of their lean-tos, kitchen and farming implements mainly, but occasionally some clever adaptation of a Terahnee toy.

But what struck him most was the silence of an encampment so large. What once had seemed as natural as breath now seemed the most unnatural thing of all. His time among the D'ni—with their incessant talk, their curiosity, their *laughter*—had changed him. Catherine particularly had encouraged him to talk, and Marrim, too, so that now he found this silence not just sorrowful but obscene—the most palpable sign of mastery. And they were done with mastery.

Or so he'd thought.

Uta raised his eyes, looking between the tents, and saw again the house and the palatial tent that stood before it, its golden banners idle in the still, warm air. And walked on, knowing that he had at last begun to see.

IN THE FIRST LIGHT OF DAWN, ATRUS STOOD TO ONE SIDE OF the big arch, watching the relyimah come through, marching in ranks as he had taught them, some of them risking a glance at him as they passed. They were in good spirits, considering, for in an hour or two at most many of them would almost certainly be dead. But that was nothing new, and at least this once those deaths would have a meaning—to maintain the freedom fate had given them.

Eedrah, standing beside him, nudged Atrus. "Look at them," he whispered. "They glow simply to see you, Atrus."

It was true. They were like candles, happy to have this one brief moment of life, this single burst of intensity. But for Atrus, there was a sadness mixed in with the pride he felt. This should not have been necessary, and he cursed Ymur for being no better than he was, and for dragging them all down to his savage level.

"How far is it?" he asked, looking past Eedrah to where Gat stood next to Hersha.

"Not far," Hersha answered him. "Our scouts inform us that their main encampment is less than an hour's march from here."

"And they are there?"

Hersha nodded. "Half a million strong."

Which meant the odds were heavily against them. But Atrus was not dismayed by that. He had organized his lesser force as well as he could given the brief time they had to prepare for this, emphasizing to them that it was strategy more than sheer numbers that would win this fight.

Or so he hoped, for neither D'ni nor Terahnee had much experience in warfare. Not in their homeworlds, nor in any of the Ages they had written. All this was new, and he could only pray that intelligence and discipline would triumph over size and brute force.

This day would tell.

As the others walked on, he joined them, silent now, brooding on the battle to come, and wondering, at the last, whether he would ever see Catherine again.

At least in that respect the relyimah were fortunate, for it was easy when there was no one to regret your passing. Easier to bear your own death when there were no ties to life.

They went on, expecting at any moment to find their enemy ahead of them, to come to the crest of a hill and find Ymur's mighty army there below them, armed and waiting. And as the minutes passed, a heavy silence fell over their ranks.

The day grew. Slowly the sun rose, the shadows shortened, and suddenly there ahead of them was the enemy.

Atrus called a halt, then stood there, just ahead of them, one hand up shielding his brow as he peered through his lenses at the distant camp.

"Well?" Eedrah asked, but Atrus put up a hand, begging for his silence. Another long moment passed, then Atrus gestured that they should move on.

Eedrah hurried to catch up with him. "Well?" he asked again. "Have they seen us yet?"

Atrus walked on in silence, striding now, so that Eedrah had almost to run to catch up with him.

"What is it?"

"They've gone."

"Gone?" Eedrah put his hand on Atrus's arm and pulled him round. "What do you mean, gone? How can an army of half a million go?"

Atrus stopped. Behind him the great host of relyimah came to a sudden halt.

"I do not know. But the camp *has* been abandoned. Their tents are all still there, and there are hundreds of huge wagons piled with food, but there is no sign of Ymur's army."

Eedrah turned, looking about him anxiously. "Then maybe it's a trap."

"I do not think so."

"But how can you be sure?"

"Because it is Ymur, and Ymur would not hesitate to try to crush us on the battlefield. He would think it shameful to set traps."

"Then what has happened?"

Stepping up to join them, Gat answered Eedrah. "I'd say our friend is dead. No other obstacle would keep him from the battlefield."

"I'd say that's so," Atrus agreed, "yet I dare not hope it true."

"Nor I," Gat said. "But let us go and see."

THEY FOUND YMUR ON THE LAWN BEFORE HIS TENT. ON HIS back, his blank eyes staring sightlessly at the unblemished sky, the knife that had taken his breath still lodged within his ribs. Close by, his own wounds all too evident, lay Uta, also dead.

Seeing the child, Atrus felt a pain so sharp it took away his breath. He groaned and wrapped his arms about himself, and Gat, not knowing what it was, called upon Hersha to tell him.

"It is the slave-child," Hersha answered, his own face creased with pain. "The boy he saved. The one who spoke out for him at the gathering."

The old man groaned, then straightened up. "Then let us honor him this day, for by his death he has saved a great many more."

Eedrah stood there, watching Atrus awhile, seeing how he went across and, lifting the boy, cradled him, as if he were his own.

Atrus turned to face them, tears on his cheeks. "Send messengers out to spread the news, and to tell the relyimah elders to come to a gathering in the capital." He looked down at the child again, then shook his head. "This is the end. There must be no more of this."

PART EIGHT

HE WHO NUMBERS BUT DOES NOT NAME:

IT IS HE WHO HERALDS THE COMING TRAGEDY.

HIS FOOTPRINTS LAY ABOUT THE MUDDIED POOL.

—FROM THE EJEMAH'TERAK, BOOK FOUR, VV. 3111–14

AT THE CENTER OF THE RAFTERED CEILING, HANGING DOWN
between the six supporting poles, was a massive inverted funnel, cunningly fashioned of wood. Beneath it a circle of earth had been excavated and filled with close-fitting stones, that pit surrounded by a built-up bank of rock, in which a huge pile of firewood had been carefully stacked.

Outside, the great plains of this new Age ran dark to the horizon, the distant mountains touched by the pale light of a tiny moon. It was late now, and the lodge house, finished hours past, was deep in shadow, its wooden walls and pillars, its sleeping stalls and meeting rooms lit only by a handful of flickering lamps, set high up on the inner walls, ancient oil lamps in iron cressets. Several hundred were gathered there in the space surrounding the pit as Eedrah struck the tinder and, raising the long pole, carried the flaming lamp across.

There was a pause as the kindling caught and then a sudden blaze of light. Sparks flew up into the darkness overhead.

There was a great cheer. In the burgeoning light, dozens of smiling faces looked to Eedrah.

"Say something!" Marrim called. She was swollen of belly now; the firelight danced in her smiling face.

Eedrah looked about him; then, casting the pole onto the blazing fire, he raised both arms for silence. "Friends," he began, "this has been a memorable day, a day of new beginnings, and I am glad to be among such company. But lest we forget, I would like to thank one person who, above all others, is responsible for our happiness . . ."

He turned, looking to where Atrus sat beside Catherine, and extending an arm, beckoned Atrus to join him.

Reluctantly, Atrus stood and came across. There was another huge cheer that went on and on until Eedrah raised a hand for silence.

"My words are brief and simple," Eedrah said, and, turning to Atrus, he bowed deeply. "On behalf of all here, we thank you, Atrus."

There were more cheers and whoops from Irras and Carrad.

Atrus looked about him, his expression for that moment stern, determined—the face they knew so well—and then he smiled. "Friends"—he turned, looking to Gat—"brothers . . . I am fortunate to be here with you tonight. Fortunate to have known you all. But now you must set out on this new venture without me."

There were cries of "No!" and "Stay!" but Atrus waved them aside.

"This is *your* world, *your* experiment in living, not mine. Yet I would offer you some words of advice before we part."

Total silence had fallen among the watching gathering. Only the crackle of the flames broke that silence as Atrus looked about him.

"When I wrote this Age, I tried to put all my experience, everything I knew about writing, into it. To make it the best I could. Yet even as I labored to do so, I was conscious that for all my skill, I could but do half the job."

"But this is a wonderful Age!" Eedrah said.

Atrus smiled. "I thank you, Eedrah, for your kind words, yet that is not what I meant. I was speaking of the new society you must build. You see, just as we take care to write our Ages, so should we take care to create—to write, if you like—the social forms and structures that we wish to adopt within those Ages; those elements that create a fair and healthy society. This I see as the one great task confronting you.

"This must be *your* world, and *you* must shape it. All I shall say is that you should learn from past mistakes and take what is best, not worst, from those systems you have knowledge of. You have a new start, a fresh chance of living, with new earth to till and new air to breathe. Take that chance, but for the Maker's sake, use it wisely."

There was a deep murmur of agreement. Atrus waited until it had died down, then spoke again.

"Tomorrow we leave the past behind. Tomorrow we close a great chapter and begin anew. Yet we must not forget from whence we have come. That was the mistake the Terahnee made." He smiled. "We are not great lords, as the Terahnee thought they were, but simple men, and we must do as simple men do and build for tomorrow, brick upon brick, stone upon stone. Yet even as we do so, it is beholden upon us to remind our children and our children's children of what was, and tell them tales of lands that are no more. That is our way, and must remain our way, until the last word is written in the last book."

Atrus took a long breath, as if about to say more, then, raising a hand, he turned and walked from the circle.

There was a moment's silence, and then a great cheer went up that went on and on while the flames leapt high into the darkness.

THAT MORNING THEY RETURNED TO TERAHNEE FOR THE LAST time.

While Atrus and the others packed, Catherine went to her room in Ro'-Jethhe's mansion. Atrus found her there an hour later, stowing the last few things into her trunk.

"Are we ready?" she asked.

"Almost." Atrus kissed her shoulder, then looked across the room. There were books open on her desk—Terahnee books by the look of them—as well as her own notebook.

"Still working?"

Catherine barely glanced at him. "Hh-hmm."

"What are you working on?"

"Oh, nothing."

"Can I see?"

She laughed. "No. Not until I've finished."

"A secret, eh?"

"A secret. Now let me finish here and then I'll join you."

"Okay, but don't be late, Catherine, or we shall go without you."

ONCE ATRUS WAS GONE, CATHERINE CROSSED THE ROOM AND, slipping the leather bookmarks back into place, picked the books up and carried them across, placing them carefully inside the trunk.

It was finally beginning to make sense. For a long time she had had nothing but snippets and vague references, tantalizing but obscure, but now, thanks to these ancient Terahnee texts, she was beginning to piece the whole of it together.

The relyimah text was a corrupted one, she knew now, and more than two-thirds of its "prophecies" were little more than doggerel added long after the originals had been framed. Not that there was one single original text of the ancient prophecies. As far as she could make out, there had been numerous so-called prophets in ancient times, back in that original homeland—Garternay—from which both Terahnee and D'ni had split off; and what was known as the Book of Prophecies was in fact a much later text, collecting together many—though not all—of the surviving prophecies.

That had been five, maybe six thousand years ago. And then had come the split and a period of forgetting so traumatic and so violent that it was a wonder anything survived to tell that tale.

Atrus, she knew, would have been angry with her had he known what she was doing. He did not believe in fate and counted the prophecies a lot of superstitious nonsense. As she, at first, had done. But circumstance had changed her mind.

A year ago, at the same time Atrus had begun work on his new Age, she had begun a deeper, more serious investigation into the matter, gathering together everything she could find on the subject, sifting through that great pile of books until she had established what was genuine and what were later additions to the canon.

But now time had caught up with her. It was time to leave Terahnee, even as she had begun to make sense of what had happened here.

Yet even that, she knew now, was as it was meant to be, for time was a circle, and the circle was about to be closed.

She closed the lid of the trunk and tightened the leather straps, then went out into the hallway and called for Irras and Carrad to help her carry it.

Time. It was indeed time.

THE SUN WAS BEGINNING TO SET AS THEY GATHERED IN THE ruins on the top of the great plateau. Most had gone through already to the new Age, but a handful still remained, along with Hersha and the old man, Gat, who, with a party of relyimah, were to help in these final moments. A new vault had been built over the old book chamber. Two holes had been cut into its top surface: one a narrow octagonal well, the other a kind of entrance, shaped like a huge arrowhead. Beside the vault two huge pulleys rested, from each of which dangled massive chains of nara, the final links of which were pinned into the marble-smooth surface of a massive wedge of stone.

Two teams of fifty relyimah waited in harness, watching as Atrus went over to greet Hersha and Gat.

"The time is here," Atrus said solemnly.

"So it is," Gat said, his long face pushing the air. "We thought you should know, Atrus. We have renamed this Age. Today it is Terahnee still. But tomorrow, when we wake, it shall be known as Devokan."

"Hope..." Atrus said, translating the ancient D'ni word. "That is a good name for a world."

Gat nodded. "We work to build a better, simpler world."

"And no more like Ymur!"

"No, thank the Ancient's words!" Old Gat grinned blindly at Atrus for a moment, then his face grew more somber. "It is a sobering lesson, Atrus, to know that gaining one's freedom is but the first step to achieving it. Nor did I guess how hard we would have to work simply to keep what we had gained. In that Ymur helped us, though he did not know it or intend it. He sent a warning to us. We have formed a great council, you know."

"I heard," Atrus said. "Oma told me."

"Oma has been a great help. And Esel, too. We shall miss them greatly."

"We shall be here in spirit, Jidar N'ram."

"That is a comfort, Atrus, but we must learn to govern ourselves now—to be our own masters."

"Then let us do what must be done." He took Gat's hands. "I am sad, old friend, and yet in my heart I know this is for the best. The child must go his own way, no?"

"So it is, Atrus. So it is."

IN THE LAST LIGHT OF THE LAST DAY OF TERAHNEE, NINE DARK figures stood atop the vault, cloaked and bare-headed at the end. Stepping out from among them, Eedrah placed the ancient Book into the carved niche within the receptacle they had fashioned, reverence in his every gesture. He stepped back and, at a signal from Atrus, Irras and Carrad began to let out the chains, lowering the Book into the deep shaft. As it touched bottom, they let go, watching, fascinated, as the fine links slithered into that eight-sided darkness.

There was a moment's stillness, and then the great slabs, which had stood like huge stone petals about the shaft, folded down, the last of the nine—a small octagon in itself—tilting over and slotting into place like a capstone, the joint between it and the others so fine, so perfectly made, it could no longer be seen.

Atrus knelt, examining their work; then, satisfied, he stood and turned back to the company.

"Sealing these Books in stone is not as secure as the entrusting of Books between friends. Yet today we do more than safeguard the Ages. We return symbolically to that very first day, ten thousand years ago, when the great Linking Books between D'ni and Terahnee were first sealed. So it was, and so it must be once again. And so we leave this land of hope, to find our own separate destinies."

Atrus turned, looking behind him at the dying sun.

A bird called, high and sweet in the silence.

They stood there, watching him—Catherine; and Eedrah and his young wife, Marrim; Carrad and Irras; Masters Tamon and Tergahn; and lastly young Allem, from Averone, who had left her parents in her native world to be Marrim's pupil.

D'ni was once again sealed from Terahnee, the two Ages as inaccessible to each other as lands behind a mirror. A dream under stone.

For a moment longer they stood there, the silence engulfing them, each of them awed by the significance of that moment. The ancient ruins lay all about and below them even as the great world of Terahnee sank slowly into darkness. Then, as the twilight shaded into night, Atrus turned and descended into the vault, the others following in silence, Eedrah alone pausing briefly to turn and look back before he, too, went down into the lamp-lit interior.

The moon now shone.

At a signal from Hersha, the relyimah began to strain, hauling upon the great chains, five thousand years of practice perfected in the ease with which they raised the capping stone, that massive arrowhead swaying gently as it lifted.

Slowly it rose, swinging up and over the vault, Hersha directing his volunteers with quiet, patient words. And then slowly, very slowly, it came down again, hovering an instant, and then sliding into the waiting gap with a sigh of polished stone against polished stone.

It was done.

Silent as shadows they stole away, leaving the two ancients alone upon the plateau. They were still a moment, both blind and seeing eyes staring at the great vault that sat amid the ruins, and then they, too, turned away.

Shadows on the silver. And silence. The circle closed.

EPILOGUE

FLOWERS IN THE DESERT. THE CHILD'S EYES OPENED WIDE.

A THOUSAND MILLION STARS DANCE

IN THE DARK MIRROR OF THE POOL.

—FROM AN UNTITLED TERAHNEE SCROLL OF ANCIENT ORIGIN.

"Standing there, amongst that small and humble company, I felt a sense of closure, as if the universe itself had taken pause before the final page was turned, the last word written.

"So it felt, as night fell, there on the plateau where our great journey had begun. Where, several thousand years before, that first great sealing-off of Ages had taken place.

"Time stood still, and as it did, the knowledge of what had happened flowed into me, filling me with the blessed light of understanding.

"The Prophecies . . .

"For five thousand years and more they had waited for him, hidden and sealed away, like some great magician's finest trick, created not to please an audience but for his delight alone.

"Yet to talk of 'magic' is to somehow belittle the achievement of whoever first drafted those prophecies, for it is now clear to me that their complex phraseology stems from the same root—maybe even from the same bold experiments—that produced the Great Art itself, and just as those words connected Age to Age, so these quite different words connected Time to Time.

"It was seen. I have no doubt about that now. Yet the fact that it was seen changes nothing. Had Atrus known—had he been aware of the awesome significance of what he did—then his actions might have taken on an air of futility, his whole life become a puppet-dance, but as it is I find his actions quite remarkable. Time and again he risked himself. Time and again he set himself against the tide of events. And to what purpose? To fulfill a prophecy? No. For at no point did he ever know the outcome of his actions. His whole life has been forged in a great furnace of not knowing, and, ultimately, it is that not knowing, that determination in him to do what he thought was right and not what was expedient, that has made his actions more than something fated: more—much, much more—than something merely 'Seen.' Written as he was, Atrus nonetheless wrote his own path, like a Linking Book back to himself.

"And it is of Atrus and D'ni that I must write. For on that day, when the picture of the prophecies came clearly into my mind's eye, I understood what only the Maker and the Great King had known. I saw the thread of happening that was stitched into every aspect of Atrus's life to bring him to that plateau at that hour. From the very first of this great history that I have written, to these last words, the purpose of events can now be followed. From the most common occurrence—the death of Ti'ana's father, which led to her journey down into D'ni—to the largest catastrophe—the fall of D'ni itself, which allowed for that unseen chamber to be discovered—it was all meant to be: to fulfill a greater good and vanquish a greater evil.

"And so, even as the prophecies speak of a great rebuilding, we now re-build D'ni, not in the great cavern, but in a new Age—an Age that is surely among the finest Books ever written in all the great history of D'ni. And it is the survivors of the old D'ni who will build that new Age. An Age of beauty and perfection and wonder that would take as many volumes to de-scribe as I have yet written.

"But you who have found my histories should know this last thing, for I have written these things only so that they might be known to future seek-ers, whether they be of D'ni or human origin—that Atrus and I live quietly on Tomahna, with a new daughter, Yeesha, cousin to Marrim's little Anna. And I rejoice and cry for joy when I dream of the life behind and the bless-ings of what is yet to come.

"And Atrus? He writes but does not lead. He advises but does not com-mand. He wonders and seeks to understand. He loves life and quietly moves to the mark that the Maker has set for him."

ABOUT THE AUTHOR AND
THE OTHER MEMBERS OF THE
D'NI TRANSLATION TEAM

RAND MILLER—WHO ALONG WITH HIS BROTHER ROBYN discovered and brought to life the secrets of the D'ni empire in the megahit CD-ROM worlds of MYST and RIVEN, and the novels *Myst: The Book of Atrus* and *Myst: The Book of Ti'ana*—rather enjoys his quiet simple life with his family in the Pacific Northwest. He continues to enjoy playing disc-golf, reading, and a carefully prepared Texas steak with a tall cool glass of peach iced tea.

David Wingrove is the author of the Chung Kuo series of novels, which include *The Middle Kingdom*, *The Broken Wheel*, *The White Mountain*, *The Stone Within*, and *Spree: The History of Science*, a volume which won the prestigious Hugo and Locus Awards for best non-fiction work in the science fiction genre. He lives in North London with his wife and four lovely children.

Chris Brandkamp, who manages Cyan's business affairs, enjoys land-scaping and furniture making, and, of course, any musical instrument.

Richard Watson is the master and keeper of D'ni. He is the expert in the D'ni culture and their language. He is a dedicated father and husband, and when not studying D'ni, shares lines from Bugs Bunny cartoons with his friends.

Ryan Miller, while anxiously awaiting Dallas' trip to the Superbowl this year, continues to uncover more of the D'ni civilization. He is also having fun hanging out with his new son.